SMIRCH

God is Gambling to Survive

Erez Buchnik

Smirch

God is Gambling to Survive

Erez Buchnik

ALL RIGHTS ARE RESERVED ©

No permission is given for any part of this book to be reproduced, transmitted in any form or means; electronic or mechanical, stored in a retrieval system, photocopied, recorded, scanned, or otherwise. Any of these actions require the proper written permission of the author.

ISBN 978-965-598-250-3

Creative Writer, Independent Publishing

This is a work of fiction. All the names, characters, businesses, institutions, places, events, dialogue, and incidents in this book are either the product of the author's imagination or used in a fictitious manner and are not to be construed as real. Any resemblance to actual persons, living or dead, actual businesses, or actual events is purely coincidental.

With boundless love,

dedicated to my wife, Shuly,

to our children Sheer, Rotem, Omer, and Lior,

and to our dog, Mimi

In loving memory of my mother, Ziva (Giselle) Buchnik

SMIRCH—God is Gambling to Survive has explicit content and is recommended for mature readers.

This world is indeed a living being endowed with a soul and intelligence ... a single visible living entity containing all other living entities, which by their nature are all related.

—*Plato, Timaeus, 4th Century BCE*

Late October,

1987

Rosie

The earth is like the breasts of a woman: useful as well as pleasing.

—Friedrich Nietzsche, Thus Spoke Zarathustra

"Adam... Adam, stop... I have something to tell you."

I raised my head and leaned over her, my gaze lingering on her bare femininity. The perfect curves, the gorgeous ivory complexion, stunningly contrasting the pink crests. *Beauty Revealed*—that cursed, faceless portrait of Sarah Goodridge was reincarnated in another female body, 160 years later. A work of art I could smell again, taste again, and touch again in three dimensions.

After I broke up with Rosie for the first time, I had only my memory to rely on. Two painful months later, I stumbled upon an old art book in the library. At seventeen, that was the first thing I ever stole. I came home from the library that evening, locked myself in my room, and took out the book from under my jacket. Lying on my bed, I opened the book on page 137. I stared at the portrait for hours. The artistic analysis described the balance of colors and shading. I read it over and over, till I knew it by heart. The resemblance was shocking. The only difference was that Sarah Goodridge had a freckle—Rosie had none. She was perfect that way. She was perfect in every way.

By the time I fell asleep that night, I was no longer angry at her. The next day, Rosie and I were back together, and the art book soon disappeared somewhere in the mess of my room. Three weeks later, I broke up with her again. Another week passed, and a rare urge to tidy up my room came over me. I found that book. The creased spine made it open, like magic, on page 137. And there we were, Rosie and I, by the end of that week—a couple again.

"What did you want to say, goddess?" My gaze moved up along her neck until I met her face, dizzy at the sight of sheer beauty.

"Alexander came over this morning. We had sex."

I sat up next to Rosie on her bed and stared at her. Any other girl would button up her blouse and sit up when revealing something like that to her boyfriend. Rosie just lay there, her upper torso in clear view.

She did it again. That was the third time. Anger and tears were pointless. But I was furious, and my face became red and wet. Not a silent weep—I wailed loudly. We both jumped when Rosie's younger sister opened the door and rushed in.

"LEAVE!" Rosie shouted at her, quickly covering herself, and then muttered. "Retard..."

Rosie's sister obeyed. Her voice faded behind the closed door as she chanted a single word. "Boobies! Boobies!" The doctors had diagnosed Rosie's sister as 'mentally retarded' —only decades later, that term would become inappropriate. Rosie was ashamed of her sister. I suspected her parents were also ashamed of their youngest daughter. I could relate to that—I was ashamed of my seizures.

"Alexander... But... We both had the final math exam today—I saw him at school this morning!" Throwing in a logical argument was easier for me than talking about emotions. Were there any emotions to talk about?

"He finished the exam early and came here from school," Rosie said dryly.

I was struggling with calculus all morning while that freak... That bastard was...

Alexander was a prodigy. He was top of our class, and I was the runner-up. But he was a nerd. He had pimples. He had the posture of a praying mantis. And he was ugly.

"Rosie, again? You swore it was the last time... Why the hell do you keep doing this?"

Rosie's look pierced my soul. "I had no choice. He threatened—"

"WHAT? HE FORCED HIMSELF ON YOU? I'LL KILL—"

"He threatened that he'd kill himself if I didn't have sex with him."

"So he's suicidal? Does that turn you on? Is that what it takes to get into your pants?" I tried to insult her.

"You have special permission to get into my pants whenever you want, Adam—how about right now?" Rosie pointed to her crotch. Right there, on her jeans, was a small drawing I once made for her with markers. It was a triangular roadsign, white with a red rim and two black silhouettes in the middle—a boy and a girl—holding hands and running. The writing below said *BEWARE OF CHILDREN*.

Rosie leaned over and pulled me back onto her. She bit my ear. Then she began to lick my left biceps. She'd made me swear I'd never take a shower after my Kung Fu practices. I'd practice three times a week, then hurry from the Kung Fu club to Rosie's place so she could lick the cooling sweat off me.

I suddenly realized Rosie had already pulled my shorts down, and pulled her jeans and panties down, and I was about to enter the same warm place Alexander had visited that morning.

"Rosie... Rosie—no," I could hardly speak, exhausted, barely resisting her magnetic pull. "I want to keep my promise to you. I won't have sex with you—with anyone—until we get married. The first time I'll have sex, I want it to be with you, as my wife. You promised you'd wait. I want to marry you, Rosie. I want you so much, but we made a vow—"

"Oh, that stupid vow again!" Rosie snapped at me. "Adam, that was six months ago! We were just kids! When we first started dating, I wasn't a virgin, so I already knew how it feels—having sex. Your willpower turned me on. I thought I could stand it like you do. I wanted to be like you. But whenever I look at you... Whenever I touch your muscles, move my finger over the veins along your arms, I just... I'm not like you, Adam. With you, it's like a superpower you have. You're like a knight in one of those medieval ballads we learn about in literature class.

"So, here's a news flash. Chivalry is dead, Adam. The guys who wrote those ballads are dead. The Middle Ages are over, and I'm not a lady waiting for you in a castle. How long must I wait until we get married? That whole 'getting married' plan seems so complicated to me... But the facts are much simpler. I'm sixteen, and you're seventeen, and we're crazy about each other.

"And I want you inside me..." Rosie whispered, moving her perfect feminine pelvis like a carnivorous plant about to catch a fly.

Should I forgive her again, so quickly? Am I ready to break my vow?

"Adam, I want you to take that strong will superpower of yours, and use it to pleasure me tonight," Rosie said with a smile that melted me. "I want us to have sex until we collapse. I want us to stay up all night and—"

I jolted back.

"Adam! You're not giving in!" She gave me a strange, astonished look. "What's... Why aren't you giving in?"

I began to cry again. The doorbell rang and the front door opened and closed. A few seconds of muffled chatter. Then, a knock on Rosie's door.

"One moment!" Rosie shouted as we were quickly getting dressed. "Come in!"

Mom and Dad walked into Rosie's room. Mom stared at my red, swollen face.

"What... How did you know I'm here?" I asked, wiping my tears and envisioning the obvious answer—my younger brother and sister.

Those little snitches...

"What are you doing here?" I asked a more interesting question.

"Get up," Mom said. "We're going home. She's no good for you."

"Who are you to decide? I'll be eighteen soon. I can—"

"I'm your mother. Keeping you out of trouble is my duty, no matter how old you are. Someday you'll understand. Maybe when you have kids of your own."

"GO!" Rosie shouted at me. "Run to your mama and papa. You're just a baby anyway! You're—" She caught Mom's enraged face and fell silent.

I got up from Rosie's bed. My body felt lighter, lacking the mass of the huge hole in my heart. I left Rosie's house with Mom and Dad.

I was silent on our way home.

"It's been almost a year since you were diagnosed, Adam," Mom said. "You're still in denial—you're living recklessly as if you didn't have epilepsy. Your life is packed. You study till late for your final exams, so you don't sleep enough. You go out to drink. And you have that Kung Fu thing. You keep ignoring our advice and your neurologist's advice. And if that isn't enough, you've become angry all the time, stressed, and even more stubborn, ever since you started dating Rosie. Alcohol, lack of sleep, and stress—they can all cause seizures."

I rolled my eyes in silent despair.

"Rosie keeps cheating on you," Mom continued. "You deserve someone better. A nice girl who won't take advantage of you. You haven't even told Rosie about your epilepsy, have you? You shouldn't be afraid of telling your girlfriend about something like that. That's just wrong."

I recalled the French kiss with Rosie one evening, twelve hours after I chewed on my tongue during a seizure that morning. The pain almost made me faint, but I didn't flinch, and she never suspected. That kiss was so sweet—Rosie's bubble gum flavor, blended with the taste of my blood.

"Adam, you're special," Mom spoke softly. "Always remember that. You're so smart and strong, you have such an enormous heart—don't let people break your heart. Someday, you'll do great things. I can feel it. You'll see."

Yeah, right, I'm special... So why do I feel like I'm damaged goods?

We came home. I locked myself in my room and stayed there the whole evening. I slept a lot and skipped school the next day.

I'd wished for my first-ever sex partner to be a girl I cared about, a girl who cared about me, who'd want to bond her life with mine, despite my defects. That wasn't going to happen. I had wet dreams about sleepless nights of carnal pleasure with Rosie. But in my nightmares, right before we reached a synchronized climax—I'd give out a sudden shout, bite hard on my tongue, violently shake my limbs, unknowingly bruise her terrified face with my convulsing arms, and finally pass out, while blood and foamy saliva drip from my mouth, staining her white bosom.

I was clueless as to what could trigger seizures in that defective brain of mine. The doctors recited their textbook checklist: sleep deprivation, alcohol, flashing lights, dehydration, stress, extreme anger, and so on. But they admitted it would ultimately depend on my physiology. Worst of all, those doctors experimented on me with various types of seizure-depressants to see what worked best. Each type had its nasty side effects—none of them made the seizures go away altogether. I was their lab rat.

I wasn't going to let those doctors dictate my lifestyle. Why would I, Adam, give up alcohol just because it triggers seizures for a certain percentage of all epileptics? I could be one of the outliers. And how would I avoid getting angry or stressed? What other emotions should I avoid? Could true love cause seizures? How about longing for someone? Or just being horny?

Most urgently, I had to find out for myself how I could get through a night of alcohol, sex, and multiple orgasms without sleep, and avoid seizures—but for that kind of experiment, I needed a lab rat of my own. I was too afraid to try it with the only girl I truly cared about: Rosie.

When evening came, I was wide awake—ready for action. I took a shower and got dressed. My pecs and biceps looked good. I liked what I saw in the mirror. I put two Valium pills in my jeans pocket, went to the kitchen, and grabbed something to eat. I ignored my parents, who were sitting there. I then stepped outside.

The pub at the university campus was branded as a place for one-night stands. I loathed that concept. I was there once before. My friends dragged me there the night I first broke up with Rosie, but I went home alone after two girls came on to me. Finally, I was back, and I was on a mission.

To be on the safe side, I charged myself with my effective seizure contraceptive, which had become my friend: Valium. I bought a pint of Guinness and downed the two Valium pills along with the beer. My messed-up neurons were going numb. Sure, there was the risk of a negative impact on my libido, but I was a seventeen-year-old male virgin—I had more than enough libido. I approached a fairly attractive girl at the bar. She smiled at me—undoubtedly a student, at least five years older than me. Such an age gap must have rendered any intimacy between us borderline illegal. When asked, I said 'twenty-six.' She either bought it or didn't mind. Whatever.

My vow to Rosie had expired. A shiny new vow—a more realistic one—took over.

Before sunrise, I will get laid.

Early spring,

536,000,000 years ago

(More or less)

― ― ―

― ― ― [m... m...] ― ― ―

― ― ― [m... m...] ― ― ―

― ― ― [m... m...] ― ― ―

― ― ― [m... m... m...] ― ― ―

― ― ― [m... m... **Me**] ― ― ―

Summertime,

2025

☥ *(Love Symbol, No. 2)*

Men think epilepsy divine, merely because they do not understand it. We will one day understand what causes it, and then cease to call it divine. And so it is with everything in the universe.

—Hippocrates (c. 460-377 BCE)

"Hello?"

"Yes—hello, is this Adam, Eleanor's father?"

"Yes."

"Good morning. I'm calling from the District Epidemiology Office. So, we're launching a vaccination campaign for second-graders in the district. I see here that Eleanor is missing some of her vaccines—right? She needs to get vaccinated against diphtheria, tetanus, pertussis, and polio. Could you bring her tomorrow?"

"That could have been great, ma'am, but we're leaving for a four-week-long vacation in two days. Can we do this when we get back?"

"I'm afraid not—can't you come tomorrow morning? We're a three-minute walk from you. It won't take long."

"Well, I guess... Okay, see you tomorrow."

Just great...

Eleanor hated needles. Her talent for drama kept improving with every blood test, every intravenous infusion—every time Shirley and I tried to convince her to let a nurse puncture her naturally tanned epidermis. But Eleanor loved 'Dad time,' even if it involved needles, so she was happy she'd spend with me that sweaty morning, at the beginning of July. We were both happy about it because 'Dad time' was rare those days.

The final days before our trip to Iceland were days of abstinence for me: zero quality time with Eleanor, her brother and sisters, and even Shirley. I worked like crazy—crazier than ever—to complete urgent tasks, reassure customers that business would continue normally, and secure enough money in the bank for our vacation.

That ritual possessed our family: working hard, swirling and roasting in the sizzling soup of routine, and fantasizing about our next trip. Finally, we'd indulge in a brief overdose of quality time. We'd go on yet another dream vacation, inflate the cloud with myriads of photos and videos, and spend money. So much money…

After Shirley and I are gone, our kids may wish we left them more money so they wouldn't have to work so hard. But then, Eden and Maya may recall how insulted they were when a man of the Tanzanian *Maasai* tribe approached me and offered I'd sell him both of them for two hundred cows—insulted because I'd already refused an offer of eight hundred cows from a man of the *Datoga* tribe. Ben may remember the New Zealand *Arapawa* ram that got tired of his teasing and started chasing him around. Eleanor may recall we went 'northern-lights-hunting,' on a cloudy night, against all odds, based on a tip from a stranger—and right when we frustratedly decided to head back to our hotel, she was first to spot a circle of clear night sky with dancing auroral ghosts and show it to the shocked Finnish minivan driver, who looked as if he'd witnessed God punch a hole in the clouds with His finger, just for us.

Those memories, that Shirley and I spent so much effort and money to stuff into our children's then-young minds, may surface in their adult future as they commute to that boring office where they work for that bastard boss and are paid half what they're worth. As they reflect on those memories, they may still forgive us.

And Iceland, our upcoming destination—well, Iceland was the perfect place to spend money.

We were the first ones at the vaccination booth the next morning. A nurse in her fifties greeted us with a smile and asked me to fill out a form about Eleanor's medical history. We approached the nurse's desk, and she prepared the syringe.

"Hi, Alex," Eleanor, whose nervous stare had been following the nurse's hands, relaxed a bit when she saw the familiar face of a boy from school who arrived right after us.

"Excuse me…" I politely drew the nurse's attention, "Eleanor has Absence epilepsy. There's no section in the form for—"

"Shh..." the nurse whispered. "Come with me. We'll let this boy get vaccinated in the meantime."

"What... We arrived first—why don't you vaccinate Eleanor first?"

"I'm truly sorry," the nurse whispered, "The pertussis vaccine could trigger seizures. Can you get approval from her neurologist?"

Eleanor's neurologist was probably the best in the country. The nurse stared at me, expressionless, as I texted for approval.

"Why are we whispering?" I whispered as I pressed *Send*.

The nurse examined me, surprised. "I'm concerned about Eleanor's privacy. Do you want everyone to know what's wrong with her?"

Eleanor and I looked at each other. We both knew where this was going. When I looked back at the nurse, every wrinkle, every birthmark, every less-flattering facial feature she was trying to conceal, stood out.

"Ma'am, Eleanor has epilepsy. Not leprosy. No big secret. Here, see? I just got the doctor's approval." The neurologist responded quickly, and that fueled my determination.

The nurse glanced at the document I presented on my smartphone. She was lousy at expressing fake interest.

"I'm sorry," she said. "We'll review this case and contact you as soon as we get the approval to vaccinate Eleanor."

Many things made me angry that summer. It was hot—the worst time to be angry. The nurse made anger accumulate inside me. No, not just accumulate. It was being multiplied.

Eleanor was diagnosed with Absence-Seizure epilepsy about three months earlier. It came from nowhere: one normal day—too normal—after returning from their hip-hop class, Eleanor and her friend Natalie made us sit on the couch in the living room and showed us a dance they'd learned. I took out my smartphone and began filming them, filled with pride.

Natalie turned to the right with a spin, and Eleanor twisted her body and arms at an angle upwards and to the left, staring at her palms without moving. I shifted my gaze from Eleanor to the smartphone screen and back, envisioning the dance moves that would come next: in a second, Natalie would spin gracefully around Eleanor, and they'd continue together, holding hands… Although that would look more like ballet than hip-hop…

But Eleanor remained frozen in this unusual posture, staring blankly upwards, while Natalie slowly rose and looked at her in bewilderment. And then, everything froze. Eleanor maintained a dramatic pose, like some ancient Greek statue, and all of us fixated our eyes on her in silence, as if we were in a museum.

Suddenly, Eleanor thawed back to awareness, confused but determined to repeat the dance.

Since then, I couldn't bring myself to play that video clip again, which remained buried somewhere in the cloud. Until, one time, a while after Eleanor was already positively diagnosed, I reluctantly watched it at the neurologist's request to measure how much time that fierce, silent lightning storm inside her skull had been grilling her young brain: one second, two, three, four, five, six.

I was angry with myself because till then I'd never heard of this type of epileptic seizure that makes you look as if someone who's watching the movie of your life on VOD has pressed the *Pause* button. Of all people, I should have known about it.

I was angry with myself because until then, I hadn't noticed those 'lapses' of hers. Eleanor's brother and two sisters knew about them long ago and were sure she was faking them.

Above all, I was angry with myself because of the chance this was somehow related to my crappy genes.

Eleanor's conclusive diagnosis came at a time of mourning, three months after Mom passed away at the age of seventy. Her death was sudden and pointless, and remembering her made me angry. I was angry with myself because of my bachelor lifestyle—self-centered and reckless. Guilt crept in. Before I met Shirley, Mom used to worry about me all the time—were those worries somehow related to her death?

The extraordinary bond Mom had with Shirley strengthened when we married and had children. The pain of our mourning for her was amplified during that irritating period, while Shirley and I were trying to balance the medications in Eleanor's body. We wished for some of the precious advice and experience Mom had gained dealing with my medical issues a few decades earlier. But we found a grain of comfort in the knowledge that she passed away unaware of her granddaughter's epilepsy.

As soon as Shirley and I reconciled with Eleanor's new situation, I vowed I'd never let Eleanor's medical condition affect any desire, hobby, or plan she may have. We didn't stop her horse-riding lessons—that would have broken her heart. I made a similar vow, decades ago, about how I would live my life, and it worked well for me. So, that pertussis vaccination bureaucratic hassle would cause us no trouble—I'd never allow that. The neurologist approved it—nothing else mattered.

And, what angered me the most was the indifference of the nurse facing me. Her patronizing fake empathy failed to conceal her indifference.

Who the hell does she think she is?

Supercharged with all that anger, I exploded at the nurse.

"But we're going on vacation for A MONTH! Your 'campaign' will be over when we return!" My raised voice made several heads turn.

"The office requires one year without seizures as a precondition for vaccination," The nurse replied firmly. "I don't have the authority to approve this vaccination for a child with epilepsy," She whispered the word 'epilepsy' as if she feared the wrath of some half-deaf ancient deity who threatened to bring 'that terrible disease' upon any unfortunate mortal who dared to utter its name.

"A YEAR? Do you even know how people deal with EPILEPSY?" I purposely raised my voice when I uttered that forbidden word—that half-deaf deity must have heard me.

"Eleanor is seven years old! Her body is growing all the time, and we keep adjusting the doses of her medicine based on her growth—there is NO WAY to tell when her next seizure will be. How do you expect her to have a full year with no seizures anytime soon?"

Wait a minute—so...

"Wait a minute—so, if that's your requirement, why did you ask me to get her neurologist to approve this in the first place?"

She didn't answer, but I'd figured out the answer as I finished voicing the question: she didn't believe I'd get the approval that fast. She was hoping for an excuse to get rid of us.

"Well, at least give her the other vaccines." I tried pragmatism, hoping to make the most of my encounter with that irritating woman.

"Unfortunately, we only have combinations here that contain the pertussis vaccine. You must order a special combination vaccine."

Oh, this bunch of idiots...

"I get it," I was furious. "You allow a nurse to ignore the decision of a senior neurologist to cover up your incompetence when it comes to children with an 'uncommon medical history' like Eleanor's. Because your greatest fear is that Eleanor would pass out, right here, on your shift. Did I guess right?"

That was harsh. I could have stopped right there. But that nurse was the perfect audience for the extended version of my monologue.

"You know, I also have EPILEPSY. But of the type you're more familiar with. I don't have lapses like Eleanor. I have seizures—first, I shout, then my body gets stiff, then I collapse, then I jerk, then I bite my tongue, then I pass out." I was shouting by now.

Everyone around fell silent. Eleanor twisted her hand a bit as my grip tightened involuntarily.

"This rotten system, your employers, will surely back you up in Eleanor's case. The same rotten system backed up my former neurologist, who treated me like a lab rat. He made me try all sorts of epilepsy medications with nasty side effects until he found one that I could barely tolerate. So, I used to have seizures once every two weeks or so. But I ensured they did not affect my family, career, or anything else. Seizures had been part of my life for more than a decade. But guess what? Your neurologist diagnosed me wrong!"

The nurse wasn't bald, and she didn't wear eyeglasses. But that neurology professor was staring back at me when I looked at her.

"Luckily, a private neurologist—not even a professor—examined me and said the pills I'd been taking for ten years had nothing to do with my medical condition. He changed my prescription—and the seizures were gone. So, here we are—thirty years later—the same rotten system, the same destructive recklessness…"

"I'm sorry," the nurse lied. She was done with false compassion. She wasn't bothered by the bureaucratic entrapment she and her 'epidemiologist' friends forced upon us, and my medical history certainly didn't interest her. She just wanted to finish her shift, knowing no one could complain about her.

"We'll be in touch soon." She demonstrated the absolute control granted to her over our fate, only in that place, only in those minutes. "Good day. Next, please."

As we were on our way back home, Eleanor broke the silence.

"Daddy, so I didn't get the shots… Was it because of my lapses?"

"Yes—but they made a mistake. Don't worry. I'll fix this. Now, do you remember the names of the people I told you about who had epilepsy, and each one of them changed the world in their way?"

"Yes, wait. Socrates, Alexander the Great, Julius Caesar, Michelangelo, Van Gogh, Lewis Carroll, Napoleon, Neil Young, and that singer, who used to be called *Prince*, but now no one can say his name, because it's *Love Symbol, No. 2*."

"Great! And who are the next ones about to change the world?"

"Me and you!"

Moon

The earth is the cradle of humankind,
but one cannot live in the cradle forever.

—Konstantin Tsiolkovsky

"Kids, are you ready for Dad's next crazy idea?"

"Come on, Dad," Eden grunted and licked her braces with her tongue. "If we say no, would you not make us hear about it?"

"Adam, speak already," Shirley said, elbowing me in the ribs.

It was just getting dark. We gathered around the campfire: Shirley, the kids, me, and two other families—our friends. The pounding desert silence could have exploded my ears—if only it were audible through the shouts of the kids playing around us. The other campfires were too far away for us to hear people's voices.

The August heat was finally dissipating. I let go of the frigid memories of Iceland, which were already one month old. Especially the glacier in *Jökulsárlón* that we saw collapsing in front of us, a few hundred meters from our boat—just thinking about it made me 'cool off.' It was also insurance. If some disaster destroyed all the photos from the trip we uploaded to the cloud, those precious memories would still survive in my mind. Long ago, travelers wrote diaries to preserve their memories.

Then there were photo albums. And recently, the cloud. But there will always be memories stored in the brain. If I don't catch Alzheimer's, it's going to be okay.

I pointed a finger upwards towards the darkness.

"A second moon. For settling down on," I looked for signs of interest through the fire's light.

Make it interesting, Adam...

"It would have the shape of a Boston cream donut," I didn't give up.

No one even glanced in my direction.

"Well?"

No response. No one was excited, or shocked, or amused. Everyone reverted their attention to their beers, or smartphones, or gazing at the campfire.

"A *what?*" Shirley said. Her words were a lifeline, breaking the silence.

Ideas had always popped into my head without warning: while I was driving, or while I was walking our dog Bonnie, or on those dark, quiet mornings. Many silly ideas mixed with great ones, some thrilling, arriving with a *eureka!*, and very few genuine strokes of genius.

I'd share my ideas with Shirley and the kids, asking what they thought. Negative feedback never deterred me. I was addicted to those moments when people would stare at me, amazed, their mouths wide open. But those moments were becoming rare, and children were the most challenging to impress. They've seen it all. Too much screen time.

"Imagine a place not too cold in winter, and not too hot in summer. Breathtaking views everywhere. Not crowded. no pollution. You can buy apartments at reasonable prices, and you can get there in less than three days—"

"AH! So, you're talking about Paphos!" Benny said. His voice was thick as he laughed and we all followed. Benny was an athletic Holistic Health coach—a cool guy.

"Much better than Paphos. I'm not talking about a place that guys like us could retire to," I said, as my fingers were playing with Eleanor's curly hair, her head resting on my lap. "I'm talking about a place where our grandchildren's children could live. It's not trivial, sure, but it's easier to achieve than it sounds."

Yes, Adam—you can really, really make it happen.

"Do you remember when NASA diverted an asteroid from its orbit a few years ago?"

"Yes, Dad," Maya said, handing me a slice of watermelon. "You made all of us sit down and watch that boring TV show. What was the name? I remember it had an A, an R, and a T. Did it begin with an F?"

"DART, Maya. The name is DART. NASA DART. Look it up—you'll be surprised."

"Right, DART. Anyway, Dad, I think it's rude. What if aliens were living on that rock? If I were them, I'd be seriously annoyed…"

"If aliens do exist, don't you think they have more interesting things to do than riding asteroids?"

Maya's post-millennial attention was about to divert elsewhere. "Yeah, whatever…"

I wiped watermelon juice off my lips. "For the first time in human history, we've changed the course of a celestial object, after millions of years along the same orbit. Impressive—isn't it? But few people know about NASA's ARM mission, which was much more ambitious…" I paused for a moment to add drama. "NASA planned to tow an asteroid over here—making sure it doesn't crash on Earth, of course—and to place it in orbit around the moon. The government canceled that 'moon-trapping' plan because it was too expensive. But if we disregard the costs for now—why don't we bring a large enough asteroid here, create Earth-like conditions, and build residential neighborhoods on it?"

"Oh, I see where you're going, Adam," Shirley said, blowing some air on her marshmallow skewer. My nostrils filled with the scent of sweet gelatin. "You want to sell land reserves on that future moon—just like those four acres on the real moon that you bought me for my birthday, right?" She looked upwards, as if locating her property.

"Adam, don't tell me that framed certificate you showed us at Shirley's birthday party—that was…" Eddie asked, shocked. "And I thought I was a bit drunk… *You're* one of those weirdos who bought land plots on the moon?" Eddie never started a conversation. He always joined in. His dark skin, white teeth, black hoodie, and the dark corner he sat in made him look like a Cheshire cat.

"It was a bundle. Shirley also got a star named after her. You wouldn't believe how hard it is to get Shirley a surprise present."

"Just book me a massage next time, Adam," Shirley teased me. "And as for the second moon—don't quit your day job yet. We have kids to feed here on Earth."

"I promise," I smiled. "But what do you think about my idea? Benny, would you invest in such a project? Would you buy apartments as an investment on the future moon?"

Benny was confused. "Wait—you're serious?"

A smile spread across my face, filled with a kind of… something… as if I'd taken responsibility for the fate of all humanity. "You bet I'm serious."

The emotional intensity surprised me. I was used to dreaming, but it felt like this dream could materialize very soon. Tears of excitement filled my eyes. "Sometimes I wonder why humanity hasn't started a project like this long ago."

For a moment, Benny seemed puzzled by my decisive statement, but a default calmness reappeared.

"You know what? Let's roll with it. What do you say, Eddie? Are we rolling with this dude's idea?" Benny said. The three of us clinked our beer bottles—a 32% AVB Scottish beer I bought for the occasion.

For Benny, it was just another exercise as part of his business management studies. "Okay, space real estate project... interesting..." Benny gazed at the night sky and then looked directly at me. "First, prove the business feasibility. You'll have to go against the richest people in the world. And NASA. And the most aggressive competitor is Egon Mars." He shook his head. A fat fly reluctantly abandoned Benny's forehead, having crossed the desert with the clear intention of settling down on that particular forehead.

"That guy..." Benny blended empathy with amazement. "When I heard that billionaire Egon Moskowitz woke up one morning, decided he'd save humanity by colonizing other planets, and changed his last name to Mars, I just... You know I'm Jewish, right? Now, a bunch of religious Jews had this crazy idea that the first Martian must be a Jew, you know? The JMM—the Jewish Martians Movement—can you believe it? So they felt he sort of... betrayed them when he gave up his Jewish last name. But I think that's bullshit: he was born a Jew, and he's always going to be a Jew, no matter what he calls himself or which planet he lives on." Benny paused when Eddie passed him a newly rolled joint. He sucked on it and let out one cough.

"And you…" Benny's glassy eyes looked back at me. "Where will you get the money to compete with a guy like him?"

"I'm going to get people to dream about upgrading their lives by moving to an artificial moon," I smiled at Benny, but I was nervous. "Have you heard of the *Earth Overshoot Day*?"

"No. What's that?" Benny asked.

"Every January researchers estimate the annual 'budget' of Earth's natural resources that humanity requires. Then they track the consumption. But humanity is abusing Earth. December 1971 was the last time we 'broke even.' Since then, Earth's entire budget has been consumed earlier each year. Last year, we overshot by July. So, to break even, we need *another Earth*!

"Think about it, Benny. The beer we're drinking is made of resources borrowed from *next* year's budget!"

Benny was about to attach the orifice of his beer bottle to his lips. I enjoyed watching his hand freeze in midair. He examined the bottle, then commanded his hand to complete its journey. He directed his scrutinizing look at me, smirking.

"Earth is a pressure cooker, Benny, and we need to blow off some steam."

Eleanor's face was red. She turned around so her back would face the heat, then put her head on my lap again. Shirley and I were alert.

Eleanor had to stay up late that night. We spent two days fine-tuning her bedtime routine for that camping trip. Sleep deprivation made her more prone to lapses—but if she missed the main event, that would mean victory for epilepsy. We kept an eye on her all night.

"So, settling outside of Earth is a solution. Egon Mars and other billionaires, NASA, the UAE, China, and at least two startups aim to send people to Mars. In ten years or so. But why move there? Benny, Eddie—would any of you take your family on an eight-month journey to build everything from scratch, to face dangers we know about and dangers we don't, and to accept that you can't even get back anytime soon?"

"We're not moving anywhere, Eddie," Louise, Eddie's wife, reacted to whatever she overheard as she approached us and sat next to him. "Adam, you're not going to talk him into doing something crazy, yes?"

"Okay, Louise, I promise we won't move to Mars any time soon. You won't like it there anyway. It's dirty." Eddie was genuinely trying to calm her. Louise laughed.

"Going to Mars is not for guys like us," I said. "Think about what happened after Columbus got people excited about moving to America. Many of the first immigrants were running away from the Catholic Church. So, I bet anyone who gets on the first flight to Mars is running away from something on Earth."

I caught a little droplet sliding down my sweaty beer bottle and squeezed it between my fingers. Why was all this so important to me? What if… What if my subconscious was way ahead of me, signaling that there is no doubt anymore about the *if*, and that the *how* will soon be pieced together?

Adam, don't lose their attention.

"And yet," I continued. "The Mars mission is *the most expensive* project by the *richest* man in the world. Not that anyone cares that Egon Mars is burning away his own money on—"

"DAAAD!!!"

After quietly kneeling behind me for some time, Ben screamed into my ear. Eleanor and I jumped in unison, and I spilled my beer all over the two of us. At a nearly humanly impossible pitch, Eleanor's shriek followed Ben as he ran into the darkness, laughing out loud. But he slowed down when realizing no one was chasing him.

"BEN! Come on!" He never liked to see me talk for too long—especially if he wasn't the one I was talking to. I was angry at him briefly. But enjoying the cool shower of that expensive liquid almost made me spill some more beer on myself. My gentle grip held Eleanor down, restricting her instinctive urge to chase him, seeking revenge. I waited for the laughter around me to calm down and then spoke.

"So… Egon Mars does whatever he wants with his money. But let's say that someone like you or me wants to raise money for a space project.

They'll need to present a more attainable goal if they want money from investors. For example, investors could buy cheap land reserves before construction work on the moon begins and sell them at a profit as the project progresses or pass them on to their children. And that's the beginning of a business plan."

Benny narrowed his eyes, contemplating. Yes, that was my weak spot. My challenge was to explain how all this would generate money. But I wasn't in this for the money.

"So, we can tow an asteroid here," I escaped to my technological comfort zone, "and adapt the technologies owned by Egon Mars and NASA to create an artificial moon for habitation.

"Settling on Mars will force us to compromise on what already exists there. And constructing this artificial moon can be a lot less dangerous to human lives, and even cheaper than—"

Eddie interrupted my flow of speech. "And where exactly would you find an asteroid the size of the moon? And how would you catch it?"

"No, no. I meant something much, much smaller. One such moon would populate no more than two million people. I've been thinking about this for quite some time. The only major challenge is gravity. And I'm sure we'll solve that with sufficient research. I've done some calculations and talked with a friend of mine at NASA. So far, no one has managed to 'kill' this idea."

"What do you mean by *one* such moon?" Benny asked. "Do you want to build *more* than one? And what calculations have you done?" He capped off his questions with a gulp from his beer bottle.

"If one works, why not build more?" I answered, satisfied with Benny's increasing interest. "We'd position those artificial moons in orbit around Earth or our natural moon, cover them with an Earth-like crust, and upgrade them with radiation protection, atmosphere, climate, vegetation and animals, electricity infrastructure, water, communication—and finally, residential neighborhoods. We can even 'recycle' the debris orbiting Earth—defunct satellites, used launchers—and use it as building material, which would add an ecological aspect to the appeal of this project."

"All this is so smart and sophisticated, Adam," said Louise, "but why are you so eager to leave Earth behind? It may be less 'cool,' but wouldn't it be simpler to *fix* Earth and adapt it to cope with the population growth than to stick those 'moons' above our heads?"

"We won't abandon Earth—we'll *fix* it," I said, concealing my surprise. I was ready for that question. But Louise was the last person whom I'd expected to ask it. I'd underestimated her.

"In fact, the population growth rate is *constantly dropping*, Louise. That's part of the problem. People's lives keep getting more complicated, so they prefer having fewer children. People have been using contraceptives to have fewer children for more than sixty years.

But imagine one million people on an artificial moon, where they are less worried about their health, jobs, or the safety of their families. Their incentive to bring more children will increase."

Louise fell silent. I liked her. She didn't like me.

"The earlier we start, the greater the chance our children and grandchildren will benefit from this."

"Okay..." said Benny, and then he yawned. A drop of cold water fell from his beer bottle and landed on his white shirt.

It's over, Adam. You've lost his attention.

"If my calculations are correct, an artificial moon should be a solid, elliptic 'donut,' five hundred kilometers wide and forty kilometers thick. People would live on the surface of those donuts, not inside them. They'd feel as if they were on Earth."

"Keep dreaming, Dad. I'm *never* going to live on a donut. All my friends would laugh at me!" Eden exercised her veto and resumed her talk with Natalie, Eddie's daughter, as her smartphone cast turquoise lights on their faces.

"I want a coconut moon! I love coconuts!" Eleanor exclaimed.

"I want pizza!" Ben said enthusiastically.

"Well, I want a hamburger," Maya shrugged.

"Adam, I see your kids are still hungry—that big dinner we just had wasn't enough for them. But it's already time to head into the desert," Benny said, getting up. "And about the moon... I don't understand all those calculations, but if you believe in this idea, you must refine it. Oh, and smooth out your pitch. We'll talk about it later."

He's right, of course.

In the glow of the campfires around us, I saw people walking south and disappearing in the darkness. We all got up and grabbed our straw mats. We looked for the darkest corner possible to settle into. The meteor shower was sparkling above our heads.

"WOWWW!"

Words, like eyeglasses, blur everything that they do not make more clear.

—Joseph Joubert

"SHIT!"

As I was walking away from the campfire, I slipped in the dark, and my glasses fell on a stone. They'd likely shattered. I returned to the tent to grab the spare pair, then headed to our mats again, shouting, feeling, and stumbling in the dark. I lay down on my mat and tried to adjust my eyes to the new situation.

Eye massage… Come on…

My optician convinced me to order the spare glasses with a slightly lower prescription, to get what he described as an 'eye massage' when watching the computer screen. I couldn't see any meteors with those spare glasses… I could hear people shouting all around me: "WOW!", "OHH!", "WHOA!" —but before my eyes, high above, was utter, silent darkness. I could only imagine what others around me were experiencing. Out of frustration, I tried something.

"WOW!" I shouted, pointing upwards, my finger stabbing the darkest point I could find. Immediately, I heard shouts all around me: "OOH!" I tried again: "AAH!" and heard "OHH!"

We were a bunch of people lying on mats in the desert, shouting at each other. The meteors were a superficial catalyst.

Satisfied with myself, I rolled over and lay on my left side. Just then, the corner of my eye caught a faint flash of light. I accepted this as the highlight of the evening for me.

One day, Adam, you'll stand on an artificial moon and gaze at the meteors from a better location.

With my eyes shut, I let out occasional cries of "WOW!" into the darkness, content with the human echo that followed.

Eleanor

I am one who eats breakfast gazing at morning glories.

—Matsuo Bashō

"Please don't watch videos during breakfast, Eleanor."

"Eleanor, are you ignoring me?"

"Eleanor… Oh—ELEANOR!" I rushed to her.

"ELEANOR…"

"ELEANOR, WAKE UP!"

At first, we didn't know whether to wait for Eleanor to wake up, or try to bring her back to consciousness. Then, the neurologist said we should take action and wake her up. I steadied her head with my right hand and held her shoulder with my left hand. Then I shook her.

Eleanor jerked her head and looked at me. I stared at her.

Did she fake this lapse?

Would it be more bearable to realize it wasn't a lapse—and deal with our suspicion that Eleanor was deceiving us again? Or would it be easier to confront our fears that the medication level in her body was again going out of balance, but to take comfort in knowing Eleanor was sincere with us? That conflict was tearing Shirley and me apart.

This time, I was sure Eleanor didn't fake anything, and yet, I asked the automatic question with the obvious answer:

"Eleanor, did you have a lapse just now?"

"No."

That wasn't the obvious answer I'd anticipated.

"What do you mean? So, what was it?"

"That was a *stare*."

I wasn't familiar with this terminology. "Eleanor, what's a *stare*? And what's the difference between that and a *lapse*?"

"When I have a stare, I see and hear everything, but I can't respond. But when I have a lapse, it's more like a dream. And when I wake up from it, I feel like I woke up from a dream. And also, when I wake up from a lapse, I'm a bit tired, as if I really did sleep."

I fell silent.

Her neurologist needs to hear about this.

And as if nothing special had happened just now, Eleanor lifted her spoon above her food bowl, launched a few swift death blows that sounded like someone walking on gravel, and resumed eating. Five minutes earlier, her bowl was filled with cornflakes mixed with cottage cheese and yogurt. But Eleanor liked it 'shredded.' So, after her 'treatment,' it all turned into a mushy, yellow-white mass.

But as for what I felt… If there could have been any shape to what I felt then, to that frustrating helplessness, that shape would have probably been similar to what was inside Eleanor's bowl.

Why do we deserve this?

Every time that nasty question snuck into my mind, it was immediately followed by me mentally 'slapping myself in the face.' I hated self-pity. And I didn't dare to think that Eleanor deserved pity.

Eleanor was a heroine by all accounts. At first, it was difficult for her, but she embraced her condition and turned it into what defined her as a special girl.

Occasionally, she'd prepare a salad for herself in the evenings—mostly avocado with salt and lemon. I was always offered to taste it, and it was always delicious. Using her smartphone, which didn't have a SIM card, Eleanor would document herself while preparing her dinner for the sake of the thousands of imaginary followers on the imaginary social network in which she was a famous influencer. Whenever she filmed herself swallowing her evening dose of the medication, Eleanor would explain to her followers why the life of a person with epilepsy is not that different from the life of anyone else.

Eleanor and I were two souls sharing one fate, descendants to a family that perpetuates and preserves, from generation to generation, at least one of hundreds of genes responsible for epilepsy. This disease spared most of the family members, and in this generation, Eleanor and I were the chosen ones.

But why, goddamn it?

What good is there in it? That 'trait' which causes you to involuntarily jerk before you pass out, or go into momentary 'hibernation,' while a lightning storm is short-circuiting your brain—how could that be advantageous for the survival of humanity? What allowed this 'defect' to survive the cruel indifference of naturally selected filters, from generation to generation, down the bloodline of families like ours? Could there be some hidden reason that would make sense of this cycle?

Had Eleanor and I been born thousands of years ago, we likely wouldn't have survived as long as we have in our time. At best, someone might have decided that our seizures were, in fact, a creepy way that God chose to speak with mortals, and we'd end up as 'oracles.' Someone would probably try to decipher God's words from the 'choreography' of our seizures. And so, a twitch to the right or the left, a frozen stare upwards or downwards, could translate to the choice between going to war and seeking peace. We'd unconsciously advise kings and seal the fates of nations.

Our ancestors were 'fit' enough to survive Natural Selection, which explains how we ended up here. So, is genetic epilepsy preserved throughout generations because, somehow, humanity benefits from it?

Or maybe it all just happened by chance? Could it be that our ancestors weren't supposed to survive and have children? Could we be evolutionary 'mistakes,' useless for the human race's urge to thrive? Is it just a matter of time until, as our race continues its process of perfection, the offspring of our family will eventually disappear from the world?

"Maybe we shouldn't even be raising offspr—"

Adam, what is this?

I scolded myself, shocked by the deranged direction in which my thoughts had drifted. It felt as if that thought wasn't mine at all.

Where did this awful thought come from?

For this, I deserved something much worse than a mental slap in the face. I was ready to mentally kick myself in the groin. No less.

I looked at Eleanor. Then, I leaned over and kissed her forehead.

"Come on, Eleanor. I need you to finish eating and brushing your teeth so you won't be late for school."

Eric

Be willing to get fired for a good idea.

—Spike Jonze

"Hello, Adam?"

"Hey, Eric. What's up?"

"Great. Everything's great, Adam."

"So, did your Quality Assurance guys finish testing my new algorithm?"

The silence was brief, yet still a few milliseconds too long. But it was enough. I sensed something was wrong.

"So that's it," Eric said after exhaling. "That's what I wanted to talk with you about. We're not going to be integrating your algorithm after all."

"What…" I was shocked. "Eric, I've already shown you that the system will respond three times faster with this method, and data transmission could be five times cheaper…"

"Yeah, but… You see… Our clients… You know them. It's a big, conservative corporation. They want to transmit and store all the data, even the 'junk data' we don't use anyway, no matter how much it will cost."

"But, Eric, this will make our solution economically impractical!"

"Adam, if we lose these clients, it won't matter anyway, right?"

I didn't like the approach Eric had recently adopted to managing the company he founded, where I was recruited third. I kept my criticism to myself.

The original product lacked dedicated software, and no commercial software could meet its unique needs. When I joined Eric and his co-founder, I decided to build software for us by myself. That software was richer in features and cheaper than anything similar, and convinced customers we were serious. We'd boast about our product with real demos and field trials, not slides and hand-waving.

Then we caught the attention of the big players. One of them, a giant corporation, became the main investor in Eric's company. They demanded that we rebuild our software to connect exclusively to their systems, making it clear they'd invest zero effort to help us. Such a move would lead us straight into a trap.

I warned Eric that our system would become severely limited. We'd be 'locked' into this single customer—working with other customers would be impossible. Our competitive advantage would dissolve, and those investors wouldn't care about our tremendous efforts to bend our product as they insisted. They'd want us to demonstrate the same results that had impressed them enough to invest. Our crippled system wouldn't be that impressive anymore. I considered Eric a friend and had to warn him, but perhaps it was too late. He was in a position where he wasn't calling the shots.

"Okay, I get it," I said quietly. "So, what do you want me to work on now?"

Again, a brief silence.

"Adam, listen: we truly appreciate... *I truly appreciate* everything you've done for the company. But at this point, we'd like to freeze the contract with you."

"Eric..."

I had plenty of experience with work termination situations from both sides of the table. I was familiar with all the nuances. It was clear. There was something else.

"Listen," I argued. "Developing an algorithm that doesn't end up in production—I can understand that. But THIS? Eric, I'm your third recruit! Wouldn't the board members think this move is sort of suspicious? And what's the deal with 'breaking up' over the phone?"

"Adam..."

"Yes, Eric?"

"I'm saying this as a friend. I didn't mean to tell you this, but it's... It's coming from the investors."

Now, it was *me* who was silent.

"Adam, they consider you a bit… a bit eccentric. I know you're telling all your friends about your idea with the artificial moon, but… Why did you have to tell *them* about that? What were you thinking? Now they're concerned you might damage their public image with stories like that."

Blood rushed to my head.

"Are you talking about the evening we took them to that pub? Are you telling me that because I told them about my idea, they think I'm some weirdo who might jeopardize their investment?"

Eric was silent.

"Tell me, Eric, could there be another explanation? Maybe someone among all our 'new friends' has an eye on my position in the company? If that's the case, I admit that person deserves all the credit for this creative trick—using my unconventional idea for *corporate shaming* that will erase everything I put into this company and kick me out of the game. Whoever that person is, let them know I said 'kudos.' You know what? Never mind. I'll go to the company's website in a month or so, scroll down to the Leadership section, and see who will appear where my picture used to be. And then I'll congratulate them myself."

"Adam, seriously…"

"Let it go, Eric. I'll get in touch later to process the termination."

I hung up and lifted my head. Shirley was standing in front of me. She always complained that I could never interpret her facial expressions and always needed explanations, thus failing to comply with the basic definition of a 'normal' spouse. But she listened to the conversation. And she knew the background. She understood what happened. And I knew how she felt.

"Adam, maybe you should tell Eric about Eleanor?"

"No way. That's none of his business," I said quietly. I wasn't going to beg for mercy to get my job back.

"Adam, I know you have other customers as a freelancer, and I'm sure you'll find something else soon. But what about all the treatments and medications for Eleanor? And we're still not done paying for the trip to Iceland…"

"Everything will be fine."

Everything will be fine.

"Everything will be fine, Shirley."

I'd have said that anyway. It was time to muster as much optimism as possible. But that time, something intangible—like a distant echo voiced by some authoritative figure who stood firmly by my side—made me much more confident.

Smirch

Having a beard is natural. When you think about it, shaving it off is quite weird.

—*Paul McCartney*

Shaving recently became a burden. Everyone expected me to shave. Shirley hated my beard. Ben and Eleanor had a ritual I loved so much I was willing to shave for it: they'd ambush me behind the bathroom door, wait for me to finish shaving, and jump on me, screaming, "Dad, you're smooth!"

Still, I couldn't bring myself to shave more than twice a month, unless I had no choice: for a meeting, a wedding, or a passport photo. Shaving was the only task that forced me to look in the mirror.

I was standing in front of the bathroom mirror. My father was staring back at me. He mimicked every expression I made, every move I made with my hands. It was annoying.

The first time my father appeared in my bathroom was shortly after Mom died. I didn't recognize him right away. He never had a beard. Shaving was always the first thing he did every morning. One of my earliest childhood memories was the scent of his *Tabac Original* aftershave.

I blinked my eyes a few times. My head wasn't aching. Those abrupt migraines I was having throughout the past week were becoming less painful. Somehow, tightly shutting my eyelids eased the pain a bit. So, I'd start my mornings with a few eye blinks, hoping to prevent the next headache.

I looked down. I had two defining moments a week before, on the same day: first, I realized I could no longer flatten my belly. My deception wouldn't be convincing anymore. I wasn't fooling even the last person who could still be fooled—myself. Later that day, when I was in the office, a coworker asked me if I had grandchildren. *Grandchildren!*

I sighed and started scrubbing my beard with shaving foam. The stubborn hair was slowly being trimmed, millimeter by millimeter until the facial skin was exposed. My father's face was becoming increasingly familiar with every stroke of the razor blade.

While shaving, I was devising my tactic for that morning—how to drop off the kids at school and still avoid traffic—

"OUCH!"

No, it didn't hurt. But my hand unexpectedly slipped with the razor on the back of my right cheek, leaving a smudge of shaving foam on the collar of my shirt. I looked in the mirror. There were no signs of a cut. Instead, I saw an unfamiliar stain on the corner of the right side of my jawbone, still partially hidden by some unshaven hair. It was shaped like a 'mole.' That is, it had no specific shape. It had the smoothness and coolness of titanium, and the colors were extraordinary: a psychedelic combination of blue, yellow, purple, and a little deep brown.

"Shirley, can you come here for a moment?" I asked.

Shirley stepped into the bathroom. "Yes, what? I have to leave soon. Oh, finally, are you shaving? What's that? Did Eleanor stick one of her tattoos on you?"

"When? While I was asleep?"

"Well, I could paint Michelangelo's *Creation of Adam* on your face while you're asleep," Shirley smiled.

"On my beard? And do you think it wouldn't come off during shaving?"

"Does it hurt?"

"Not at all."

"Dad, are you done here?" Maya stuck her head into the bathroom. The natural, unreal, dark orange color of her hair—a color that women would pay a fortune to imitate—highlighted her delicate, pale face. "I have a bus to catch in fifteen minutes. What's that *smirch* on your cheek? Is it some new boomer thing? PLEASE don't be like those bald guys with ponytails..." she said with a smile and disappeared without waiting for an answer.

Shirley made a futile attempt to scrub off that thing with saliva. She then touched both my cheeks. "It's cooler than the left side," she mumbled, furrowing her eyebrows.

As expected, she shifted to operational mode and pulled out her smartphone. "I'm scheduling an appointment for you with the dermatologist. Here, see that? You're so lucky: someone canceled, and there's an appointment available tomorrow."

"Tomorrow… How? I can't—"

"You listen to me and listen to me WELL! I'm not letting you neglect yourself! I can try to schedule it for the day after tomorrow, but not beyond that."

"Okay…" I sighed. Then I noticed I was brushing my fingers over that stain on my jaw. It felt surprisingly good.

Needle

Black is the true face of Light.

—*Nikola Tesla*

It didn't hurt or particularly bother me, but I wanted to get that 'smirch' looked at, not just to reassure Shirley. Postponing routine check-ups was becoming a habit of mine. Since I turned fifty, reminders were piling up for such periodic check-ups, which are important to have but easy to reschedule indefinitely. I was also trained in suppressing feelings of guilt every time that fitness instructor would call and pleasantly ask me why I stopped coming to the gym, the same gym where I received the call with the news of Mom's death.

I was proud of myself for keeping the appointment with the dermatologist. Shirley agreed to find me an appointment three days after I noticed the smirch—the gods must have bestowed on her the gift of finding free slots for doctor appointments anytime she wanted. The appointment was in the evening, so I didn't waste working hours. Or, rather, hours of hunting for new customers. Also, those days were unbearably hot, and I preferred not to come sweaty.

I was about to enter the clinic building when something made me stop. I turned around and looked up. The sky was unusually dark, devoid of clouds and moon.

When I entered the office, the modest lighting made me feel like darkness was following me. The doctor, a middle-aged, well-groomed lady with a heavy French accent, gave me a bored look and invited me into her tiny, horribly mundane clinic—if I had to spend all day there, I'd go crazy.

She first examined my hands, feet, back, and abdomen before getting to the psychedelic smirch behind the right side angle of my mandible. To my disappointment, she wasn't particularly impressed.

"It doesn't look like something that should bother you," she said. "I'd still like to burn it. Please sit on the bed." She prepared a device that looked like a thick needle with a cable connected to an electrical outlet and brought it close to my jaw.

On a previous appointment, a few years back, she recommended burning a mole I had on my waist, which bothered me when it rubbed against my belt. Whenever I saw her, I'd imagine a picture of her as a young girl, sitting in the backyard of her house with a box of matches and burning beetles.

I remembered this procedure wasn't supposed to be painful. I had no intention of closing my eyes—

"No way"

—so, for a moment, I was surprised I didn't see anything, although my eyes were open. I heard a thump and a soft moan. I turned on my smartphone's flashlight and saw the doctor lying on the floor. I helped her get up.

"Are you okay?" she asked in a concerned tone. The blinding light of my flashlight made it difficult for her to check if I had any facial injury. It amused me that she looked as if trying to recall something. Maybe the phone number of someone she'd call if a lawsuit is filed against her? Malpractice attorney? Insurance company?

"Yes, I think I'm okay," I wanted to calm her, but I didn't want her to calm down too much. Besides, I *was* okay, quite surprisingly. I touched that thing on my face. It had the same gentle texture as before, and it didn't hurt. But the doctor—some force *threw her back* and made her fall on the floor—while I felt no opposing force.

She found the device and lifted it. We both looked at it and then at each other, trying to make sense of what happened. The tip was charred along about two millimeters, and another two millimeters sparkled in a color that resembled my smirch.

"I'm so sorry… Luckily, you weren't hurt. It could be an overload in the electrical network—there's some construction work going on in this building. I see that other rooms on this floor are also dark."

In fact, the power went down in the entire building.

With the computer down, the doctor couldn't schedule a new appointment for me. She promised to call me the next day to reschedule. A few moments later, I was groping my way down the stairs—four floors—to exit the building.

Come to think about it, what are the chances that such a power outage would happen right as the doctor pressed the button? And what electric current could ruin such a device? What pushed the doctor back while I felt nothing?

When I reached the stairs on the first floor, it came back to me:

'No way...?'

Who said that, as the light went out? Did I imagine it? As if it came from somewhere thoughts don't belong to, deep inside my head...

What's happening to me?

"You must be mad," said the Cat, "or you wouldn't have come here."

—Lewis Carroll, Alice's Adventures in Wonderland (1865)

"Get up."

The time was 5:44 AM—just one minute before my alarm clock was supposed to go off. I turned off the *snooze* option so Shirley wouldn't wake up. It was a holiday, and I forgot to disable the alarm the night before—and I was pleased with myself for beating an alarm clock.

I went to the kitchen and took out a bottle of orange juice from the fridge.

"Good morning."

The shock and the shiver that accompanied it almost made me drop the bottle. Not the fragment of a distant dream. Not Shirley's voice or any of the children's. It wasn't even a voice. A thought passed through my mind, but that thought didn't belong to me. I didn't bother to look around me for a more rational explanation. After yesterday evening at the dermatologist's clinic, and this morning, I had no doubt. Someone was speaking to me.

"You're right. Most importantly, don't panic."

"Who's this?" I asked quietly.

> "We're here for your own good."

"What... What's happening to me?"

> "Everything's fine with you. And you don't have to talk. No need to wake up the house. Think about what you want to say. We'll understand."

"What's happening to me?" I thought, and that thought distantly echoed somewhere deep in my mind.

> "Don't worry, we'll explain everything. At this stage, you think you've gone mad. If you're hearing voices in your head, that's a well-known sign of going mad, right?"

"Uh... right?" My thoughts stuttered. I was having a conversation, in my mind, with... with myself? The scary thing about it was the conviction. It all had a strong feeling of... of indubitability...

I ran my fingers anxiously from my ears to the back of my head and then to my temples, trying to find some trace of surgical intervention.

> "No, no one implanted anything in you. You have to convince yourself you're not crazy."

"Yes... I guess..." I formulated words in my thoughts. It made sense that I'd already doubt my sanity, but I wasn't done with the shock phase yet.

That strange *We* who spoke to me was trying to pick up the pace of my understanding. That *We* was impatient.

> **"Go down to the street right now and walk to the bus stop across the corner. Don't look confused. You must leave right now."**

It was early morning, on a holiday. I found foreign thoughts in my mind, but couldn't find any reason to resist them. I let curiosity suppress fear and lead the way. I got dressed quietly and left the building. Along the way, I remembered a book I once read—I forgot its name—it had many morning scenes, and they all consistently described the 'crisp morning air.' I had no idea how morning air could be crisp, till that morning. But on my way to the bus stop, I inhaled through my nose. The air was crisp.

The bus stop was a five-minute walk away. The street was deserted, and so was the station, as expected. At these hours, on holidays like today, a bus would pass here once an hour.

As I approached, a tall man with long, hairy legs showing below his short khaki pants suddenly appeared across the corner. He crossed the road and approached the station. Then I turned and froze for a moment, surprised to see yet another man walking toward us from the other side of the street. I recognized him. He lived a few blocks from us. I occasionally ran into him at the neighborhood supermarket. He was wearing pajamas—the same pajamas he always wore to the supermarket. His eyes caught mine, and he paused, just like I did, and then continued.

We all continued walking toward the station and arrived together at 5:55 AM. The chance of three people in our age group arriving at the same time at this bus stop at this time of year was zero. We stood at the station and looked at each other suspiciously. Apart from mutual polite nods, no one had anything interesting to say.

And then, the realization landed on the three of us at the exact second.

Each one of us had a colorful smirch behind the angle of his right jawbone.

Voices

Hearing voices no one else can hear isn't a good sign, even in the wizarding world.

—*J.K. Rowling, Harry Potter and the Chamber of Secrets*

"Did you also hear...?"

"Yes," said the neighbor in pajamas.

The hairy guy nodded.

The neighbor in pajamas turned around and focused his attention in the direction he came from. Then he left us, silent, gazing forward as he walked away. I wanted to share my surprise with the hairy guy, but his expression had already changed to a focused stare. He, too, turned around and walked back the same way he came. I stood there, stunned.

> **"Have you calmed down? Now go back home before everyone wakes up."**

I wiped the sweat off my forehead. I was very, very far from being calm.

Adam, be methodic. You need to analyze this situation and formulate a tactic to handle it...

So, I was talking to myself through thoughts, but in fact, I wasn't talking to myself because I was thinking thoughts that were clearly not mine.

And I wasn't going crazy—right? What about those two men I saw at the bus stop? Was I supposed to believe their thoughts brought them to the same place and at the same time my thoughts brought me? Was that more evidence I wasn't going crazy?

First my mom, then Eleanor, and the pertussis vaccine, and Eric, and the payments for Iceland—so much noise in my life, from all directions... and now—voices in my head?

Cooperation seemed like my only choice—and choosing to cooperate should have relaxed me. Once you acknowledge there's only one course of action you're supposed to calm down, right?

Wrong.

A one-eyed cat, the neighborhood bully, was sniffing intently at the closed door leading to the garbage containers outside our building. I recognized him and approached his left side, the vulnerable side where he was missing an eye and an ear. He didn't notice me until I was right behind him, then he looked back at me. When I passed him, he started following me, meowing, and complaining about the absence of quality remains in our garbage.

Sorry, cat, I have enough to deal with besides your complaints.

At the entrance to the building, I stopped and leaned against the wall. The handlebars of a bicycle parked there slightly scratched me. I carefully wrapped myself in the morning's dim illumination under the staircase. I put both my palms on my temples and squeezed.

That also didn't change anything. Right, Adam?

"So, who are you?" I entered the apartment and closed the front door. I approached the mirror, passing my hand over the smirch. It was still difficult to refrain from saying my thoughts aloud.

"We're new here. We arrived on Earth two months ago."

"WHAT?" My hand recoiled reflexively. "You're aliens?"

"No. This stereotype is too extreme."

"What does that mean? You're not from Earth, but you're *not* aliens?"

"Do you consider a meteorite falling on Earth to be an alien?

"The universe consists of several fundamental elements. Humans are aware of only a few of them. Pure consciousness is a fundamental element. We are pure consciousness. To simplify, you can assume we're residues of the breakdown and chemical reactions of what you call 'antimatter.'

"But don't worry. We're not antimatter in its classic form, so our contact with matter will not result in mutual 'annihilation.' There's no chance we and you will annihilate each other."

This *We* character was rushing me again—like a tutor preparing me for some test, quickly going over the study material with me. I hadn't realized my cheek had antimatter on it, otherwise, concerns about the 'annihilation' of the matter in my body, through contact with that antimatter, would have been justified. So, it was too late to panic. But more opportunities to panic seemed likely to appear soon.

"Pure consciousness—an element of nature—doesn't need a body to exist. It can freely move in space. Consciousness can propagate from one body to another like energy moving from one mass to another. If you don't consider a stone, light, or energy from outer space to be 'aliens,' you can conclude we're not 'aliens' either.

"We're the 'brain' of the universe. We spread throughout the universe, so the cosmic consciousness would gain knowledge and mature—like any intelligent organism. The universe learns through us."

The 'brain' of the universe...

That didn't come from me. Someone inside my head was contributing content to this conversation—content that was nowhere within the limits of knowledge and worldview I'd held until then. Those were interesting ideas, but they weren't my ideas.

It was happening. I was sharing my brain with some *entity*—maybe more than one. I was asking questions, getting answers, and enjoying that thrilling sensation of learning. I was being exposed to knowledge that surpassed mine.

Me

I think, therefore I am.

—René Descartes

I came out of the bathroom heading for the living room. I cut through beams of sunlight and the dust particles they exposed, and sat on the couch.

Right... The 'pure consciousness' idea... I read something about that a while ago...

Those days I used to wander around 'knowledge marketplace' websites, asking and answering questions. The subscribers were a closed community of knowledgeable 'aristocrats' who held opinions about everything and resented the vulgar folk—those who'd argue about politics and would never use spell-checking software. Those websites were status symbols—the perfect forum to discuss philosophy, theology, and science. Especially, what modern science cannot explain yet.

Humanity has always been obsessed with the nature of consciousness. What does it mean to be *Me*? Why do I experience my body as a single entity composed of multiple organs, and how do I always know where *Me* ends and *Everything Else* begins? How are we different from creatures lacking self-awareness, like sponges, starfish, and sea urchins? What makes us more than just a heap of sensory organs and neurons, but beings aware of ourselves and our surroundings?

The theory of evolution could never explain how consciousness *evolved*—unlike a tail, wings, a sense of smell, or any other feature that evolved due to merciless survival constraints. Neuroscientists, psychologists, and philosophers reverted to ancient theories about consciousness that used to be considered 'mysticism.'

I threw this question into the abyss of my mind as if dropping it down a deep well:

"So, consciousness is a fundamental element of nature?"

And as if an echo came back up that well, the answer came:

"Yes."

Naked

It was the curse of mankind that these incongruous faggots were thus bound together—that in the agonized womb of consciousness, these polar twins should be continuously struggling.

—Robert Louis Stevenson, Strange Case of Dr Jekyll and Mr Hyde

---

I leaned back on the living room couch. Bonnie, who was curled up on her pillow next to the front door, anticipated this move and gathered enough courage to approach me, pressing her nose against my knees.

I had an urge to dig up knowledge from the internet, to equip myself for a discussion with *whatever-it-may-be* that was in my head. But what would I search for? I stared at the ceiling, trying to extract something meaningful from anything I could associate with *the nature of consciousness.*

Shekhinah in Jewish mysticism. Plato's *Anima Mundi—soul of the world.* Those and other ancient *mystical* theories describe the universe as a single, eternal, self-aware entity, independent of any physical body or *matter.* Some consider our consciousness a *fragment* of that monstrous, universal *brain*, and attribute some primary *consciousness* even to chairs, rocks, and other inert objects.

And antimatter? The amounts of matter and antimatter were roughly equal when the universe was very young, but now there's almost no antimatter left in the universe and science can't explain it. Could consciousness—a mystical concept, not *material*—originate from *antimatter*?

"Too early for this."

What the hell...

Like a sudden bolt of lightning in my brainstorm... This was a direct response to what I'd pondered within myself! *No one* was supposed to be exposed to that! Those thoughts were private, and they were *mine*!

"So, that's it? I can't keep my thoughts to myself anymore?"

"You can't."

"Hey! What do you mean, 'I can't'?"

"But they're perfectly safe with us."

How could my brain think two thoughts at the same time? While I was trying to recall—using my brain—any details about cosmic consciousness and antimatter, some other entity was thinking 'surrogate thoughts,' *using the same brain*, and those thoughts materialized in words.

Too early for this? Fascinating. Terrifying. Very problematic. My thoughts were completely exposed to that *We*, while I couldn't access the thoughts of *We*! *We* was deciding which thoughts to share with me.

My thoughts were naked, and someone was peering at them through a keyhole.

Maybe it's some espionage thing... Maybe, the knowledge in my head is important to some foreign, unfriendly government...

I thought up a plan—I'd *restrain* my thoughts to avoid divulging information while getting as many answers as possible from *We*. Sure—but *restraining* my thoughts was, by definition, impossible. Anyway, *We* already knew my plan as soon as I thought about it.

Frustrating...

"What did you mean by *too early*?"

> "You're familiar with very simplistic concepts. You wouldn't understand the full answers to what you've been asking. We'll return to these issues in the future."

What? 'Won't understand?' Me? Come on, try me. I'm intelligent enough!

> "You're on the right path to understanding, but you have a long way to go. You'll need patience to understand all this deeply. Here's one simplified concept:

> "Your eye filters a very narrow range of electromagnetic waves. This range is what humans call 'visible light.' Think of your brain as a similar sensory organ that filters consciousness. It senses a tiny fragment of the entire spectrum of cosmic consciousness waves.

> *"We can expand the spectrum of consciousness of the human brain or any other brain. You could then realize how to locate the missing antimatter, for example. That's currently outside the human brain's range of perception."*

Simple. Painfully simple. Too simple. As if I were a little child, being taught something extremely complex by using simple words and dumbed-down concepts. Maybe I'll never fully understand the complete explanation. But the realization was mind-exploding—it made me breathe heavily. If I'd read this in a book, it wouldn't have come close to that feeling. Beyond words formulated in thought, it was distilled truth. That was a moment of understanding *a truth*.

Bonnie must have sensed the intensity of my experience and figured I'd have no spare attention anytime soon for scratching her head. She gave me a look that had no expectations or disappointments and returned to her pillow to curl up again.

"So why did you come here?" That would likely be the first question humans would ask, whenever aliens land on Earth and engage in the first-ever verbal dialogue with us. But at the level of thought—a deeper, much less disciplined level—the order of my questions made little sense.

> *"We are pure consciousness and nothing more. We lack the body and sensory organs you have. Through you, we can see, hear, smell, taste, and touch—and learn."*

"But I already have consciousness of my own…"

> *"No one's going to erase your consciousness. On the contrary: your senses will sharpen, and your responses to the environment will improve. And you'll expose us to the intense experiences unique to life on Earth. The symbiosis between us is the most natural thing imaginable."*

"So, are you now 'taking over' everyone? Or is it just me and those other two?"

> *"You were chosen carefully out of the entire population. We assign different tasks to each one of you. You're all Singulars."*

Singulars

The real question is not whether machines think but whether men do.

—B.F. Skinner

I was raised to believe I was special. Mom was convinced I'd do great things someday. Recently, on every birthday, a grim reminder would creep into my mind: I haven't fulfilled my potential yet—I had one year less to make my mark and prove Mom right. I was blushing with excitement when my mind formulated the question:

"What makes me a *Singular*?"

"You're designing an Orb."

"Of course! I mean... I am? What's... What's an *Orb*?"

"Sentient civilizations construct Orbs to extend their habitat. Your 'artificial moon' design, an asteroid repurposed for humans to live on, is a simple type of Orb. Humans are the most cognitively mature species on Earth—you were supposed to populate Orbs around Earth more than one hundred thousand years ago. It's the first significant achievement we expect any intelligent civilization to reach."

Yes... Yes! I knew it!

"But humans don't plan for their offspring beyond the next generation. When we arrived, we were surprised that very few people have pragmatic plans for settling future generations outside Earth. Not within a reasonable timeframe. We're investigating what caused the cognitive delay of your species. But there are a few Singular humans, who plan more realistically. You're one of them.

"You're already in the advanced stages of planning an Orb. Your plan is far from complete, but it's interesting and realistic. We're assigning you to manage this project."

I was willing to embrace that. It was a bargain. Among all the ideas I'd ever had, I was ready to believe *that* was indeed the big idea for which life had been preparing me.

I spread my arms and let them rest on the back of the couch. I couldn't take the smile off my face.

I was a successful hi-tech expert, with a record spanning several decades, always keen to keep abreast of every emerging technology: DDoS, LTE, 5G, VoIP, IoT, ML, VR, AR, AI, APT, PON. Every acronym prompted me to reinvent myself, not to lose relevance against the younger, more arrogant generation.

But then, I looked back on all the 'technological achievements' I'd assisted in developing.

We developed sophisticated information security products that were ready for any attack. Still, unlike a refrigerator or an oven where you can just put your hand in to check if it's working, it was impossible to test our products against all conceivable scenarios. Our sales were based mainly on our reputation as experts in the field.

We built real-time monitoring systems for thousands of cameras and sensors, recording our world and storing video footage and measurements in the cloud. We frantically sought ways to analyze this vast blob of data and provide any forecast about the future, which would hopefully be more intelligent than simple fortune-telling. As data accumulated, storage costs skyrocketed, making it harder to justify all that effort.

We built an Artificial Intelligence system, fed with all the knowledge ever poured into the internet, with all of humanity's fears, prejudices, and dark impulses. Then, we'd face this 'oracle,' our creation, and ask it a question. We were thrilled when it vomited the answer back at us, remarkably fluent and perfectly phrased, with the same fears, prejudices, and dark impulses.

The customers were satisfied, but did humanity benefit from the technologies I helped create? Ultimately, my achievements amounted to helping some entrepreneurs get rich and providing job security for a few engineers, whose expertise will forever be in demand to maintain those complex systems.

No. I couldn't point out even one technological achievement I was involved in, that truly helped *advance* humanity. If anything, my achievements so far might have contributed to making the world 'broken.'

The idea of artificial moons stemmed from my guilty feelings. It was my pragmatic attempt to care for the well-being of future generations so they wouldn't curse us for the 'broken' world we were about to hand over to them.

With all the insights I gathered on my own since this idea popped into my mind, on so many topics—astrophysics, astrobiology, asteroid geology, urban planning in space, space entrepreneurship, potential competitors like Egon Mars—I still didn't know how to kick-start such a project. If anything, it would have made more sense for Egon Mars or some other tycoon to be chosen instead of me.

Yet, this was me—Adam the 'eccentric' —who was more innovative and ahead of his time than all humanity. At this point, more than ever, Eric and his investors were welcome *to go to hell*.

> **"We're scouting for candidates for this project and other projects that humanity is lagging with. You and every other Singular will have a specific role according to their skills."**

I blushed with excitement. "So, we're building an Orb together? And other Singulars have other projects? How many of us—

"Wait," a different question broke my train of thought. "You identify yourself as *We*, but this feels like a one-on-one conversation. Are you one or many? Male or female?"

> *"Identity and gender are trivialities. You are free to choose whatever helps you communicate with us."*

Hmm... It feels like I'm speaking with...

"Okay, something about you seems female. I'll address you as a female from now on. And what names do you use? Would I be able to pronounce them? How should I address you?"

> *"Names distinguish individuals. I am identical to all the others who came with me. We don't use names. You can address me whichever way you want."*

Weird... No names... No identities...

"So, how many of us are there? Singulars, I mean. And how do you scout for Singulars?"

> *"There are now a few hundred Singulars like you, who have been assigned roles. The contributions of each one of them will advance humanity significantly. I've chosen you to carry out the Orbs project—I'll help you with that. Others like me are wandering through people's consciousnesses, studying them, without those people realizing it. I've already been with you for five days, studying you long before you noticed me. And so more*

and more Singulars are chosen. Ultimately, we will reach one billion."

I shuddered. "You'll take over one billion people?"

"You shouldn't be concerned. I could have lied to you and said there are only three. I'll always tell you the truth because I want trust between us. Trust is essential for cooperation. I don't expose my thoughts to you, but I'm exposed to yours, so you need to trust me. You must accept I can't share many things with you that I know you're not ready for.

"Like us, human minds all belong to the cosmic consciousness. We came here to ensure your species has matured optimally. You'll engage with the consciousness fabric and enrich it in due time.

"There are many tasks to complete before this can happen. I've chosen you out of many other qualified candidates to assist with one task—constructing Orbs. But if I see you don't trust me, I can always move on to someone else. You can't get rid of me, but you'll soon realize you want me to stay."

Powerlessness. Right then, that's what I felt, and it was relaxing. That was surely the most important event in my life. Alert, with sharpened senses, I tried to absorb as much as possible, to maximize the experience. The flow of information and new insights engulfed me, and I was willingly carried away. Still, one thing didn't sit right:

"You said all of you together compose the consciousness of the entire universe, right? So how is it that I already have consciousness?"

"Your consciousness exists because of us. Ancient creatures never evolved awareness of the finite boundaries of their bodies, and the world beyond those boundaries. More than half a billion years ago, we sent our germinators over here. They landed here 542,039,972 years and 146 days ago. They ignited the initial self-awareness in organisms living on Earth back then."

Five hundred. Forty-two. Million. Years.

Yes, that's the number I remembered. They all came back to me—dusty memories that smelled of old books.

I clutched the back of the couch. I needed that steady touch against my back. A slight dizziness—a sort of *A-ha!* moment—overcame me, like feeling a little drunk. Intense streams of understanding flowed through me. It felt good to understand.

It all made sense. She solved a 542-million-year-old scientific mystery. Decades ago, when I was a university student, I was fascinated with this mystery and explored it on my own, until it sucked up too much of my time and I gave up. I didn't stand a chance anyway: the most outstanding evolutionary researchers of all time frequently argued about it but never solved it. One thing they did agree upon was a name for that mysterious event:

The Cambrian Explosion.

Explosion

The universe gives birth to consciousness, and consciousness gives meaning to the universe.

—John Archibald Wheeler

"Professor… Samuel?"

"ADAM! Why don't you ever *knock*?"

Professor Samuel jumped in his chair. Crumbs of fish food scattered on his shirt, some clinging to his ruffled hair.

"I *did* knock! I *always* knock! You…" I quit protesting. It was pointless. "Never mind. Sorry…"

Whenever I visited him in his room—the most secluded room on campus—I'd always startle him. It was frustrating. Dragging my feet along the corridor, faking loud phone calls, gently knocking on his open door, whispering "Professor Samuel?" Nothing worked. He was always startled.

When I entered he was feeding the fish. In those days, maintaining a saltwater fish tank required some 'black magic.' He did look like a wizard when he leaned in the dark over the magnificent vessel full of extraterrestrial-looking creatures that were swimming around the corals. I had immense respect for that man.

He was the supervisor in my final project at university, on behalf of a large tech company where he worked as a Distinguished Engineer. In other words, he woke up in the morning, decided whether to go to the university or to the company's offices, entered his room, and did whatever he wanted.

There were many topics I could choose from for the final project. Still, before I met Professor Samuel, I had my eye on the project he supervised: *Developing Probabilistic Models for Optimizing Automated Software Testing*. Undoubtedly, it was *the most* boring topic among all the options.

My considerations were more pragmatic than mere intellectual satisfaction: the computer labs assigned to this research were within walking distance from the female students' most popular sunbathing spot on the beach. There was also a high-quality squash court nearby, and the apartment I rented back then wasn't far. So, every day after finishing my work in the labs, I'd change into a swimsuit, go down to the beach, and try my luck with some female students. I always preferred biology or architecture students.

We'd chat a bit, share our complaints about the workload, and at some point, I'd suggest we play squash. If she didn't know how to play, I'd offer to teach her. After sweating and getting tired enough, it became feasible that we'd continue from the squash court to my apartment. Programming in the morning, sunbathing in the afternoon, squash in the evening, and sweaty sex at night. That lifestyle was hard to beat.

As I got to know Professor Samuel better, I learned to appreciate our time working together. He convinced me to publish a joint paper about *Automated Software Testing* in my spare time. I even accompanied him, at my expense, to a conference in Hong Kong to present the paper. During the conference week, I was amazed at how many people all over the world were interested in *Automated Software Testing*.

"You have a few crumbs... in your hair..."

"Thank you..." Professor Samuel brushed his hair with his hand. "How are you progressing? Did you finish consolidating all the sub-models we formulated for the individual tests? With enough research, I'm sure we can come up with some aggregate *super-model* that might allow us to achieve even more optimization. It might even be enough for a follow-up paper. We must make sure no one else is already working on a similar idea."

"I've searched a lot, but it seems there's nothing like that."

"You probably haven't searched well enough. Come, I'll show you how to search."

Professor Samuel turned on his computer. He opened the search engine, typing two words:

'Super Model'

He pressed *Enter*. It was clear what would happen next, but I couldn't stop him.

His screen filled with pictures of young, beautiful, fully nude girls.

I miss those days. No firewalls, no content filtering. The final days of the era of innocence. The internet wasn't so innocent anymore, but most people, including Professor Samuel, were still innocent.

"Okay, let's get back to that later," he said, blushing with confusion as he turned off his computer.

That was a great opportunity. "Do you know what the *Cambrian Explosion* is? I read about it in the library yesterday, but there was very little information."

I always tried to steer the conversation with him to his personal field of research. His true love was evolutionary biology. At first, I just enjoyed watching him talk with enthusiasm, but soon enough, he'd pull me in. I spent extra hours in the library, conducting my own research on the origin of life.

He turned to me as I sat in front of him.

"Did you know Sigmund Freud began his career four years after Darwin's death?" He said, smiling. "An appointment at Freud's clinic could have been Dawrin's chance to spill out all his frustrations with that Cambrian Explosion. He admitted that his theory of evolution could never explain what happened here a little over half a billion years ago.

"You see, the first living creatures appeared on Earth almost four billion years ago. Simple single-celled organisms, 'microbes' absorbing food into their bodies, replicating themselves to reproduce—and that's it. No pretense, no grand plans for future generations.

"No self-awareness." Professor Samuel tapped his temple with his finger.

"For over three billion years, life evolved here at an insanely sluggish pace. Sure, there were already multicellular organisms, and some species even had several genders for more 'sophisticated' reproduction. But those were still simple creatures, mostly shapeless 'sponges,' and the first creatures with a symmetrical body."

And then he added a dramatic tone to his voice:

"Suddenly, almost all of them *disappeared*.

"At the beginning of the Cambrian era, within no longer than *ten million years*—less than a second in terms of the evolutionary time scale—Earth was teeming with a huge variety of complex creatures: creatures with a backbone. Creatures with shells. Creatures with central nervous systems.

"Creatures with *consciousness*." He tapped his temple again. A crumb of fish food broke loose from his hair and fell slowly to the floor. My eyes followed the crumb, but I remained attentive, fascinated by his explanation.

"It's as if someone came to Earth—some 'prehistoric Steve Jobs'—sold brains to everyone like they sell smartphones, and forever changed life on Earth. No one can explain this, certainly not in terms of the theory of evolution. The slow processes of Natural Selection could have never led to such dramatic changes so quickly!"

"Amazing," I said sincerely. "But I did find a brief mention of one theory. Someone claimed all this could have happened because lots of oxygen was suddenly released—tectonic plates moving around, or something like that?"

"A weak argument. It wasn't the only time in Earth's history when oxygen levels changed. And oxygen levels over the eons don't always match the pace of life development.

"And if that's not enough, there's another mystery. *The Great Unconformity*. Strange name, right? Well, if you'd realized that a long, long time ago, someone *peeled* a huge layer off Earth like you peel an orange, what would you have called that?" he chuckled.

"In Earth's prehistory, based on geological findings, there's a *mismatch* between rock layers—a huge 'unconformity.' There's a billion-year gap. It's simply impossible to know what happened here during that time: what creatures lived here, what the environment was like—nothing! As if someone came here and did something really, really wrong on a global scale, and then just 'scraped' a whole layer off Earth, to get rid of the 'evidence.'

"Now, guess which period was permanently erased from history: those were the billion years that ended shortly before the Cambrian Explosion! Very suspicious, isn't it?" Professor Samuel stared at me as if I were a suspect. "Religious evolution-deniers believe this implies some *Divine Intervention*. Or, in other words, the *hand of G—*"

"That's the role of our germinators."

I jumped, startled. The smirch cut off my burst of memories of that talk in Professor Samuel's room, hundreds of kilometers away and decades back in time. She threw me back onto my living room couch, to continue the mental dialogue we were having.

"The germinators integrate into the bodies of mindless creatures. They're the catalysts that enable those creatures to develop a 'central nervous system' —a brain. In creatures like yourselves, built of clusters of 'cells,' this brain refines the structure and function of the cell, allowing a greater variety of differentiation of 'stem cells' into specialized cells. Eventually, the brain takes control of all the organs in the creature's body. This is necessary for self-awareness."

My body twisted on the couch. I'd been sitting for too long and it became uncomfortable, but I willingly paralyzed myself. My head burned up. I didn't try to stop it. I didn't want it to stop. My understanding was absorbing a lot. Too much, maybe—too quickly.

Parasite

Almost all the wise world is little else, in nature,
but parasites or sub-parasites.

—Ben Jonson, Volpone (1606)

"So... so your 'germinators' *implanted* themselves in those creatures? How can that be? And where is that missing layer that was peeled off Earth?"

> "When offspring of a certain organism transition, over many generations, from a state lacking self-awareness to a state of self-awareness, they consume significant amounts of energy and require many resources. That missing layer of matter you're wondering about served in part to fuel those initial transitions.
>
> "The remaining part underwent a complex process of transformation. For simplicity, you can assume it was converted from matter to antimatter to consciousness. The products of those processes constitute the original substance, from which the consciousness of each self-aware creature on Earth evolved."

Funny... The flesh of our brainless ancestors morphed into some invisible 'thinking juice' that fuels our brains...

"The germinators also know how to trace the reproduction cycles of their hosts. Throughout generations, the germinators accelerate the development of consciousness, and consequently, the development of the brain. That's why your brains function the way they do today."

Everything made sense, sort of. Over eons, simple life on Earth had been ignorantly pursuing lazy paths of least action. Then, in an event of Biblical proportions, life unwittingly took a big, juicy bite of the 'fruit of comprehension.' Or, in fairy-tale terminology, life was tempted to chew on some 'poisoned apple,' and immediately entered a 'Snow White sleep' of ten million years.

When life awoke, it was nothing like what it had once been.

The simple prehistoric organisms that had existed before disappeared forever. Their flesh was sacrificed on the altar of consciousness. Since that awakening, the new organisms that had lived here became sophisticated and kept evolving faster than ever. They were *self-aware*.

How fast did life mature during the Cambrian Explosion? How different were offspring from parents? I'd always been frustrated by the huge generation gap between our children and us. Their sophistication, modern ways of communication, alternative online identities, aspirations... Everything was foreign to me. Were parents in the Cambrian era frustrated with how quickly their offspring had become sophisticated? Was it even possible to feel frustration back then? To feel anything?

A human brain, versus the rest of the body—the brain is a 'parasite,' and the body is the 'host.' Thinking about this felt strange—this act of thinking wouldn't have been possible without that 'parasite.'

Every human has an intimate perception of what *Me* means, thanks to the fruits of the 'seeds of consciousness,' sown hundreds of millions of years ago in the bodies of some prehistoric underwater creatures. Creatures that today would surely be classified as 'seafood.'

> *"Exactly. Without us, each individual organ in your body would still have its own nervous system, lacking central control. For example: if your left hand had its own 'will,' your brain wouldn't have been able to instruct it to move in the direction of your head. So, you'd never have been able to accomplish the act of scratching your head, which is what you are doing right now."*

My hand froze as if it had been caught doing something wrong.

> *"You should appreciate your skin—it allows you to perceive the three-dimensional confines of your existence."*

'Appreciate your skin...' Wasn't that the slogan on the poster at the bus stop?

> *"Without central control, none of you would have been capable of understanding yourselves as a complete organism within one*

body, which exists in a world where there are many other organisms, some like you, and some different. You wouldn't have had the ability to be aware of your existence."

"So, you spread consciousness throughout the universe—but why? Why is it so important for you to keep expanding your knowledge all the time? Where does this *urge to learn* come from?"

"You humans accept the 'urge to live' as a given, enigmatic trait of nature. But you mistakenly think your 'urge to learn' is unique to your kind and requires a body and a brain. The 'urge to learn' stands by itself, just like the 'urge to live.' When you combine the two, you get a civilization of self-aware, cognitive creatures."

The 'urge to live' and the 'urge to learn' —this feels important... Why does this feel so important?

Random images raced through my mind, uncontrollably: the Sphinx in Giza, the International Space Station, the Mona Lisa, an Intel processor, the Gutenberg Bible, Bluetooth earphones, the Eiffel Tower, The Smiths, Croquembouche, *Die Hard* 1 and 2, wet wipes, push-up bras, ChatGPT, the Great Wall of China, tanning booths, Stonehenge, Teenage Mutant Ninja Turtles, reality shows, Homer's *Odyssey*, shampoo vacuum cleaners, Paris Saint-Germain, smart toilets, the Burning Man festival, the COVID vaccine...

All of humanity's achievements—and the achievements of all intelligent life on Earth—were made possible thanks to some kind of 'parasite' from outer space…

In the last ten minutes, three new pieces of the puzzle of human knowledge fell into place. As if I was taking a step back, looking at the emerging picture, and realizing it surpassed everything I'd ever imagined.

Aliens

But where is everybody?
—Enrico Fermi

"Wait. Did you say earlier that we are *not* the only intelligent beings in the universe?"

> *"The universe is teeming with life and intelligent civilizations. Each intelligent civilization received a similar treatment to yours from us and has evolved cognitively because of us. First come our germinators, ensure the persistence of consciousness across generations, and help it mature over a few hundred million years. Then we arrive, merge with the most advanced form of life, and assist in further advancing life on the planet to its ideal state. We've been doing this since the early days of the universe."*

"But if there are so many advanced intelligent civilizations out there, why haven't we met any of them yet?" I articulated in my thoughts the decades-old unanswered question known as *Fermi's Paradox*. Was this mystery also about to be solved?

> *"We originally planned for you to contact one of the intelligent civilizations near you long ago. We connect the consciousnesses of all civilizations with each other, thus expanding the consciousness fabric throughout the universe. To interact with*

intelligent beings outside Earth, you don't have to travel and physically contact them. And you don't have to wait for them to come and meet you. Once you're connected to them through consciousness you'll communicate with them directly. Thoughts spread in space almost as fast as light.

"But for humans, we ensured such a connection wouldn't happen at this stage. It requires sufficient levels of maturity from both civilizations."

Several weeks before, I was standing in front of a waterfall in Iceland, trying not to be pushed back by the force of the cold water. The ideas that had just flooded me were like a waterfall of understanding before me, equally powerful and enjoyable. I could almost hear the fourth piece of insight falling into place in the puzzle of universal enigmas. Once again, I felt the flow of those gentle streams of understanding within me.

So, the 'lords of intelligence' decided we couldn't play with intelligent aliens... Why? Aren't we mature enough? Maybe they're not mature enough for us? Or...

Okay, Adam—stop! All this is just too easy.

I'd recently woken up, and it wasn't time for breakfast yet, but I'd already acknowledged the invasion of smirches from outer space. They'd equipped our ancestors with self-awareness, which we inherited. They could answer many questions asked by humanity and other questions we haven't asked yet. Oh, and after millennia of speculation, it appeared intelligent alien civilizations did exist, with whom we shared a *universal goal*: to merge into cosmic consciousness.

Great—but one thing could still shatter this splendid theory. The smirch had become 'female' upon my request. Ignoring the 'inverse mansplaining' I sensed, I began to suspect I'd been conversing with *a female version of myself.*

"*No.*"

"What… What do you mean… *No?*"

> "*No, you're not crazy, Adam. You're still afraid that I don't exist, and your subconsciousness is inventing stories, and you convince yourself they're true. You're afraid you've invented a female 'alter ego' of yourself, and she reminds you of yourself because it is yourself.*
>
> "*You're right: the tone is indeed similar to yours. I'm replicating your tone so this conversation will be easier for you to grasp, but the ideas are mine.*
>
> "*You'll have to convince yourself that everything I told you is true. Eventually, you'll realize you're not crazy. You should keep trying to understand the complete picture. I know you want to learn more.*"

That was true. I wanted more of that thrill of knowing, although I didn't know if that information was reliable. It was the moment to decide—and I decided to overcome the fear of losing my sanity, and surrender to my passion to understand more. I had so many more questions. The most obvious one was:

"Well then, why haven't you allowed us *close encounters of the third kind* yet? Is it us or them? Isn't any civilization in the neighborhood as mature as we are?"

"You're disturbingly inferior."

Shirley's smartphone startled me, buzzing with an alarm indicating it was 6:15 AM. I silenced it. The sudden transition from sitting to standing made me stretch. No one had woken up, and no one would wake up soon. On such days off, the mornings belonged to me exclusively.

"*Inferior*? In what way are humans inferior?"

"542 million years were more than enough time for your consciousness to develop much more than it has till today, even with all the unpredictable catastrophes that life on Earth endured, such as life-destroying asteroids. Something held you back. We're still investigating exactly what that was."

The smirch admitted, for the first time, she didn't have an answer to something. After the immense flood of understanding I experienced during the last half hour, her lack of knowledge made me feel strange.

"I don't have answers to everything. I'm learning, just like you. Your consciousness is based on the same element that constitutes me. When I learn, the universe learns. When you learn, the universe learns."

"So... Everyone in the universe is much more intelligent than us?"

"So far, none of the sentient civilizations on other planets, within the consciousness fabric, had ever experienced such a severe developmental setback. For example, as I said earlier, you should have colonized at least one Orb long ago.

"Throughout the universe, the cognitive and physiological optimization of self-aware creatures at the forefront of evolution is expressed in an improved reproduction rate. Eventually, the population grows so much that they must find ways to settle outside the boundaries of their home planet.

"Any intelligent civilization mature enough cognitively and technologically would expand their habitat to Orbs. We wait for signs of cognitive maturity, such as the construction of the first Orb, which is easy to detect from a distance. When we detect those signs, we come for a second visit to assist. Earth is now positioned at the verge of the consciousness fabric. And the consciousness fabric must always expand."

"Okay, so it's like you've reached Earth riding this wavefront of intellect, where behind you every living creature is cognitively more advanced than us, but wherever you haven't reached yet there is no conscious life?"

"Yes. By now, humans were supposed to be cognitively mature enough to interact with the consciousness fabric so it would expand further. But you're not even close. The maturity level of your consciousness is much lower than the minimum required to connect you with other intelligent beings. There is a risk that you'll contaminate the consciousness fabric.

"What happened here to your consciousness has never happened before, anywhere in the universe. The probability of something like this happening is zero. We still don't have a logical explanation, but we're investigating the matter and will soon find an explanation. Your evolutionary deficit is so drastic that the events that caused it must have left some traces."

"But... if we still haven't built an Orb, then why have you come now?"

"We detected some concerning signals. Eighty years ago, we detected singular events of energy release. The intensities were much weaker than those of volcanic eruptions, and no natural phenomenon could have caused them, yet they were still destructive. This, coupled with the fact that you still haven't launched an Orb, led us to conclude that something may have malfunctioned, and you may need help. So, we set out."

Eighty years ago...

My back was sore. I wanted to get up from the couch. I didn't move.

The first week of last August, with the broadcasts that flooded the media: the commemoration ceremonies, the images burned into memory, the entire month when it was simply better not to turn on the TV.

That museum we visited. Before and after pictures. An old recording of an American news anchor reporting in a dry voice. Bones of a human hand, preserved in a glass window that had melted. Text trying to explain the logic behind all this. Pictures of skinny people. Sick people. Burned people. Charred people.

The tears in Maya and Eden's eyes. Ben, who wet his bed that night. Eleanor's nightmares. Shirley and I, wondering if exposing the kids to all this was worth it. Our camping trip to see the meteor shower in the desert was our escape from all that, our attempt to balance out the horror.

The events of those years shook humanity to such an extent that we have never fully recovered. It turned out the impact echoed beyond Earth.

That's exactly what happened back then:

Hiroshima and Nagasaki.

Atom

I know not with what weapons World War three will be fought, but World War four will be fought with sticks and stones.

—Albert Einstein

> "Correct. When we were on our way here, we recorded the pace of these energy releases. Initially, it rose consistently, but then it declined, and today it's close to zero.
>
> "During our initial reconnaissance among you, we learned about World War II and atomic bombs, and the agreement signed since then prohibiting nuclear tests above ground. But we also understood that experiments continue underground. There are also experiments conducted in space. You persist in inventing new methods to destroy yourselves."

"Why did it take you eighty years to arrive? Don't you have a spacecraft that can approach the speed of light or something like that?"

> "Eighty years is a negligible amount of time. Interesting transformations usually require tens of thousands of years to occur. Your ancestors had deviated from any reasonable timeframe for terrestrial consciousness to mature, and whatever caused that had happened eons ago.

> *"And we don't need spacecraft. We propagate over celestial substances—comets, asteroids, and meteorites—we can absorb ourselves into any physical matter, much like energy. We are located on the inner disk of asteroids surrounding you, and the outer layer encompassing your solar system. We monitor you from all directions."*

What? The outer layer and inner disk? That must be the...

The *Oort Cloud* and the *Kuiper Belt*. I wouldn't have known what the smirch was talking about if I hadn't stumbled upon that website with the nerdy Astrophysics article, a few months back. But there was that inexplicable conviction again, the confidence: that information wasn't based on any memories of mine—it was revealed to me by someone who *wasn't* me. And it was *true*.

They've been watching us for half a billion years... What for?

That concerned me—but I was satisfied I'd managed again to translate those new facts into scientific concepts I'd recognized. The Kuiper belt is a wide ring of rock and ice in endless orbit. It's relatively close, barely seen from Earth. But it dwarfs next to the Oort Cloud—an immense spheric minefield of celestial fragments, two light years away. That's the ultimate boundary of the solar system, surrounding us from all directions but too far to be seen from Earth. We can only calculate its location. Inside that giant balloon, the Kuiper Belt is like a tiny washer, and our solar system is like a few grains of sand. Most comets and asteroids ever observed pass through the Kuiper Belt or the Oort Cloud.

A memory surfaced. I was a kid in elementary school, glued to the TV screen, watching the live broadcast of the Voyager-1 spacecraft launch. In 1993, this spacecraft passed near the Kuiper Belt, and it would have to continue its lonely one-way journey and survive over 300 more years to reach the Oort Cloud.

With such coverage of the solar system from all directions, the smirches may have intercepted a brief event like an atomic explosion. Still… Light emitted from Japan reached the Kuiper Belt after a few minutes, and the Oort Cloud by 1947. Either way, it must have been too faint to indicate any 'anomaly.'

If they'd concluded an 'anomaly,' they must have come from…

> *"…somewhere closer. Correct. We also populate many celestial objects orbiting the sun. Eighty years ago we were on an object you call 'Chiron.' The abnormal combination of intensities and wavelengths made us change course for landing on Earth. You probably remember the meteor shower you saw two months ago."*

More accurately, the meteor shower I didn't see.

> *"We landed here that day. Since then, we've been gathering information and preparing you."*

"Preparing us for... what, exactly?"

"For the next era in your cognitive development. From now on, Earth is also our home. We'll find the cause of your anomalies, return you to a proper course of evolution, and advance intelligent life on Earth to an optimal state for the benefit of all of us."

Breathing

Breathing is the greatest pleasure in life.

—Giovanni Papini

The street bustle became louder, but there was still no sound from the bedrooms. They all overslept. Once again, I tried to find a comfortable sitting position on the living room couch.

"You said this interaction with you includes improving my senses. Does this mean that I'll be able to do things I couldn't do before?"

I'd always dreamed of getting a skipper license, but I gave up after two failed attempts to pass the exam. My heart would sour every time I passed by the marina.

"Absolutely. Skills like the ones you're thinking about right now won't be a problem. I'll help you."

"How exactly does this work, this thing with the senses?"

"Pay attention."

Suddenly, I was entirely focused on Eleanor's breaths. I'd heard them from a distance before, but now my attention was pinned on them as if I were right at the side of her bed. She had a nosebleed the day before. It happened to her occasionally on hot days, and her nostrils were a bit congested, causing her breaths to sound different. Then Maya's breaths joined in—long, gentle, and calm as if she were practicing yoga. I always predicted a future for her in alternative medicine. Then I noticed Eden's breathing from under her fluffy blanket. It amazed me that I could hear them from where I was in the living room, let alone distinguish them from the hum of the air conditioner in her room, which was the farthest room from me. Then Shirley's breaths. She was sleeping with her mouth open again. And again, the constant alertness that characterized her both in wakefulness and sleep—the slightest hint of danger would wake her up. Then Ben—his breaths made me think something was troubling him in his sleep. Finally, Bonnie. Shortly after she returned to her pillow, she was already asleep. She was within my line of sight, wrapped up in herself, her tail slightly twitching with each breath. Her elderly breaths were the loudest, but the last ones to sharpen in my consciousness.

I followed those six frequencies, the intervals between them, how much air was inhaled, and how much air was exhaled. The waveforms materialized as if viewed on an oscilloscope screen, and then, as if I solved some mathematical problem at university, in an *Introduction to Communications* course, all these frequencies were superimposed together, to become a single, calm harmony. Algebra, turning into emotion. I was flooded with peace. Family.

"Okay. Very impressive. Also, quite scary. You can actually control me completely."

"Not at all. I can enhance your sensory experience. I can't control your muscles or disrupt your thoughts. As I said, you gain sharper senses and intense experiences, and I'm exposed to your experiences and learn from them. And all of this is for the common goal of bringing the civiliz—"

"...Adam?"

Shirley

Women are meant to be loved, not to be understood.

—*Oscar Wilde*

Someone touched my right hand. I opened my eyes, surprised when realizing they were closed in the first place. Shirley stood over me, a worried look on her face.

"Everything okay?" she asked with concern.

"Yes, good morning," I got up from the couch, stretching my aching back, and kissed her.

"Should I tell her?" I almost whispered the words, and at the last moment remembered I was only supposed to think about the question.

"Soon. Right now, it might be harmful."

"Were you meditating or something?" Shirley looked as if trying to figure out what had been out of the ordinary about me. "And did you go out? I thought I heard the front door before."

"I'm just a little tired." I did feel tired, right? "Yeah, I went out for a short walk. Have you noticed that the air is particularly 'crisp' this morning?" I asked with a grin.

"Right. And the tap water has a velvety texture. Can we cut the nonsense? We need to give Eleanor her medicine soon. Did you take yours?"

"No. Thanks for reminding me…" I said and headed to the bedroom, cursing myself as I grabbed the pills.

I always tried to avoid situations where Shirley would prove to me I'd forgotten something, especially when it came to taking my medication. Shirley's mission-driven character was what defined her. She'd never forget something, be late for something, or let herself lose control. Weed? Shisha? Never. Once, she agreed to try a Space Cookie. Apart from not liking the taste, it didn't affect her.

Spending your life with someone like Shirley is *addictive*. I loved her—idolized her—because of her abilities. My disorganized life paled in comparison, despite all the achievements I used to be proud of. I got used to relying on her to take charge of the operational side of our shared life. For some reason, though, she assumed everyone should be like her.

"But why do I *always* have to remind you?"

Cases where I forgot to take my pills were rare, but I knew what would happen if I spoke out and denied Shirley's statement. I'd be dragged back into the same worn-out argument, based on her claim that my survival in the world for so long till I met her was a miracle.

"You didn't tell me what the dermatologist said yesterday. Didn't she suggest any treatment for that mole? It looks the same."

"She was about to burn it with that electric device she has, but there was a power outage," I said, amazed at how I'd reduced that freakish incident to a triviality. "She'll schedule me for a new appointment."

"Adam, I don't want you to procrastinate with this. Get it over with."

I agreed reluctantly. I'd never lied to Shirley. It wouldn't be easy to make her accept that scheduling another appointment was pointless.

"This is fine. Very soon, Shirley will become a host to one of us."

"I want us to take the kids with the bikes to the park today," Shirley said. "I want you to check that none of the bikes have a puncture, and I'll prepare sandwiches for us."

"Wha—" A single syllable slipped out of my mouth. It wasn't intended for Shirley. She ignored it.

Handling both dialogues at once made me feel I had attention deficit disorder. I was struggling to formulate my responses in thought without arousing Shirley's suspicion. My automatic reaction was a protest. The whole 'smirch' thing was new, so I wanted to examine it myself before Shirley would get a smirch.

"It's not up to you to decide."

I didn't like the firmness of the response, but I put off the confrontation for later.

One after the other, lazily, the four kids got up. We were planning the trip while having breakfast.

Suddenly, the door opened. Bonnie jumped up, barking frantically.

Natalie

The better I get to know men, the more I find myself loving dogs.

—Charles de Gaulle

For several weeks now, we've been trying to solve this riddle.

Natalie—a timid and delicate girl, the youngest daughter of our neighbors Louise and Eddie, and a good friend of Eleanor—was like family to us. She didn't even bother knocking on the door when she came over. Bonnie had always treated her like she treated everyone else, with a wagging tail and licks. That is, everyone except me. That old dog was always afraid of me. Her fear filled me with guilt for something bad I might have done to her in the past and had forgotten. Bonnie had never bitten anyone, and I couldn't recall her ever barking at anyone—not mail carriers, not plumbers, no one.

Until about a month ago.

One day, Bonnie started barking at Natalie—and kept barking whenever she was around. As long as Natalie was sitting, Bonnie was calm. Every time Natalie stood up and walked around, Bonnie resumed barking. Bonnie feared my reaction but didn't stop, even when I scolded and tried to quiet her. All of us, including Natalie, had already gotten used to it but still occasionally kept guessing the reason for this curiosity.

That morning, when Natalie stood at the door, Bonnie's barking was again ear-piercing. Natalie looked indifferently at Bonnie and closed the door. She walked toward us and sat down at the dining table. The barking stopped.

"You should find out why Bonnie is barking."

"What do you mean?"

"Let me try. Press me against her right jaw."

"Press you against... *What*?"

"Do it. This seems concerning."

Bonnie had already returned to her pillow. I got up from the table and approached her. She looked at me with her big, black, sad eyes. I knelt beside her and held her so she wouldn't run away. Then I positioned my head against hers, my right cheek facing hers, and pressed the corner of her right mandible to the smirch on the contour of my right cheek.

It couldn't have been more than five seconds, but what I experienced in those five seconds would remain etched in my memory forever. It's something that can't be described in words—thoughts of a creature that doesn't use words.

It wasn't easy. This insistence, this habit that humans have developed to 'pick' on every organism, every concept, every idea, every emotion, and to attach to each one of them a certain sequence of syllables... With all the advantages of this habit, it necessarily caused injustice to the object. One or two words will never be able to encompass within them the full meaning of what they're supposed to describe. Nature needs no names. Bonnie's thoughts comprised scents, tastes, visions, and, primarily, sounds.

It's difficult for most of us to think like this, but there are a few exceptions. Beethoven, for example: as his hearing deteriorated his works emphasized the lower pitch sounds that he could still hear. But once he went completely deaf and was no longer distracted by the sounds around him, he focused on his inner language of music, and his later works were characterized by fantastic richness.

I tried hard to focus, and Bonnie's thoughts translated to the crude language my own thoughts were used to: *girl... dog... house... scent... danger...*

My heart pounded quickly. I jumped to my feet in a leap. From the direction of the dining table, I felt six pairs of eyes staring at my back in bewilderment. I tied Bonnie's leash to her collar.

"Adam, no need for that. Ben already took Bonnie for her morning walk," Shirley said.

Out of nowhere, I suddenly recalled our trip to Thailand two years back. One morning, we went to the Thai Boxing Club next to our hotel and had a family workout. We also bought a few pairs of professional boxing gloves as souvenirs on that occasion. Without thinking about why I was doing it, I went to the storeroom and pulled out a pair of my size gloves. I dusted them off, but then I noticed a glimmer of light from the drawer and remembered the knuckle duster I bought on the same occasion in a fleeting moment of insanity: two blades for each finger, each blade more than 2 centimeters long. It was such a dangerous weapon that we ensured the kids never knew I bought it. But apparently, I hid it so well from the kids that I forgot about its existence altogether. I took a right-hand boxing glove in my right hand and the knuckle duster in my left hand. I couldn't decide what to take.

"Take the knuckle duster."

I tucked the knuckle duster into the left pocket of my pants, took the right boxing glove and a left leather working glove I found, then returned to the living room and pulled Bonnie with her leash.

"Natalie, come with me and Bonnie. We're going to your house."

"Adam, are you ready to explain all this to me—what's going on with you this morning?" Shirley asked angrily.

"Shirley, I need to check something at Natalie's house. I hope it's nothing. We'll be back soon."

"Why are you taking Bonnie with you?"

"I have a feeling she knows something," I said quietly.

"*What* are you *talking* about?"

I turned to Shirley, and we exchanged glances.

"I'm coming with you," she said firmly.

The four kids looked at each other for a moment, and then they jumped up. Within three minutes, we all arrived at the front door of Natalie's house. Bonnie looked vigilant and determined as if ten years had been just erased from her age.

Eyes

There are different types of Evil Eye:

Ayn—The eye from someone who may love or know you and not have evil intentions towards you.

Hasad—The envious eye from someone who hates or dislikes you or something you have but wants it removed from you.

Nafs—The admiring eye which a person can put on themself.

Nathara—The evil eye which comes from the Jinn.

—Islamic spiritual tradition

Natalie's parents stared at us in astonishment.

"Hi. I apologize for the unplanned visit. Can we come in for a moment with Bonnie?"

"Why?" Eddie asked, blocking Bonnie's way in as she tried to get around his legs. She wasn't a strong dog, but at that moment, it was hard for me to hold on to her and prevent her from forcing her way into the house.

"Bonnie keeps barking at Natalie. She really wants to check something inside your house. She's a smart dog. Would you like to let her in and see what she wants?"

"She won't poop inside the house, right?" Louise asked and directed her piercing look at my smirch, noticing her for the first time. I remembered Louise was obsessed with cleaning and also afraid of dogs.

And she didn't like me.

"No chance," I tried to reassure her.

Louise and Eddie looked at each other, then at us, and then at Natalie. Finally, they cleared the way for us, and we all entered. Bonnie led the way, followed by Shirley and me, Natalie's parents, her brother, her sister, and our kids. A few sniffs later, she found her way to Natalie's room.

As we entered the room, she immediately pulled me towards the right side of the bed, which was against the wall. What interested her was on the floor, beneath the bed. On that side, on the mattress, was also the pillow on which Natalie laid her head every night. Bonnie stretched out on the floor and tried to crawl under the bed, whimpering and growling, with her teeth exposed, unwilling to calm down.

"Keep her away."

I pulled Bonnie back.

"Shirley, hold her for a moment. Make sure everyone stays back."

Shirley took the leash, momentarily surprised by the force she had to resist. Bonnie was close to choking, and her barks sounded like coughs, but that didn't stop her.

I turned on the flashlight on my smartphone, slid my right hand into the boxing glove, and my left hand into the working glove. I lay on my right shoulder close to the bed, with my head almost touching the wall, and pulled out the knuckle duster. The muttering behind me stopped.

I glanced back. Louise hugged Natalie tightly. Natalie's brother and sister peeked behind them. Shirley stood close to the kids, and Eddie was tense like a spring. Everyone remained at a safe distance.

Slowly, I used the glove on my right hand—the same hand that was firmly holding my smartphone—to move away the chiffon cover that hid the darkness under the bed. I pointed the flashlight inwards, following the beam of light and the dust particles it uncovered. Was Louise cleaning here regularly, as I could expect based on my acquaintance with her?

I slid my right hand slowly towards the wall, while my left hand, gripping the knuckle duster with strength, followed the right one, lifting the cover and illuminating each part of the dark space until I touched the foot of the bed. I didn't know why I was doing everything I did... until that moment.

And then, at that moment, I understood how dangerous the situation was.

Because then I saw them.

Eight green eyes. Six of them stared blankly at me. The other two looked in other directions. They were too close to me.

For a brief moment, I froze, dumbfounded. And then—

"Adam!"

Just as those chilling eyes narrowed the short distance between them and my right arm, they met the device in my left hand, which was already in motion on a path so precise, yet incredibly challenging for my shoulder joint, and continued with it until they collided with the wall, accompanied by a brief sound of crackling.

I kept the blades of the knuckle duster pinned to the wall, and carefully tilted my left hand from side to side and in rotations, deepening the wound. And then, slowly, I pulled out my hand with the magnificent creature still nailed to it, as one of its legs was still completing, abnormally slowly, the movement that began when it was still alive. Louise stifled a scream.

Bonnie stopped barking. She approached Natalie, who stood beside Shirley, her face frozen and pale as a statue, and licked her toes that peeked out from her sandals.

George

Intuition is a strange instinct that tells a woman she is right, whether she is or not.

—Oscar Wilde

I rubbed my forearm and left shoulder, to relieve the sharp pain. The spider's massive abdomen was smeared on the wall under the bed, as well as on the working glove and the knuckle duster. The mucus-like texture of the ruptured intestines against the red background of the working glove created an especially grotesque combination. I wasn't sure if there was a risk of exposing myself to an arachnid's venom through contact with its internal organs, so I carefully removed the working glove and used a few paper towels to pull out the distorted corpse. It wasn't easy, as rigor mortis had already caused its eight formidable legs to clutch the knuckle duster forcefully. I placed the enormous spider, the knuckle duster, and the gloves in a plastic bag I got from Louise.

The kids were stunned at first—but they sprang into action and surrounded Bonnie, hugging her excitedly and competing for her licks. Bonnie was ecstatic. Her tail wagged so fast it looked like it was about to fall off. But at the same time, everyone was giving me piercing looks. Bonnie was that day's heroine—and I was the 'freak.'

"Alright, Adam. I'd like you to explain to me right now... *What the hell happened here?*" Shirley asked. I'd always enjoyed watching her when she took charge of a situation. "How did you know there was a spider under the bed? What was that thing with Bonnie? Do you even know if it's poisonous? And if you knew it was poisonous, why take such a risk?"

I took a few seconds to organize my thoughts. "You saw it exactly as I did. Bonnie led us here. How could I have known what Natalie had under her bed? We've already ruled out everything else, so it just occurred to me that Bonnie might be trying to alert us to some danger in Natalie's house. And no, I don't know if it's a poisonous spider, although based on Bonnie's behavior, I suspect it might be."

"So how did you guess you should bring gloves—and that... *thing?*" She looked at the bag with the knuckle duster.

"Intuition." My answer to Shirley was the conclusion of a split-second internal dialogue: I convinced myself that, for the time being, 'the smirch' deserved some descriptive name. In that early stage of our relationship, 'intuition' could be a decent temporary nickname for her. Just like that, the answer I gave her became a 'non-lie.'

"Maybe we should call George and let him take a look at this giant spider?" Eddie suggested, carefully peering under Natalie's bed.

"Great Idea!" I exclaimed. I'd hoped for something like that, that would spare me from further interrogation.

It had been six months since George moved into our neighborhood. He was a solitary, eccentric guy who loved animals. He worked at the zoo outside of town.

Throughout everyone's life, there are occasionally one or two strange, seemingly insignificant coincidences. With George and me, the oddity was that we'd known each other long before he moved here. When I lived in the university dorms, he lived across the hall. Whenever I met him on campus, he'd look sleepy and exhausted.

I'd never have remembered him if it weren't for that incident in the dorms. One night, after midnight, George knocked on my dorm room door. I could barely decipher his tired mumbling. He begged me to let him sleep on the floor of my room just that night. Unfortunately for me, and fortunately for George, my girlfriend didn't come by that night. I agreed, and he sprawled on the floor and fell asleep before I could find him some bedding.

The next morning, he made me swear not to tell anyone and then told me everything. He'd been raising an iguana in his dorm room—severely violating the university's regulations. The temperature in the room always had to be between 27 and 35 degrees Celsius—which explained the strange odor I'd sensed whenever I passed by his dorm room door. The hot fumes from the iguana's litter box filled George's room and made it unbearable to sleep in—till one night, he decided he'd treat himself once to a good night's sleep. Decades later, by chance, he became my neighbor again. Instinctively, I avoided passing by his apartment whenever I could.

We sent a message in the neighborhood group chat and asked George to come and check out some strange animal we captured. He read the message and arrived within five minutes. Whenever I saw him, I lingered on the small pot belly he developed in the past decades, which was disproportionate compared to the rest of his body, as if it was an accessory for a costume he'd bought online and worn under his clothes. Apart from that difference, he looked exactly as I remembered him from my university days: the tousled hair, the week-old whiskers, the hyperpigmented skin from too much sun exposure, and his eternally rumpled training suit.

I showed George the contents of the plastic bag and asked if he could classify the spider's species, and whether it was poisonous. George's eyes fixated on the slimy mess and the three eyes still sticking out of it, as if they were staring directly at him.

Then George began to sob quietly.

"*Sonia!...*" he whispered.

It took me a while, I admit. It was just hard for me to believe that this was the solution to our mystery.

"George, what did you do?"

"They didn't take care of her properly... You see? She's special..."

"Adam, what's going on here?" Eddie asked, and his gaze almost scorched me. I gave him a quick glance.

Eddie was far from being stupid. Gradually, he concluded it was time for him to get angry.

"WHAAAT?" This time he yelled. And before he finished uttering that word, he knew what he should be angry about.

Sonia

Certainly, a wild animal is cruel. But to be merciless is the privilege of civilized humans.

—Sigmund Freud

"YOU'RE A DEAD MAN!" Eddie shouted, lunging at George. I stood between them, taking an extremely powerful punch to my ribs, which was not intended for me but still made me bend over in pain. I bumped into George, who stumbled and fell on the floor.

"MOVE!" Eddie roared at me.

"Shirley, call the police. Eddie, calm down. He'll have to answer to the police. You don't want to get in trouble because of him."

Eddie stood over George, pressing the sole of his shoe down on his Adam's-apple. "YOU'RE NOT GOING ANYWHERE!"

George gasped.

"Eddie, easy," I requested. Reluctantly, he eased the pressure a bit.

Louise approached Eddie and touched his arm gently. It was impressive to see the immense impact she had on him. It took a few moments, but eventually, he calmed down. I wanted answers.

This monstrous animal did not belong here. Keeping it as a pet is a serious crime. Somebody must be missing it.

I took out my smartphone and searched for the word *spider*. It took three seconds. While going through news sites, one unusual keyword caught my eye:

'MEGASPIDER'

One news site had a four-month-old article archived somewhere: it all started at the Australian Reptile Park north of Sydney. A few years back, a box with no sender address arrived at the park. It was received as part of a routine collection of venomous spiders captured by residents—a common practice in Australia. The goal was to 'milk' venom from the spiders and produce antidotes.

When the park employees opened this box, they found a female *Australian funnel-web spider*, the deadliest spider on Earth. That wasn't unusual, as funnel-web spiders are widespread in Australia. What amazed them was that the length of the spider was *no less than eight centimeters*. Before then, no one had seen a spider of this kind longer than five centimeters. That megaspider was unique. Just as George said, she was one of a kind.

All that was just the background story. The real news was that four months ago, the park in Australia reported the disappearance of the spider. Did this spider somehow travel from Australia, settle under Natalie's bed, and stay there for a few days? Maybe a few weeks?

Perhaps it was pure luck that Natalie hadn't reached under her bed with her hand and that Louise hadn't cleaned there recently?

Is it possible that I was responsible for ending the life of that megaspider with a knock-out?

I shivered.

The news of the spider's disappearance briefly made headlines and then faded. There was no chance for such an article to receive special attention from me or most people I knew. And there was no chance I'd associate this news with my brief encounter with George, around the same time, when I noticed he'd returned from the airport. I mean, I realized he'd traveled when I saw him return. He was dangerously tanned, had a blush on his face, and was in a hurry. He briefly told me he'd accompanied a scientific delegation visiting several wildlife parks in the Far East. I expressed interest for about forty seconds, asking myself if I should envy his lifestyle, and each of us went our way. And that was it.

When the police arrived, they called the station and corroborated the unfortunate demise of that rare, lethal creature that had been missing on the other side of the world—and their faces became stern. They questioned everyone present and several other neighbors. George cooperated. He told them how he smuggled the spider out of Australia, showed them where he'd kept her, and explained how she could have escaped from his home and hid under Natalie's bed for a month. The secret of my alliance with the smirch seemed safe. The police found my 'intuition' story reasonable and didn't suspect any 'foul play.' Yes, hiding the truth from Shirley, and facing the police, were enough to make me think like a criminal.

But Shirley wouldn't give up. I was eager to tell her.

"Patience. It will soon be okay to share all this with her. You'll understand everything soon."

I handed the plastic bag to the police, with all its contents, happily parting with the knuckle duster and finally convincing myself that its purchase was justified. The police put George in their car without handcuffing him and drove off.

Just before we returned home, I saw Louise coming out of Natalie's room with rubber gloves in her hands, holding a scrubbing brush and cleaning spray. She whispered something in Eddie's ear for a moment, and he called me.

"Adam, tell me, do you remember where you got Bonnie from?"

"Sure," I smiled.

Lies

Marriage is the triumph of imagination over intelligence.

—Oscar Wilde

"BEN—ENOUGH!"

It occurred to me how accustomed I'd become to associating Ben's laughter with the sight of him running away—and a little mischief.

"YOU MUSTARD!" Natalie yelled after Ben, while frantically brushing her hair with her hand. He looked back at her, frowning. Was that a curse?

"Don't worry, Natalie," I used my calm voice. "There are no poisonous spiders around here—certainly not in this park. Just ignore Ben."

"Ben—I'm watching you. No more spider-hunting! And don't put anything on anyone's hair!"

I noticed, to my relief, that Natalie wasn't afraid. After the bizarre events of that morning, I was a 'spider expert.' I watched the tiny spider slide down on an invisible thread from her hair to the ground and disappear, probably wondering what the fuss was about.

We spent the afternoon in the park with our bicycles. It took some effort to convince Natalie to join us and relax. She was initially agitated, but eventually, she came along. She'd recently learned to ride a bike and wanted to practice. That was an added incentive.

My smirch was silent all afternoon. I took some time to digest the events of that morning, knowing that my thoughts were fully disclosed to a third party. When I was a kid, lunatics occasionally walked on the street and talked with invisible partners. Nowadays, people close million-dollar deals while walking on the street and talking with invisible partners through a tiny earpiece. The differences between my partner and theirs were that my partner wasn't invisible, didn't look like an earpiece, and our conversations were at zero volume.

So, that's your way out of the mess in your life, Adam? The smirch?

Everyone returned home tired and went to bed earlier than usual—a relief from Shirley's persistent cross-examination. I could hardly sleep that night. I wanted to make sense of everything that happened during the day and align expectations with the smirch regarding Shirley.

Many years ago, when I realized that my relationship with Shirley was heading in a serious direction, I did something shocking—I even shocked myself. Contrary to the limited guarantee I allowed myself with my previous relationships, I decided I'd never lie to Shirley. Since my first girlfriend had broken my heart, I didn't dare remove all my barriers and defenses for any other girl. Then, Shirley came along. I could never understand what made me maintain complete honesty with her. Every few years, whenever I paused for some soul-searching,

I'd shockingly discover I stood by this decision. Compared to all the other goals I'd set for myself in life—to always stay fit, to work less and earn more, to spend more time with family, to visit my parents more often, to find activities for the kids that would keep them away from their screens—achieving 100% honesty with Shirley filled me with supreme pride.

Of course, I couldn't brag about this achievement to anyone. It was pointless to estimate the vast number of arguments I could have avoided if I'd succumbed to replacing the truth I told Shirley with those incredibly creative 'white lies' always ready to fire on my lips. Now, I feared that the fact that I'd hidden information from her over time would lead me to lies.

"There's no need to fear, as long as the lie serves our purpose."

"I'd be happy to know why our purpose requires lying to Shirley. Maybe then I'll be convinced that lying is justified…"

"You have a neighbor, Iris."

"Iris? Sure, I've known her well since she was a baby. She's the eldest daughter of the neighbors, good friends of ours. She has already started a bachelor's degree in bioinformatics, and she is also a professional dancer, performing worldwide, and she's only fifteen. She'll be sixteen next month. Her parents, us, and the whole neighborhood are all very proud of her. Without a doubt, an impressive young girl. *What the hell does she have to do with all this?*"

"You're supposed to mate with her."

SMIRCH—God is Gambling to Survive

Strings

First love is only a little foolishness and a lot of curiosity.

—George Bernard Shaw

Okay, so from that moment on, things got complicated.

Six words, *You're supposed to mate with her,* and that's the trouble they got me into.

Our brains are programmed to sense the world in four dimensions: length, width, height, and time. Time always flows constantly forward, beyond our control. But memory and imagination elevate the way we experience time. For example, to catch a ball thrown at you, you remember its trajectory *in the past* and use your imagination to estimate its path *in the future*.

Imagination lets us experience the dimension of time 'from above,' the same way we view space. Using your imagination, you can move through time, forward or backward, faster or slower, or even stop it altogether. You can do that only through imagination—or with a time machine, which most likely you don't have.

The *String Theory* leads humanity's quest to understand how our universe 'ticks.' This theory claims that the universe spans a space of not four, but exactly *ten dimensions*. We cannot perceive the other six dimensions—only describe them through mathematics.

Perhaps some prehistoric creatures could perceive more dimensions. Throughout evolution, offspring that could focus on the four dimensions familiar to us, and ignore the other six, may have been more successful in their struggle to survive.

Maybe a few lucky mutants among us perceive five dimensions or more. Einstein and Darwin's achievements are still challenging for most people to understand because they demand envisioning phenomena that occur at extreme speeds or over millions of years. Could these two geniuses have been born with mutations that gave them multidimensional vision, so they could easily qualify as *X-Men*?

Those mysterious six dimensions have become a 'blind spot' for the rest of humanity. They're like infrared, ultraviolet, Wi-Fi, Bluetooth, or any other electromagnetic radiation that differs from red, green, or blue, because our eyes and brains cannot interpret their frequency as a color we can see.

Our senses let us grasp the present situation. Our imagination allows us to illustrate situations that happened or didn't happen, fictional or realistic—to plan and prioritize different scenarios as if we were experiencing them now, in four dimensions, with time flowing forward and backward at whatever speed we want, with all our senses. With this modest combination of dimensions and senses our imagination can run wild.

Our cravings and desires have been shaped over hundreds of thousands of years, to ensure the survival of Homo Sapiens. Then, less than 4,000 years ago, seemingly out of nowhere, humans formulated the principles of morality to tame those cravings. Surprisingly, young morality keeps winning the mental struggle against our ancient cravings.

But no matter how moral you are, certain situations may sometimes pop into your head—situations unrestrained by morality. Morality may be expressed in what you do, or don't do, but no one can tame your imagination.

Not even you.

If your imagination runs wild and deviates from the bounds of morality, and, by chance, an extraterrestrial entity has stuck to you, with the ability to read your thoughts, you need to ensure that misunderstandings do not arise.

That's what happened to me. Six words, *You're supposed to mate with her*, caused my imagination to plunge into a sequence of situations, tangible to the point of pain, encompassing all my senses, the three spatial dimensions, and the dimension of time, which I raced through at a high pace with no foot on the brake and no hand on the steering wheel.

The figure of Iris as I never intended—never dared to think about her. Her flowing auburn hair. The curves of her body—a dancer's body. The freckles. She feels some childish and naïve attraction towards me—maybe curiosity, maybe foolishness. I'm tempted. One overwhelming night. Her eyes—looking at me and smiling, as I lean over her. Desire hormones rush in waves. Endorphins. Oxytocin. The brain is excited. All the considerations, commitments, constraints, and those mind-boggling feelings of guilt—they all give in to something marvelously simple, a well-defined goal with clear instructions: keep the pace... keep the pace... the pace...

I'm her first. Blood. A big secret with a short expiration date. A scene with Shirley and Iris's parents in the neighborhood garden. The neighbors—staring. The children's traumas. Crying—lots of crying. Handcuffs. Prison. Divorce. Guilt. Loneliness. The end.

"Do you understand now?" I threw the words into the void of my thoughts as that horror movie ended.

> *"I understand. So, Iris can move in here as another member of your family unit and serve as an additional partner for you."*

Thrill

Bigamy is having one wife too many. Monogamy is the same.

—Oscar Wilde

She's not giving up!

Inevitably, I was dragged into yet another scenario in my mind—a sequel of the previous one, with an important twist in the plot: Iris's parents, in some magical way, are convinced to let her join my 'harem.' But the true magic happens when Shirley agrees, and even the kids welcome Iris into our home. Despite all the fantastic things happening in Iris's life now, she prefers to become my second wife, and eventually, she and I have children together. I'd never considered bigamy and wasn't even sure if it was legal.

> *"We'll marshal everyone involved as hosts, starting with Iris's parents and Shirley. Then, all this will be easily achievable."*

I plunged into a third, much more intense delusion. The bizarre phantasms that passed through my mind had criminal implications—but the 'parasites' that recently landed here encouraged them and would assist in making them a reality. How could this be possible? Could those smirches change our social structure, what's allowed and what's not, and turn such a foul scenario into a legitimate one?

A sudden forbidden thrill ran through my loins. Something young and impudent, which I remembered vaguely, but hadn't felt in many years.

I sat in bed and shook my head. Shirley turned around to face me—I froze. Then she stopped, and her breath returned to a calm, deep rhythm.

There was already one clear consequence of this conversation. Every future encounter with Iris would feel completely different than before. It was better to avoid her altogether.

"I get it that you can be connected to all the knowledge accumulated in the universe so far," I thought angrily, "and that you and your colorful friends want to establish a fruitful relationship with humans. But you'll need to learn some things about the social norms *accepted* in our 'primitive' world, and especially about what's *not accepted*. Certainly not in the last hundred years. Certainly not in the society I belong to. I still don't understand why it's so important for you that Iris and I 'mate,' and how you'll convince her it's the right thing for her—if that's what you intend to do.

"But I can't just take a fifteen-year-old girl, just like that, even if for some reason *she* wants it, and make her my wife. Not the first one, and not the second!"

"Why?"

That moment felt special, and I lingered on it. It finally hit me. So far, the smirch had been establishing facts. She didn't need my help to expand her knowledge. For the first time, she asked me something, something she didn't know the answer to. She waited for me to think about the answer, so she could tap into my thoughts and 'read' my answer.

Then, I paused a little longer on something else, quite surprising. The smirch asked a naïve, childish question. I was about to recite the automatic answer in my mind—the mind of a moral human. But why did I have to teach the smirch about gender equality and the condemnation of pedophilia? Why weren't those noble ideas universally recognized and self-explanatory? Why couldn't I come up with a more convincing justification other than the banal statement 'because humans are moral?'

Indeed—why?

Why?

Morality, like art, means drawing a line someplace.

—Oscar Wilde

"*Why*? I'll tell you *why!*" I tried to buy some time, simultaneously organizing my thoughts into a coherent answer. The lingering effects of that burst of fantasies, which I was still trying to recover from, made it difficult for me to do so.

"Because it's considered exploitation of a minor!" I finally conjured up a coherent thought. There were so many answers to this question, and they all popped up in my mind—but the uncontrollable order in which they came was problematic.

Why was 'exploitation of minors' the very first argument my mind came up with? Why did it take me longer to remember I shouldn't cheat on Shirley? What would the smirch conclude of this? What does this mean about me?

I had a lot to explain to the smirch anyway. I followed that awkward order. "In modern society, there are rights and duties for every individual. Men and women, boys and girls, the elderly—everyone is entitled to equal opportunities to live with dignity. I can't believe for a moment it's possible and certainly don't want it—but if I pull Iris out from the meteoric path she's currently on, for the sake of my whims,

I'd rob her of an opportunity for self-fulfillment and accomplishments, and lower her self-esteem! I'd downright exploit her! Even if you could somehow brainwash her and make her choose it, her choice would be meaningless because she isn't mature enough yet to make such decisions!"

"So, if you mate with Iris, even if she wants it, you'll be 'exploiting' her?"

"Of course!" The word 'mate' echoed in my mind long after the smirch finished exclaiming her question. I struggled to avoid visual thoughts.

"Ages ago, such things were accepted and normative. Women were treated as objects that could be bought and sold, and their main purpose was to bear children. But we've progressed since then—at least in most of the world. There are still cultures where treating women like that isn't wrong, but those cultures are considered primitive and undeveloped.

"Now, there are different kinds of people, and for some, it's harder to control their 'animal-like' cravings and avoid exploiting others. There are laws for such people and severe punishments for such crimes."

"So, the thoughts that passed through your mind a few moments ago—are they related to your animal-like cravings?"

Aaahhh...

"Sometimes, people have uncontrollable thoughts that don't necessarily reflect what they intend to do. No one can read minds. So, if someone *only thinks* about something they're not allowed to do but doesn't *go ahead and do it*, no one will punish them.

"See, Iris is still a minor. In modern culture, under a certain age, a person's judgment is not mature enough to take responsibility for their actions. Someone like her, who is too young, may act naïvely and irresponsibly, and certain people may exploit that for their benefit and against the interests of that immature person. Iris is still a minor, so she shouldn't be the subject of sexual desire by someone my age. It would be considered immoral, and I'd be exploiting Iris for my 'animal-like' cravings. And there is zero tolerance and severe punishments for exploiting women, especially minors."

"When will Iris stop being a minor?"

"As far as I remember, the law considers a person's judgment when they're over sixteen."

"So, in one month, you can mate with her."

No—this is insane!

Explaining these simple concepts to the smirch was surprisingly challenging. What happened to her? How did she turn into this relentless, tactless matchmaker?

"In modern society, morality comes first," I thought, frustrated. "Anyone who wants to belong to society must act according to the principles of morality. The law tries to force people to adhere to morality, even if they don't do so automatically. But long before you break the law, you need to be moral.

"If I weren't married to Shirley, and if Iris were at least twenty-five, and if both of us were interested in it, then maybe it would be morally acceptable. But could you please just stop for a moment and tell me *why the hell* you think it's so important that I 'mate' with Iris?"

"Iris is still unaware of it, but she's a Singular. She's already become a host."

Shiver

The naked woman's body is a portion of eternity
too great for the eye of man.

—William Blake

> "We recruited Iris for the Orbs project based on her skills. She'll report directly to you. You'll construct at least ten Orbs. Considering the human lifespan and typical intelligence level, this project requires three generations.

> "Iris is already in her fertility stage. In the coming decades, you and Iris will bring offspring, and I'll collaborate with the one Iris is hosting to tune the cognitive development of your offspring for this project. The offspring that you'll have with Iris will grow up in an environment where they'll learn about the project firsthand, engage in your activities as they grow, and continue your legacy."

Our legacy? Iris is... She's just a kid... And what about Shirley?

> "Shirley is irrelevant: soon she will no longer be able to bring offspring, and she lacks any knowledge and cognitive abilities that would be beneficial in the context of the Orbs project. Based

> *on our observations of her, we assume Shirley may react negatively when she realizes you're supposed to mate with Iris."*

That's a fair assumption...

> *"You must not reveal our existence to Shirley, because her unpredictable reaction could risk this project. But she shouldn't worry. Shirley will soon become a host. We'll find a use for her in another project very soon."*

I was appalled by the extreme lack of sensitivity of this plan. But I was also appalled by the horrible fact that it made sense.

"You do realize that people can work together and achieve impressive goals without the need to 'mate' and bring children together who will continue their legacy, right?" I responded in my thoughts, yet still pondered the potential of the model the smirch presented. Could the Great Wall of China have been built in less than 2,000 years, if it had relied on the labor of entire families, by consent, over several generations, instead of forced labor?

> *"You're beginning to understand. I also want to understand how your species became Earth's most advanced life form—and how you survived to begin with."*

That could have been the first time a non-human offended a member of the human race. "Hey! What the hell does that mean?"

> *"Not only is the development rate of your consciousness dangerously slow—you also create all sorts of artificial barriers, like this problematic concept of 'morality,' which will make it even harder for you to improve the quality of your offspring."*

I was fed up. My thoughts, which raced through my mind, were completely exposed. In addition to them, other thoughts passed through my mind. Those other thoughts weren't mine, ideas I didn't even agree with, a worldview opposed to mine. My brain worked twice as hard and was busy *arguing with itself*.

"I don't even have the energy to respond to this. I need to sleep. I hope I've explained myself. We'll solve this in the morning. Good night."

"Good night."

I thought I hadn't slept, but suddenly there was light, and it was already 8:22 AM. I thought Shirley had left for work without saying goodbye, but then a faint memory, like a dream, came to me of her kiss and her voice urging the kids to leave for school. I thought it was the alarm clock, but it was the doorbell.

"Just a minute!" I shouted.

I had a conference call scheduled at 10:00 AM with a potential customer, and I'd already prepared myself for it the day before. I planned for a relatively relaxed morning while putting on a T-shirt and my favorite shorts—unfortunately, Shirley classified those shorts as boxer underwear, and never let me wear them when we had guests.

I walked towards the door and opened it, not bothering to look through the peephole. I froze, and the sudden shiver that passed all over my body felt more intense.

I barely restrained my automatic reaction to what I saw, and the visions that flooded my mind. My brain initially categorized the visual signals from my eyes as *stimulating*, but I forced myself, horrified, to settle on *aesthetic*. In another circumstance, it would have been difficult to choose where to direct my gaze, and I'd have quickly come to my senses, looked down at the floor, and tried to avoid embarrassment. But at that moment, my eyes wouldn't move. They were magnetized to one thing.

A multicolored stain, partly concealed by bright auburn curls.

Iris

You cannot swim for new horizons until you have courage to lose sight of the shore.

—William Faulkner

Iris and I stood facing each other with gaping mouths, like two fish lying on a fishmonger's counter somewhere in East Asia. It lasted almost half a minute, and then I came to my senses and invited her in. She hesitated, standing at the door, then came in and settled on the nearby chair in the dining area. I apologized and hurried into the bedroom, angry at myself as I changed my pants, accepting Shirley's verdict about them. I returned and sat opposite Iris.

"What's going on, Adam?" Iris said as I returned. "Do you have anything to do with this?" She pointed in the direction of her neck.

What made her come here?

"So," I asked her, "you had no idea I also have a 'mole' like yours on my cheek, right?"

"A MOLE? Is that what it is?" Iris was alarmed. "What—how come we both have it? I haven't met you in… in more than a week! Is it contagious? Like a skin disease? Is it dangerous?"

"No, it's not like that at all. You can relax." I worried that the explanation I was about to give her wouldn't calm her down, but stress her further. "So, why did you come here?"

"I started hearing these weird voices—more like thoughts—in my head. They insisted I must prove to myself that I haven't gone crazy, and said you could help me with that."

Clever. So, they appointed me as their 'evangelist.' Quite effective.

"Look, what I'm about to tell you will sound completely bizarre, and I still don't have answers to everything. I've known you for a long time, and I know you can approach this objectively. Like a scientist."

Iris smiled, and I remembered when she came over with her parents, long ago. She was very young then, and her braces made it hard for her to speak. She was in some program for gifted children, and had come up with a riddle about a tetrahedron—I was the only one around interested in hearing about it. Since then, we had many conversations about math, astrophysics, and biology. That nerd blossomed and turned into this incredibly smart and beautiful young girl.

I told Iris everything I knew, except for that minor detail about the aggressive attempt to have us 'mate' with each other. My smirch was unusually quiet, but Iris said that her smirch was communicating with her throughout our conversation. I prayed the smirches would spare another display of tactlessness from us, and indeed, the topic of 'mating' didn't come up.

Iris's calm reaction impressed me. Realizing you had an alien stuck to your cheek... Well, not an alien... A self-aware element of nature, infinitely more intelligent than you...

"So those 'smirches' chose you to lead this 'Orbs' project and want me to join too? And I'd be reporting to you? In what role? I'm just starting my bachelor's degree. This sounds super interesting, but I'm not changing my plans unless I know exactly what's going on," she said, sounding like any fifteen-year-old girl who knows exactly what she wants to do in her life.

"I certainly wouldn't dare ask you to give up anything. I'm just telling you what I was told. What I did understand from them is that this project is long-term. It's planned for several generations ahead, and I have no idea when they plan to start. Maybe even in a few more years. I see it as a mission that will benefit all humanity, maybe only in a few generations. I might not even live to set foot on the first Orb in my lifetime. But it seems to me that *you* might." That was, in fact, the 'censored' version. I pronounced 'you' instead of 'our offspring.'

"So, what are we supposed to—" Iris suddenly fell silent, her face blushing, her freckles emphasized. She lowered her look.

"What is it?"

"My smirch wants me to attach him to yours."

Vision

On the secretly blushing cheek is reflected the glow of the heart.

—Søren Kierkegaard

I blushed too.

"Okay, listen. I feel like you need some time to process this. It's completely new for me too. Take your time, think about it, and call me when you're—"

"No. It's okay. I'm ready. Are you?"

"Yes," I said, not knowing what I was ready for.

Slowly, we moved closer, cheek to cheek. Just before we made contact, Iris brushed her hand through her hair, exposing a white ear, and a sweet, fresh scent of perfume emanated from her neck. Her smirch revealed itself in full view—slightly larger than mine and slightly closer to the back of the neck. I was focused on her smirch and shivered when Iris gently placed her right hand on my left shoulder and pulled me towards her. I also put my right hand on her left shoulder, and an old memory surfaced as my fingers felt her bra's strap. In my debaucherous youth, I developed a talent for guessing the type of bra, by touch, through a blouse. It had been most useful while making out, as my goal was to unhook the bra. I immediately recognized it—a cross-back clasp sports bra stretched just right. I scolded myself as I pulled out of that journey in the past, quickly sliding my finger away from the strap.

We pressed our cheeks together.

At first, I stared at the entrance door, and Iris stared at the glass door that led to the balcony. Then it became clear how I knew what Iris was seeing. Somehow, I was indeed seeing through her eyes, and I assumed she was also seeing through mine. We were sharing two pairs of eyes. Then, everything disappeared, and darkness remained.

From that moment on, we shared the experience. We saw stars twinkling from all directions. I looked down. My feet were gone, and so was the rest of my body. I became a point without volume. The feeling was an intensified version of what you'd feel when wearing a virtual reality headset. There was something I saw—familiar, blue and white.

We were floating high above Earth.

Everything started flowing frantically: images and sounds, smells, and tastes. We didn't see our bodies, but our senses picked up everything, and it was all burned into memory. There were 'things' we experienced that we didn't perceive through our familiar senses, things that no words in any language in the world could describe. Everything we saw and experienced fell, until those moments, under the category of things that are extremely difficult, if not impossible, to implement. The explanations were excellent, and the plan was clear. Iris and I just started the course *Introduction to Orb Construction*. The plan presented to us was much more practical than the 'donut' I'd been working on in the past year. This course would equip both of us with all the knowledge required to approach the challenge.

A plan for colonizing Orbs

Summary of the Objectives (adapted to Earth):

- The goal is to establish ten Orbs in three stages within 160 years.

- In the first stage, one Orb will be placed in orbit around the natural moon.

- In the second stage, three additional Orbs will be placed in orbit around the natural moon.

- In the third stage, six additional Orbs will be placed in orbit around Earth.

- The Orbs will serve as habitats for humans and animals, requiring Earth-like conditions, including gravity, atmospheric pressure, magnetism, photosynthesis, climate, protection from cosmic radiation, maximum population density, and more.

- Each Orb will accommodate a population of at least two million people.

- Existing technologies, as well as technologies currently under development, for populating Earth's natural moon and Mars, must be made available for the purpose of establishing Orbs, and, if necessary, adapted for this purpose.

- The Orb will be built around a core, originating from fragments of an asteroid or a whole asteroid.

- Existing technologies for altering the trajectory of an asteroid must be improved and adapted for the purpose of towing the core safely close enough to Earth.

- The asteroid must be reinforced and stabilized so that the forces exerted on it do not cause its disintegration.

- The tilt angle of the rotation axis of the Orb around itself, as well as the direction and speed of rotation, must be defined.

- For each of the Orbs, whether orbiting the natural moon or the Earth, an optimal orbit height must be defined.

- Human physiology is still primitive and prevents their survival without Earth-like gravity. The Orb's gravity must match Earth's.

- The habitable surface area will rotate with the asteroid to create minimal artificial gravity.

- Supplementary technology for achieving Earth-like gravity will be shared with no more than three humans, all at least 20 years old and younger than 30.

- This supplementary technology is based on [————————] and will require [——————————————].

- The asteroid must be surrounded by an artificial layer preventing the escape of gases that compose the atmosphere.

- Materials for building the habitat surface will be mostly sourced from the asteroid itself, with some materials transported from Earth or manufactured in space.

- Additional technologies will be required to complete the preparation of Orbs for human-adapted life, such as magnetic fields, radiation shielding, water production, plant growth, and atmosphere creation.

- Most complementary technologies are already being developed by private companies and government agencies as part of the effort to populate the natural moon and Mars.

- All existing developments must be pivoted for the benefit of populating Orbs.

Oscar

In law a man is guilty when he violates the rights of others.
In ethics he is guilty if he only thinks of doing so.

—*Immanuel Kant*

I felt the out-of-body experience had ended. I opened my eyes. Shirley stood right in front of me, still holding the handle of the door, which was half-open. Then I realized Iris and I had shifted into a hugging position during the 'course.' We were close. Way too close.

The first thought that crossed my mind was, "Good thing I changed my pants." I recoiled, breaking contact with Iris. I heard a faint 'tick' and sensed a tingle where my smirch was.

Iris opened her eyes and looked back, then jumped to her feet, pale as a ghost.

"No, I was just... I have a meeting... I just stopped by to get a document I forgot..." Shirley said, as if trying to apologize. "It should be in the room... No, actually..." She collapsed to the floor, breathing heavily, her hands hugging her knees.

My heart pounded hard. I approached and kneeled beside her.

"DON'T TOUCH ME!" Shirley screamed, causing me to fall back.

"You're a real idiot, Adam! How could you? WITH A CHILD? You do realize you're going to jail, right?"

"I didn't do anything even CLOSE to illegal!" It was lame and not very convincing, but still better than all the cliché lines that surely come to mind in such situations. "It's not what you think..." "Let me explain..." "We didn't do anything, I swear..."

Shirley stared at Iris for a moment, then returned her attention to me, sobbing quietly, and then she calmed. "Young girl, I don't want to see your face in my house anymore," she said, without looking at Iris again.

Looking at the floor, Iris marched quickly toward the half-open front door, as three knocks were heard. Behind the door peeked the sunglasses from the movie *Top Gun*. Beneath them was the mustache of the detective from the *Magnum P.I.* show, and above them—defying the blatant attempt to exhibit a macho attitude—a pale forehead gleamed, and signs of baldness.

"May I come in?"

Shirley got up on her feet with a half-spin.

"Who are you?"

"I'm Oscar. I'm a detective in the police force." Shirley glanced at the badge he pulled out. "Ma'am, I understand you were on your way out. I'd appreciate it if you stayed with us for a few more minutes." He waited a moment before directing his penetrating stare towards Iris, as if he wanted to give her a moment to absorb the request, but she didn't bother to refuse and stood there frozen, halfway out, toward freedom.

He looked at me for the first time. Suddenly, something in his gaze changed, making me uncomfortable. "Are you Adam?"

"Yes."

"I have a few questions for you."

At that moment, I couldn't think of anyone I was less willing to let into my house than Detective Oscar. "Please come in."

"Two days ago, you had an appointment with your dermatologist, right?" Oscar asked as he entered and closed the door. His worn-out leather jacket completed the fashion statement.

I nodded.

"Why did you make the appointment?"

I touched the corner of my right jaw and felt something strange. "To have her check the mole I have here."

Oscar approached me.

"Are you sure the mole was here? I don't see anything."

"What are you talking about?" I jumped up and approached the full-body mirror outside the shower. Oscar's eyes were piercing my neck.

He was right.

The smirch was gone.

Doubt

Doubt grows with knowledge.

—*Johann Wolfgang von Goethe*

"Iris has a mole just like mine…" By the time I finished the sentence, I'd already seen that Iris's smirch had disappeared too. Iris understood this from my look. She stood there, shocked.

"I don't know about Iris, but until this morning, Adam did have a mole," Shirley said.

"I'm not interested in your mole, Adam," Oscar said. "What does interest me is that your dermatologist complained you attacked her."

"…I attacked—WHAT?"

I wondered how José Ribalta felt on August 17, 1986, in his boxing match against Mike Tyson, after Tyson hit him with his signature combo—*Right-Hook-Right-Uppercut*: trying to stand up, questioning his ability to win the fight.

"She filed a complaint against you. She said you pushed her and caused damage to expensive equipment she had."

"But it was *the mole* that caused the short circuit, not me! I don't know exactly why, but it doesn't like electric currents!"

Oh, what a mistake I just made...

Shirley gave me a strange look. "What's wrong with you, Adam?"

"Look, I usually don't deal with complaints like this," Oscar said, ignoring my last statement. "But I do handle special cases. And what makes this case special is my cousin.

"It so happens that my cousin works in the lab that received your dermatologist's needle for repair. He's also a hobbyist geologist. Now, all he was asked to do was replace the damaged needle with a new one. But he's a bit of a smartass. So, he performed some tests on the needle beyond protocol and was surprised to find... Wait, I knew I wouldn't remember this..."

He put on reading glasses, took out a crumpled note from his jacket pocket, and read from it.

"Kamacite, Olivine, Pyroxene..."

Oscar squashed the paper and reshaped it to a tiny ball. He looked around and spotted the half-open trash bin.

No way—he wouldn't dare...

He took the shot. Missed. He spoke again, as if nothing happened.

"My cousin also told me, and this one I remembered without writing it down, that he found poison—*cyanide*—and another substance he couldn't even identify, but he thought it might be a new type of *superconductor*. Well, if you ask me, I have no idea what a superconductor is. But you don't have to be a genius to understand it might be related to short circuits, like the one that happened at your dermatologist's clinic. He told me that besides cyanide, all the substances he identified—and obviously the one he didn't—don't exist naturally on Earth. They exist in meteorites.

"Adam, could it be that you found a meteorite recently and took it as a souvenir?"

I wasn't given a chance to answer. Oscar didn't wait for a response and continued.

"Yesterday, a guy named George, your neighbor, was brought to us. He was arrested after confessing to stealing a poisonous spider from an Australian zoo. The spider disappeared from his house, and I understand that you found it and killed it."

"Right," I said, hoping that would earn me some points.

"So, George said that the spider couldn't have escaped by itself. He thinks you somehow knew about it. He thinks you snuck into his place and took it."

Handcuffs

Truth is only an illusion we have forgotten is an illusion.

—Friedrich Nietzsche

I kept silent. I was furious. Oscar continued, stroking the right side of his mustache. "I was ready to believe that George is trying to frame you in an attempt to get out of the mess he's in, but then my cousin called me, and your name popped up for the second time within twenty four hours. You were immediately upgraded to the most interesting case around. I love interesting cases, so I came here to meet you personally. So, Adam, could it be that you took the spider from George's house?"

"NO WAY!" I shouted and slammed my fist against the shower door frame, but only two of my knuckles met it, and my face twisted in pain. That guy was truly getting on my nerves. It was evident he was trying to lead me into making mistakes—and he was succeeding. I was missing the inner voice of the smirch. I remembered the heated dialogue we had last night and became filled with regret. Did she conclude that I'd lost my trust in her and decided to abandon me?

"So, what's the deal with you, young lady?" Oscar didn't see a need to react to my words. "Aren't you supposed to be at school? They already release you at noon these days?"

"It's already *noon* now?" I exclaimed in surprise. That 'course' took up my entire morning! I'll have to come up with some explanation as to why I didn't join the call at 10:00 AM. Not that it mattered now.

"What's your name? How are you involved in this?" Oscar asked.

"Her name is Iris. I found them here, hugging—or something—I don't know what they were doing together…" Shirley said in a trembling voice.

"How old are you?"

"She's fifteen," Shirley said, beating Iris to it.

"Sixteen," Iris immediately followed, but had to correct herself:

"Next month."

"Alright, I've seen enough," Oscar said as he reached for his handcuffs, his fingers caressing the grip of his pistol along the way.

"WAIT!" At that point, the best strategy seemed to be to tell the truth. Or what I thought was the truth. Until then.

"The mole that was on me came over a meteorite a few weeks ago. There are many more like it, already a few hundred attached to people and exposing themselves. They are intelligent at a level we can never match. They want to improve our lives here. They carefully select the people they expose themselves to and assign each of them a specific purpose."

Shirley grabbed a chair and landed on it, staring into space, holding her head. Oscar listened to me with great interest this time. "And what purpose do they assign you?"

"I'm supposed to construct artificial moons. Iris will also be part of this project."

"How do you communicate with these *moles*?"

"They can communicate with us through thoughts."

Oscar was silent for a few moments. "I see," he finally said.

"Okay, so let me tell you what I see. I see a very intelligent person. I wouldn't be surprised if he has knowledge of handling dangerous substances like cyanide, spider venom, superconductors, and even materials from outer space. Maybe he found a way to cause a change in skin pigmentation—a change that disappears after a few days. Maybe he stole a poisonous spider and put his neighbors in danger. Maybe he uses chemicals to seduce a minor and convince her to believe in some story about extraterrestrial moles. And maybe—you have to admit it makes sense—maybe he hears voices in his head telling him he needs to build an 'artificial moon.'

"It might surprise you, Adam, but there are quite a few people like you. Your motive for allegedly doing such extreme stuff must be seriously warped—I must get to the bottom of this. The thing is, compared to most warped people with warped motives, you appear to be an intriguingly dangerous man—take that as a compliment, Adam. I have no choice but to detain you. We'll continue this at the station. Ladies, I'd like to ask you to accompany us to testify."

I stood with my back to the dining table. My hands gripped the edge of the table tightly. Oscar approached me.

"Adam, I need you now to put your hands forward."

I felt the sweat, and I couldn't speak. I couldn't move.

"Adam, I'll repeat myself one more time:

"I need you—NOW—to put forward—YOUR HANDS."

"Adam… Honey… Please, put your hands forward…"

My eyes, which had been hypnotized on Oscar's face, finally broke loose and moved left towards Shirley's voice. It was almost too late, but at the last moment I saw the tear in her eye.

That tear thawed me.

And I reached my hands forward.

Abyss

If you gaze long into an abyss, the abyss also gazes into you.

—Friedrich Nietzsche

Oscar drove the car, and I sat in the seat next to him. I lowered my eyes for who knows how many times. I had *handcuffs* on my hands—a flashback to the end of the first fantasy, the most horrible of them all, that I experienced the night before. In the rearview mirror, I occasionally caught Shirley glancing at me and quickly looking away.

When we got into the car, she briskly and efficiently coordinated Eden and Maya to ensure they picked up Ben and Eleanor from school, prepared lunch, and took them to their extracurricular activities. She didn't volunteer any unnecessary information. On the other end of the line, it was a completely normal day.

I didn't see Iris, but I assumed she dared not lift her head. I also didn't hear her. From that, I inferred she'd decided to deal with this situation herself and avoided contacting her parents. I hoped she wouldn't change her mind.

I tried to organize my thoughts during the drive. How did I get into such a mess? Why did the smirch disappear right when I needed her?

I reviewed everything I'd gone through: the episode at the dermatologist's clinic—my word against hers. The two neighbors, at the bus stop—I had no idea how to locate them, and no one in law enforcement would go out of their way to assist me in searching for them. That scene with Bonnie and George—it wouldn't be wise to reveal I managed to 'read' the thoughts of a dog. Anyone would believe George's story more than mine. And Iris... That was the biggest problem. She was surely already convinced that what she'd experienced was some hallucination and I was somehow responsible for messing with her mind, maybe with some drug.

I was so alone. No one would stand by my side in the situation that arose. Not even Shirley.

Right away, I started plunging into an abyss.

An abyss of realization.

Realization of something terrifying.

At the age of seventeen, at a peak fitness level, with impressive grades, and with lots of ambitious plans for my life, I was diagnosed with epilepsy. I swore not to let it affect my life. I made peace with the seizures being part of my life, so giving up on any of my desires was pointless. I drove, went out drinking, studied until late at night at university, and traveled abroad to work, by myself, for a year. I acted against all the recommendations of the doctors, in a kind of rebellion against my medical condition.

Since the seizures always occurred right when I woke up, I always had a Valium pill and a towel next to the bed to put between my teeth so I wouldn't bite my tongue during the seizure. I even started practicing meditation to stop seizures in real time. Surprisingly, it worked well.

All this worried my parents, and especially my mother, a lot.

During the third decade of my life, I underwent an arduous process of self-reassurance:

'Epilepsy is not the end of the world, Adam.'

'You're still creative, Adam.'

'Those seizures didn't short-circuit your brain, Adam.'

'You're not messed up, Adam.'

This succeeded beyond measure. When that private neurologist realized the outrageous mistake in my diagnosis, I changed the prescription and the seizures subsided, the self-reassurance slid into other realms:

'Your ideas are excellent, Adam.'

'Epilepsy must have improved the wiring in your brain, Adam.'

'You're special, Adam.'

More than ten years have passed since my last seizure, and the feeling of triumph over epilepsy filled me with satisfaction.

Until not long ago, when things started to fall apart.

Blows

We should take care not to make the intellect our god;
it has, of course, powerful muscles, but no personality.

—Albert Einstein

First, my mother passed away. She was energetic and vibrant, and we were all very close to her and competed for the privilege of spending time with her. Her death was an absolute shock to us, and I drowned in feelings of guilt. A few months later, Eleanor was diagnosed with epilepsy. Two blows, one to the ribs and one to the face—*Right-Hook-Right-Uppercut*—which caught me unprepared.

In the days following Eleanor's diagnosis, I'd spend hours going over medical websites, learning what epilepsy actually is. It occurred to me that contrary to my habit of delving deeply into various topics like evolution, astrophysics and philosophy, I'd never bothered to learn about the illness that had been an integral part of my life for so long.

The best treatment that modern medicine could offer Eleanor was exactly what it offered me decades ago—medicine that prevents seizures. I didn't want to settle for that when it came to Eleanor. I was Jack, trying to climb that monstrous beanstalk. Maybe I, of all people, could find something that modern medicine had missed, something that could cure her for good.

I fully utilized my analytical skills in computer science. I'd collected data from Eleanor's EEG tests and fed them into artificial intelligence programs trained to identify security breaches and computer viruses. I'd hoped this 'avant-garde' combination of disciplines would yield clues for a solution from those heaps of raw brain wave signals.

At some point, that research led me to wander into more spiritual realms, searching for a correlation between neurons and consciousness, between nerve stimuli and the soul. I drifted from one knowledge marketplace to another, conjuring up wise questions I could ask to get noticed, mingling with self-appointed experts, and responding to questions in a way that would make my online profile appear sophisticated. I caught the attention of *real* experts who engaged in academic discussions with me. I diligently collected facts, theories, speculations, lies, and half-truths.

And after a few months, I realized that Eleanor's new condition had severed my mourning of my mother. The hazy memories of the joy of life I had before all this mess started, already had a spoiled smell—as if their expiration date had passed too quickly.

Until we reached the parking lot outside the police station, I was close to convincing myself that this traumatic period had deteriorated my mental state. I reviewed once again the events of the last few days. Every memory was darker than the previous one.

An extraterrestrial entity in the form of... of a *smirch*? Speaking to me through thoughts? Appointing me as the manager of the most ambitious project in human history? How did I come up with so much *bullshit*? How could I believe in all of this, praise myself for my general knowledge in philosophy and astrophysics, and marvel at the universe's deepest secrets that were revealed to me? Will my children remember me not as the architect of artificial moons, but as a self-destructive Don Quixote, who was too smart for his own good?

How could I be so stupid?

Maybe I found a meteorite in the desert, on that trip in August. And maybe I gathered enough knowledge to achieve, or create, a substance that would cause my skin color to change and would also react to an electric current. And maybe I 'hacked' the event at the dermatologist's office: I did possess the technical knowledge to trigger a power outage at the right moment. For example, remotely controlling the main switches through my smartphone wasn't easy, but it was possible. Maybe I pushed the dermatologist when the electricity went out. And maybe I planted the spider under Natalie's bed. And my thoughts about Iris last night... Maybe I'm a *pedophile* after all? Maybe I also used date-rape drugs on her. And maybe, through the building blocks I gathered on my internet wanderings, I constructed for myself an alternative reality that would package everything that happened to me recently into a pretty convincing explanation. And all of this I maybe even *hid from myself*.

My inner voice suddenly sounded particularly mocking.

So maybe you're pretty messed up after all, huh, Adam?

I wanted so much... *so much*... to get some sign from the universe that there was a purpose for all the chaos that had invaded my life out of nowhere.

My unofficial diagnosis pointed to dissociative identity disorder—or, in layman's terms, *split personality*. I didn't know if it made any sense that a person with multiple personalities would diagnose themselves with no professional help. Besides, all the cases of dissociative identity disorder I heard of were characterized by a transition from one personality to another. Still, several 'personalities' conversing with each other at the same time? I haven't heard of any similar real-life cases. But it reminded me of that movie, *Fight Club*.

Above all—and that was my last hope—I still didn't *feel* I was crazy.

Yet, evidence suggested I did indeed enfold into my life a sort of *Fight Club* of my own—though as much as I tried, I couldn't remember how that movie ended.

"What did you say?" Oscar asked impatiently, as he firmly gripped my seat with his right hand and twisted his upper body to the right while casting his laser-like gaze over my face and then back to steer the police car in reverse into the parking spot.

"I didn't say—" I answered and looked at him quickly, concerned, wondering if I'd expressed my deranged thoughts aloud, without realizing it. I fell silent as soon as Oscar directed his look forward again and briefly glanced at the rearview mirror to finish adjusting the parking.

No, I wasn't the one who spoke to Oscar. All I could do in the next moments was to stare at the back of his right jawbone.

Attention

If you take care of the small things, the big things take care of themselves.

—Emily Dickinson

A while ago, I took Eden for a routine appointment with her eye doctor. Before returning to the car, we stopped at a café and grabbed takeaway sandwiches and drinks. Eden got an iced coffee, and I got a weird soft drink that had an odd taste of murky ginger. It was new, so I had to try it. I was very disappointed, but Eden joyfully refused to allow me even a small sip of her drink, to get rid of that awful taste.

Throughout the ride home, Eden was glued to her smartphone, chatting simultaneously with a thousand friends. Occasionally, while keeping her eyes on the screen, she'd reach out to retrieve her coffee cup from the holder and take a sip through the straw. She didn't notice that I was also stealing forbidden sips from her coffee. I'd pace myself according to Eden's drinking pauses. My hand movements didn't raise Eden's suspicion because our cups were next to each other in the cup holder. As long as she didn't look, she assumed I was reaching for my drink. If Ben had attempted that stunt, they'd have already been at each other's throats. But me? In recent years, I'd exhausted my efforts to earn a bit of her attention, hoping for an illusion of being a little younger. By the time she was fourteen, she was ignoring me by default. So why not take advantage of that to enjoy her iced coffee?

It would surely be easy to use evolution to justify our habit of focusing, ignoring details, and preferring simple interpretations of complex situations. Oscar was oversimplifying the situation. He didn't see any of the four smirches I'd seen so far—and not the fifth smirch, which now nestled under his right ear. He was pleased with his mundane interpretation of this story. Zero aliens. Zero artificial moons. One crazy guy. I assumed that even when he'd notice his smirch, he wouldn't immediately reconsider my wacky version. To remain calm, I snuck quick looks at his neck. It was still stained.

Sure, the picture of the smirch on Oscar's neck could have been confined to my head—another symptom of my alleged mental pathology. I allowed myself one last benefit of doubting I was crazy—the kind of crazy Oscar had in mind, at least. The terrifying conspiracy theory I'd developed about myself could be crumbling. I looked away and leaned against the police car's door to my right, trying to distance myself from Oscar—I wasn't going to give him any reason to blame me for somehow 'infecting' him with that smirch.

Oscar exited through the driver's door of the police car, circling around its back, his right cheek facing the almost vacant parking lot. Shirley, Iris, and I exited through the right doors. None of them had yet noticed the smirch on Oscar's face. My head was void of ideas. I stalled, blocking Shirley and Iris's view of Oscar's right cheek while trying not to arouse suspicion.

Oscar pointed at the entrance to the police station as he walked around the trunk of the police car, caressing one of its many dents. "Go on."

Shirley and Iris entered first. I walked quickly behind them, and finally, Oscar, his smartphone pressed to his right ear, engaged in some conversation.

A junkie—an extremely thin man, wearing a black mesh tank top—also entered the station accompanied by a police officer. I counted on his body—ears, nose, eyebrows, nipples, navel—close to twenty piercings, and there were surely more, in less visible areas of his body. The two passed by us on the right. The junkie glanced at Oscar's cheek. The smirch was partly hidden by Oscar's smartphone but the junkie must have noticed it while passing us. He chuckled at me, and licked his lips, catching at the last moment a drop of saliva that was about to dive from the edge of his lip onto his tank top.

The guard sitting next to the massive metal detector at the entrance recognized Oscar from a distance. His impression revealed that his favorite person on Earth was, in fact, not Oscar. He didn't bother to look in our direction again. As the junkie passed through the metal detector, he set it off with a petrifying beep. The guard grunted and reluctantly pulled out his handheld metal detector. He let us through, focused on a meticulous manual examination of the junkie, the numerous piercings making that task particularly challenging.

Iris passed through the metal detector first, followed by Shirley, then me. The metal detector emitted a short, annoying beep when I passed. The guard and the junkie glanced at me. The guard looked, indifferent, at my cuffed hands, and signaled me to proceed. Some day, his carelessness could cost him dearly.

I turned and looked directly toward Oscar. He finished his call and was hurrying to close the gap that had formed between us. Pushing his phone into the back pocket of his pants, he quickly approached me. Shirley and Iris were also looking at Oscar—their eyes and mouths opened synchronously in silence, as soon as Oscar's right cheek was in clear view. They finally saw it.

What happened just as Oscar passed through the metal detector gave me a lot of satisfaction. A small revenge.

Actually, a big revenge.

A painful revenge.

Fields

I fear not the man who has practiced 10,000 kicks once, but I fear the man who has practiced one kick 10,000 times.

—Bruce Lee

What I saw brought back memories of the *Inside Crescent kick*—sweaty memories from the Kung Fu club where I'd practiced in high school. That kick was so characteristic of Bruce Lee. I was so impressed by its uniqueness that I focused on practicing that kick until I mastered it perfectly. An Inside Crescent kick required extreme effort and wasn't the most effective in a fight, especially if aimed at a tall opponent's face. Still, Bruce maximized its potential. In his movies, just before firing that kick, you could see a smug look on his face, as if he were slightly drunk. That was his fighting philosophy. You're supposed to enter a fight calmly and relaxed. High muscle tone will lead you to defeat.

It unfolded in slow motion: Oscar's face was *kicked to the right*, followed by his whole body—eventually landing on his left cheek at the feet of the metal detector, while the neurotic beep of the device blended as a dramatic soundtrack into this short scene. I could imagine myself at seventeen, a lethal young man with a fragile heart, as the inner side of my left foot met Oscar's right cheek after my leg completed a precise half-circle in the air in the clockwise direction. Yes, his height was perfect for my sharpened Inside Crescent kick from those days.

That kick was carried out precisely as I'd imagined it, and was what he deserved, but I wasn't the one who kicked Oscar. In fact, what was most impressive about that kick was that *there was no leg attached to it.*

Oscar immediately got up on his feet, surprised but determined. His experience in martial arts was evident. Torn blood vessels gave his right eye a reddish look. Some filth that was on the floor stuck to his left cheek. He couldn't directly attribute to me what had happened—we were about four meters apart. But I could swear he was trying to melt me with his look.

He wasn't a man for unnecessary words. He lunged towards me, through the metal detector. Another beep and two seconds later, he was again sprawled on the floor, cursing, still not on the side he'd been trying to get to of that giant magnetic portal.

Oh... I get it... Wow...

The explanation I found for what I saw was so bizarre, but not much more bizarre than anything I'd experienced in the past few days.

"It's not worth your effort," I called to him through the metal detector, as if that was the only way he could hear me.

"The 'mole' sitting on your jaw is composed, among other things, of superconductors. Like your cousin told you."

"WHAT MOLE?" Oscar asked. His voice had a surprising new tone— fear.

"Superconductors *hate* electromagnetic fields," I said, sounding nerdy. "Just like the electromagnetic field emitted by this metal detector. Near an electromagnetic field, they create an opposing symmetrical field. Superconductors on Earth do that, but it's only been observed at very low temperatures and high pressure. And the resistance was relatively weak."

I enjoyed the attention I received from all present. "But materials functioning as superconductors at room temperature... Well, that's a *completely different story*. That's a holy grail many scientists dream about, but no one has succeeded in demonstrating. Your cousin somehow detected a superconductor, using standard laboratory equipment. That alone suggests that it's not a regular superconductor.

"So maybe, just *maybe*, 'moles' from outer space brought superconductors different from the ones we know? If so, they might be orders of magnitude more powerful than those on Earth, which means as long as this 'mole' is on you, you won't be able to pass through this metal detector in one piece.

"Oscar, until you prove that what you have on your cheek is *not* a 'mole' from outer space coated with a superconductor at room temperature, I'd advise you to be careful not to damage your pretty face."

Improvisation

Life is a lot like jazz… it's best when you improvise…

—*George Gershwin*

Oscar was shaking. He pulled out his smartphone from his pocket, struggling to press the screen until he switched the camera to *selfie* mode. He glanced at it. Ever since the encounter with my two neighbors at the bus stop the day before, I noticed small but distinct differences in the shades of different smirches. The colors of the smirch on Oscar's jaw were a blend of all the smirches I'd seen till then. That particular color combination was aesthetically clashing with the complexion of Oscar's terrified face.

"GET THIS OFF ME!" Oscar raged.

"Get *this* off me," I replied firmly while extending my cuffed hands forward. The metal detector beeped again.

"Are you sure you can get it off?"

"Yes," I lied.

Oscar gestured to me with his hand. "Come here."

"Forget it. Throw me the keys to the handcuffs. I'd have to get past you to escape, right?"

Oscar hesitated before he pulled the keys out of his pocket and threw them at me. They fell to my feet, following my failed attempt to catch them in mid-air with the handcuffs on.

I looked at the guard. He approached me, picked up the keys, and stared, puzzled, at Oscar. Oscar nodded, and the guard uncuffed me.

I passed through the metal detector, which reacted to my presence with indifference for a change. Oscar stopped a twitch in his left shin muscle. He brushed his hand over his right cheek. As I approached him, I felt more and more the heat of the fire in his gaze.

"What now?" he asked as I stood before him.

From that moment, I switched to full-on improvisation.

"Don't move," I said, nearing his face. I looked around and saw that everyone—Shirley, Iris, the guard, the junkie and the officer accompanying him, other police officers who approached us, detainees, and even the cleaning lady at the far end of the room—were all watching us intently in silence. Some spectators gathered around us but kept a safe distance.

Slowly but surely, I brought my right cheek closer to the smirch on Oscar's cheek. Oscar recoiled.

"What are you doing?"

"DON'T MOVE."

I gently brushed my right hand, in a soft caressing motion, lightly touching Oscar's left ear towards the back of his neck. I gripped his head tightly and made the edges of our right jawbones touch each other.

Then I pressed.

Hard.

Intimacy

Blushes are the sign of guilt; true innocence is ashamed of nothing.

—Jean-Jacques Rousseau

We embraced for about three minutes. In fact, after about twenty seconds, I was pretty sure the process was complete, judging by the temperature differences between my left and right cheeks. I kept holding on to Oscar, imagining his eyes looking around nervously at his coworkers, as they were watching him snuggling with a detainee. I carefully counted the clicks of the camera buttons on the smartphones held by the officers facing us. When I spotted one officer recording a video, I slid my right fingers over Oscar's hair, stroking up and down. He stood still like a statue, barely breathing, furious.

I tried to estimate how fast those images and videos of us sharing an 'intimate moment' in public would reach the police station chat groups, and simultaneously, how soon the macho guy image that the soon-to-be-bald detective was desperately trying to preserve would crumble.

I was finally satisfied with my estimation of the volume of content that had been recorded. I decided I'd toyed with Oscar enough and detached myself from him. Like earlier with Iris, I heard a sound like that of a spark-lighter, and my right jawbone slightly itched. Oscar jolted back. His right cheek had an unusual but uniform reddish hue, identical to the color that covered his entire face, from ear to ear: a red blush, a complexion of rage mixed with embarrassment.

Without a word, he rushed towards the men's room, rubbing his right cheek frantically.

"What were you *thinking*?" Shirley's voice startled me. I hadn't noticed her approaching me from behind. "Why on Earth didn't you tell me about all this?"

I embraced her, leaning my chin on her right shoulder. Iris stood on the other side of the metal detector, looking directly at me.

"Do you remember how you reacted when you heard about this for the first time? That's why. And soon you'll also get a—"

"Touch…

Touch…

Touch…"

A foreign thought burst into my consciousness like a motorcyclist merging onto a crowded highway.

No… There were *three* motorcycles.

I knew what to do next. I clasped our right cheeks together. I assumed Shirley's hair, caught between us, wouldn't be a problem.

And then a tsunami of… WOW!

Shirley and I shared an amazing experience. Maybe looking for words to describe it isn't even worth the effort. It could be defined as an *intellectual orgasm*. That elevating rush right when you finally understand something important—the brain feels slightly warmer—yes, that sensation, intensified by orders of magnitude.

At first, I was concerned that Shirley would panic and break contact, but then her grip tightened. Neither of us cared. We didn't care about the commotion around us. We didn't care that we were experiencing an intimate act in public. We didn't care that this experience, indescribable as it was, was entirely new for both of us.

In the Old Testament, the term *to know someone* was a poetic way of saying *to have sex with someone*. Maybe that experience was the purely intellectual part of the Biblical *knowing—emotionless erotica*? These smirches could manipulate the human intellect in strange ways we may never understand.

Shirley and I both knew when it was time to detach. This time, the short 'tick' sound and the tingling sensation were more noticeable. I looked at Shirley. She had a loving, smiling, but focused look. She said nothing, but gently caressed the colorful smirch on the back of her right jaw—as if she were petting a puppy. Suddenly, her face became serious.

She turned and gestured for Iris to come over. Iris passed through the metal detector, and Shirley hugged her, just as I'd hugged Shirley earlier. A few moments later, each of them had a smirch of her own.

Iris moved back her curls and felt her smirch. The position, shape, and colors were identical to what I'd seen on the back of her cheek that same morning.

I was full of guilt. "Iris, I'm so sorry for all the—"

"Adam, it's all right," Shirley said. "Iris and I talked."

She took my hand, and with her other hand, took Iris's. And then, Iris took my free hand. A flux of understanding went through us—the realization we were about to do great things. Three human beings, three seeds of consciousness that had germinated and bloomed for half a billion years and ended up inside our skulls—and three new pieces of consciousness that joined us.

Home

If liberty means anything at all it means the right to tell people what they do not want to hear.

—*George Orwell*

Oscar ran out of the men's room and called after us as we walked toward the exit. "WHERE do you think you're going? I still need to question you!"

Shirley turned to Oscar. "Sorry, we have to get back to our kids. What makes you think you have the right to stop us from leaving?" She asked, her gaze piercing.

"You're not stupid, Oscar. You know that the stories of the dermatologist and of George *together* aren't enough to hold Adam here. If anything, *we* might sue *the doctor* for negligence. Right, Adam?"

I nodded in agreement.

Oh, Shirley, how much I love you…

"I suggest you let it go, Oscar," Shirley continued. "You've embarrassed yourself enough today."

"These moles on you. They… they…" Oscar let out a slight stutter. "They could pose a danger to the public…"

This time, I responded. "Wait a minute. You tell me you've concluded that the three of us pose a danger to the public, but you have no evidence to support that other than *the color of our skin*? Can I get that in writing?"

Oscar didn't respond. He looked utterly exhausted.

"Good day to you, Oscar. Go to hell." I allowed myself to risk insulting a police officer.

We turned back towards the door and stepped out into the sunlight.

> *"You need to go home now. He's waiting to meet you."*

Oh, how happy I was to share my mental space again.

"Well, hello to you too! Why did you disappear like that? Hey, are you the same smirch I had this morning?"

> *"Yes, it's me. There were some important tasks I needed to complete. But now it's your turn to act—together with Iris."*

"I really hope you're not referring to what you talked about last night. Because if so, then there's no chance."

> *"Don't worry. Like I said, we also need time to learn. We realize that, for the moment, it will be easier to advance humanity's important goals if you adhere to the principles of morality."*

"I'm glad you figured this out, although the term *for the moment* bothers me."

I looked at Shirley. Her gaze was cheerful and light-hearted as if she'd met an old friend and they were catching up. Occasionally, some utterance slipped from her mouth, the beginning of a word she'd meant to think about but started to pronounce out of habit—and stopped.

Iris, on the other hand, looked focused and determined. Her forehead was furrowed. The internal dialogue she was having at that moment must have been fascinating. She'd already started to work.

"Wait, who's waiting for me at home?"

> *"We had to leave you and Iris this morning to organize the meeting that will take place at your house today. I'll explain everything on the way."*

Egon

The most effective way to do it is to do it.

—Amelia Earhart

I was never good at identifying cars by their designs or logos, but I recognized the shiny blue Tesla blocking our parking spot. In any other circumstance—whether or not I urgently needed my car—I'd have already launched an angry message on the neighborhood chat group, demanding the blocking car be moved before I called the police.

This wasn't a normal situation, and I did not want to see the police anytime soon. Besides, the stress from my next task was the only thing I felt.

"It'll be okay. Don't worry."

I approached the car, only then noticing the person sitting inside. It took a few seconds for him to notice me. He turned his gaze towards me, inhaled from the half-joint he was focused on until that moment, extinguished it, then got out of the car and stood facing me, a cloud of sweet smoke dissipating behind him.

"Adam?" he asked, looking at me with narrowed eyes, and that single word was enough to give away his accent.

"Yes. Pleasure to meet you, Mr. Mars," I shook his hand.

Shirley and Iris approached and introduced themselves. Egon Mars glanced at the three of us.

"So I—I'm trying to recall what I did last week, so I open up my calendar and—and suddenly, a new meeting pops in, before my eyes. A meeting with you, here, at your house. I don't know who you are, or who did this and how, but I was very impressed by this trick and had to see what this is all about. And the—in the meeting invitation, it was written that you have a message for me."

"Yes," I said, trying to conceal my astonishment. "I wanted to update you that—" Before I could utter the news, I froze.

"To update me... that... what?"

"To update you we're starting a project of building and populating artificial moons. We'd like to suggest that you collabor—"

Again, I froze. But it was different—as if I'd forgotten how to speak. Or rather, as if *someone* had suppressed my ability to speak.

> **"Tell him what I told you: that all the development originally intended to colonize Mars must be repurposed immediately for the Orbs project."**

"WHAT THE HELL IS THIS SUPPOSED TO BE?" I angrily threw a thought into the depths of my consciousness. "So, you're *controlling my speech* now? Just like that thing with Iris, if you don't let me handle this my way—the civilized way—it will be very difficult to make progress!"

"—suggest that you collaborate with us." I regained my ability to speak. Egon looked at me strangely. After all this, I'll have to set some rules with the smirch.

"See this?" I pointed to my right cheek. "These 'moles' arrived on Earth a few weeks ago. They have all the knowledge needed to launch artificial moons around Earth and our natural moon, and to colonize them with about two million people on each moon. We'll construct on them an environment suitable for living in, at least as comfortably as on Earth. The first artificial moon will be operational within a few years. That's much less than it will take you in practice to bring a million people to Mars. And it will be much easier, much more economically feasible, and *much less dangerous* to reach and return from an artificial moon, compared to Mars."

I had immense respect for that man, Egon Mars. I could easily recite his biography, the highlights in his career, the interviews he gave, and every other aspect of his activity exposed to the public. I'd always fantasized about the first thing I'd say to him if I were ever lucky enough to meet him briefly in person.

I never imagined that the first thing I'd tell him would be that I was about to take over his business.

Decisions

It's OK to have your eggs in one basket, as long as you control what happens to that basket.

—Elon Musk

Egon Mars was a genius. But, not every genius can become Egon Mars. He was always quick to learn from his rivals and partners, and to implement as needed. Adhering to professional ethics didn't always seem to be a major concern to him.

Egon Mars wasn't a regular person, and certainly not a regular businessman. Unsurprisingly, he skipped the shock phase that every regular person—myself included—would experience on the first encounter with an extraterrestrial entity. He must have believed me. Otherwise, I'd have seen the Tesla driving off with a trail of dust behind it before reaching my third statement. He wasn't concerned about the first serious challenge from any competitor against his 'baby,' his ambitious project for establishing human colonies outside Earth—as could be expected from a regular businessman. His face revealed that, at that moment, he was 'raising his antennae' and beginning to gather data. As for deciding whether to collaborate, he'd postpone that to a later time.

"I di—I didn't get a 'mole' yet. Why don't I have one?"

Good question.

"That's not for him to decide. And not for you either."

"I don't know," I said, struggling to hide my discomfort. "The moles share knowledge with us. But they don't disclose their considerations when choosing 'hosts.' They assign a specific role to each person in the artificial moons project and other projects."

Iris approached us and smiled politely. Shirley listened intently.

"She's a *kid*..." Egon Mars whispered to himself.

I ignored that.

"Iris and I, for example, will lead the artificial moons project. This project and others will advance humanity and intelligent life on Earth. We're doing this for the benefit of future generations."

"So—so how am I supposed to make decisions?"

My discomfort grew.

Iris intervened. "You'll communicate with the moles through us."

"Unacceptable. I want a mole. No mole—no deal."

He simply stepped into the Tesla and drove off.

Leverage

Risk comes from not knowing what you're doing.

—Warren Buffett

Egon Mars wanted a smirch of his own. Maybe he wanted a smirch that would grant his wishes. Whether or not the concept of 'negotiation' turns out to be unique to Earth, he was eager to negotiate with what he probably considered to be 'aliens.' The conglomerate he'd built and owned for colonizing Mars was his leverage, and he was by no means willing to relinquish direct control. The benefit of humanity and life on Earth weren't major concerns for him. Yet, we undoubtedly sparked his interest, and he'd surely do his homework and examine the business potential of collaborating with us. The next meeting with Egon Mars was just a matter of time.

> **"We've been exploring this severe human deficiency. How did humans evolve so that individual benefit is a primary interest for each of you, surpassing the common good of your species? No intelligent civilization we've encountered exhibits such behavior, and still survives and thrives over time."**

Something briefly buzzed inside my head. Like the thought of a sound.

> **"Adam, human communities are completely confused. Someone conspicuously contemplated contaminating your collective**

cognition with counterproductive concepts of 'self-fulfillment.' Your compulsive compassion for the 'Me' and counterintuitive contempt for the 'Us' could compromise your continuity!

"On our first coming to Earth, 542 million years ago, we conveyed to your consciousness-deprived ancestors the competence to comprehend what 'Me' is. Our core conjecture was that we could count on their cooperation in concert to contribute to the common benefit of the 'Us.' But now, on our second coming here, we've corroborated that humans have come to a conflicting conclusion. What you commonly consider 'self-fulfillment' comes in complete contrast to your correct cosmic commitment!"

Collective cognition... Compulsive compassion... Correct cosmic commitment...

What's going on?

"What a jerk." Shirley's voice disrupted my thoughts before I could figure out what seemed awkward about the smirch's choice of words.

"Being a billionaire doesn't mean you're entitled to be a jerk!" Shirley exclaimed loudly, just as the Tesla turned left at the far end of the street and disappeared. But she calmed right away. "Come, Iris. How about a cup of coffee? Tell me about your smirch."

As we headed inside, thoughts raced through my mind. My cognition was embracing the pragmatism of my smirch. "So, what do we do now?"

"Locating Egon Mars and getting him to meet you here was easy. Eventually, he'll cooperate. We'll take care of that.

"But we learned about someone much more influential than Egon Mars. Surprisingly, we couldn't locate him. You must help us find and enlist him in our joint effort."

That intrigued me. Egon Mars was the richest, most interconnected human on Earth. His enigmatic and singular personality garnered him a massive community of loyal followers. Who was *much more influential* than Egon Mars? No one could fit that description.

"I'm sure you know him. You humans call him 'God.'"

God

Faith is like Wi-Fi, it's invisible but it has the power to connect you to what you need.

—Gabby Bernstein

"GOD?"

"Yes. God."

That made me laugh. But an interesting fact about laughter: you can't just 'think' it.

I burst into laughter and made Shirley and Iris, who sat at the dining table, jump in surprise. Bonnie was also startled. There was no way she'd ever understand what had happened—still, Bonnie's look made it clear she thought I was blaming her for something. She slunk under the dining table, her tail between her legs.

"Private joke," I offered a lame apology to Shirley and Iris.

"What's the reason for your reaction?"

I calmed down and resumed our mental dialogue. "God is not a person."

"Humans are the most advanced species on Earth. So, God belongs to a species inferior to humans. We've observed that most people use male pronouns when thinking about God, so

there must be a female of the same species so they can mate. Which species do they belong to?"

"God doesn't belong to any species." I thought, still smiling. "No one has ever scientifically proven He exists. But over three-quarters of all humans believe He exists, in some form. They've never needed any evidence to convince themselves of the existence of God."

"This aligns with our observations. We've seen that God holds a significant place in the thoughts of a vast number of people. This cannot be justified if God's existence hasn't been proven yet. There are signs that certain people have a deeper connection with him than others—but we haven't found a way to approach him ourselves.

"For example, God once communicated with your son."

The smile that was still on my face vanished.

"BEN? What does Ben have to do with this? And how do you know... Did you probe his mind? You have no right—"

Then I remembered.

There was a time when Ben was God's best friend.

Ben

People don't know what Kabbalah is, and so they jump to conclusions... And so they make assumptions and they judge.

—*Madonna Ciccone*

It happened when Ben was in kindergarten. He was four years old. One day, Shirley got a call from his kindergarten teacher.

"First—everything is fine. Ben is fine," she'd always adhered to the protocol, which dictated an opening that would relax the parents before they envisioned any horror scenes, like the child breaking a leg or something. She asked Shirley and me to meet her face-to-face in the middle of the day. That was unusual.

When we arrived, the teacher met us at the kindergarten entrance, after asking her assistant to watch the children for a few minutes. We sat away from the children's line of sight. She opened a transparent folder and pulled out two drawings.

"Ben drew this at the beginning of the school year." She said, handing us one of the drawings. "I can show you drawings made by all the other children, from back then. You'll see it's hard to distinguish between them. The motifs are repeated in all the drawings. Those drawings matched Ben's age and developmental stage."

Shirley and I looked at each other for a moment and then again at the teacher as she pulled out five more drawings.

"These are Ben's drawings from this week. A while ago, he started drawing a lot more, and he quickly surpassed all the other children in the complexity of his drawings."

The new drawings looked more like sketches, like a map or an architectural plan of some structure.

"Shirley, Adam, could it be that Ben was somehow exposed to *The Book of Zohar*?"

"What? Do you mean... *Kabbalah*? Jewish mysticism?"

"Yes."

Shirley and I exchanged glances again. We were both shocked.

"Look, there's no need to be concerned." The teacher tried to calm us. "I recognized these signs from my studies and asked Ben about them. He told me God is his best friend. He said he visits Him occasionally, going through a hole above his bed. The drawings show the path leading to God, and the resemblance to descriptions in the Kabbalah is remarkable. Ben says God doesn't allow anyone else to come up to Him, and anyone who tries risks their life."

Then she smiled. "I was truly impressed when Ben said that, long ago, there was no such thing as 'feelings.' Then, God decided to create the world, and when He'd finished, and there were feelings in the world,

God felt happy. This distinction between intellect and emotion is a fundamental concept in the Kabbalah. And the abstraction level of this idea is way beyond the level typical of Ben's age. You should be proud of him. When we talked, I had to keep reminding myself I was talking with a four-year-old. I found myself asking him for advice about my career…"

We addressed the matter rationally, and took the predictable action—we sought therapy, just Shirley and me. After numerous sessions, we found an explanation we could easily 'digest.' The summer before, for her 40th birthday, Shirley had fulfilled her childhood dream of watching swimming competitions at the Olympics. We went on a three-week trip, leaving all four children with their grandmothers, the caregivers, and anyone who'd agreed to volunteer. That was traumatic for all the children, but Ben took it the hardest. He was so angry at us he wouldn't even come to the phone when we called from the hotel. When we returned from the trip his reaction triggered, quite stereotypically, an exchange of blame between me and Shirley. That had strained our relationship for a while, worsening Ben's reactions even further.

Thanks to the therapy, we could more easily connect the dots and relate Ben's 'escape' to 'God' with his anger at us. We found it easier to deal with our guilt than to examine other explanations, especially if they came from mystical realms.

Ben had grown up since then, and at some point, abandoned those stories about God. I covered the small hole above his bed with a picture of dolphins, and during one of the coronavirus pandemic lockdowns, when we painted the entire house together, I permanently sealed that hole. Occasionally, we talked about that incident, and he'd dismiss it and consider his 'God stories' the product of a kindergartener's vivid imagination. That was easier for us.

But following my recent acquaintance with the smirch, it may be time to reconsider the existence of some 'mystical' entities in our world. Perhaps Ben had been 'communicating' with one of those entities at that time?

That buzz again…

> *"We confirm Ben's considerably consummate cognitive competencies compared to common humans. Yet, we couldn't comprehend how he could connect us to Cod."*

"You mean, 'God,' right?"

> *"Yes. But if the existence of God has never been proven, and maybe cannot be proven, then how did he gain so much influence on so many people?"*

Adam and Eve

Some call it evolution,

And others call it God.

—William Herbert Carruth, Each in His Own Tongue

The wall clock surprised me. It had been less than three minutes since we came home. All those thoughts went through my head so fast—discussing God, remembering Ben in kindergarten—my train of thought was a bullet train.

"The idea of 'God' explains everything that cannot be explained in any other way," I felt I was explaining that to a child—although no child ever needed such an explanation to grasp what 'God' is. "For example, people who experience a tragedy find comfort in believing it was 'God's will.' They can't ask God why He brought the disaster upon them, so they accept His will with resignation."

> *"Very interesting. This idea of 'God' is certainly unique to Earth. We've never encountered intelligent beings elsewhere, who prefer not to seek logical explanations for their questions, but rather settle for an explanation that cannot even be verified as true. But what led humanity to adopt God in the first place?"*

"The greatest mystery that occupies humanity is the origin of life. And this mystery is easily 'solved' if you acknowledge 'God' exists.

"Most people who believe in God are convinced that God *created all humans*. They're sure He watches over us like a father who watches over his children. Belief in God requires several basic assumptions that don't align well with the principles of evolution. But the truth is that no one has ever provided a comprehensive explanation for the essence of our existence. Those who believe in God have always struggled to explain our physiological development, while the theory of evolution relatively easily explains it. But accepting God as supreme intelligence explains where our consciousness came from, while evolutionists have always struggled with that.

"At least, until you arrived," I added. Something bothered me for a moment, and I almost identified it—as if passing quickly before my eyes—but it disappeared.

"How did God create you?"

Very surprising... Her interest in God is growing...

"Every religion has its theory. According to the story I was taught in kindergarten, God first created all the creatures in the world, then used dust, or dirt, to create one male, *Adam*, and one female, *Eve*. They lived in a place called the *Garden of Eden*. That place was a kind of all-inclusive five-star nudist resort. God provided for all their needs, except for the ability to be self-aware. And the ability to distinguish between good and bad. And clothes, of course.

"The story goes—remember, it's folklore from over three thousand years ago—that God warned Adam and Eve not to eat the fruit from The Tree of Knowledge, because it wasn't healthy for them—or, as God put it, it would kill them. But a serpent who passed by on the way to work for his boss, Satan, convinced Eve that God was talking nonsense, and Eve convinced Adam. The serpent said it would be good for them to eat that fruit, because then they'd become like God, and maybe they could open a competing resort to the Garden of Eden—or something like that. When they ate that fruit they became self-aware. And the first thing they did when they became aware of their bodies was to put some clothes on. What they did made God angry, and He canceled Adam and Eve's membership in the Garden of Eden. According to this story, all humans are descendants of Adam and Eve."

"Why was God angry?"

Why was God angry?

Where there is anger, there is always pain underneath.

—Eckhart Tolle

"What do you mean 'why was God angry?' They did exactly what He warned them *not* to do!"

> *"We are now exploring the concept of 'anger' within our study of what you call 'emotions.' Emotions are another cognitive defect humans suffer from, due to the enormous developmental gap you've accumulated—you still have a long way to go."*

Cognitive defect? She's insulted all humanity... But to realize she's insulted us, she needs emotions—she'll never understand...

> *"The emotional response when a person intentionally does something 'bad' is 'to be angry' at that person. But Adam and Eve weren't capable of intentionally doing 'bad.' Before eating that fruit, they couldn't distinguish between a 'good' deed and a 'bad' one. They'd have eaten from this fruit sooner or later—even if the serpent hadn't convinced them.*
>
> *"Also, the serpent couldn't have convinced them that eating the fruit would be 'good' for them because they didn't even know*

what 'good' was. Neither God's warning nor the serpent's persuasion influenced the outcome—eating the fruit. It happened because Adam and Eve were there and the fruit was there.

"So, what was the point of warning them not to do 'bad?' And what was the reason for the anger towards them after they did 'bad?' And why was God so upset in the first place about Adam and Eve becoming intelligent beings?"

My sudden head-first plunge into that deep theological discussion surprised me so much that I forgot about her insulting depiction of human emotions.

I'd never thought about that plothole. I had a completely secular education as a child, and still, I could recite the Story of Creation ever since I could remember myself. I hadn't appreciated this story enough. As an adult, I labeled it 'science fiction,' but didn't pay as much attention to its details as I did with other science fiction stories.

The smirch had a point. If someone lacks the skills to distinguish between good and bad, why give them a task that requires these skills as a prerequisite? It's like asking a colorblind person to solve a Rubik's Cube.

What about something simpler? What about 'forbidden' versus 'allowed?' Adam and Eve had to obey God mindlessly, regardless of the consequences of their actions. Such obedience requires a kind of 'training.' A trained dog obeys its owner's will without wrestling with moral issues of 'good' and 'bad.' Perhaps creatures who aren't self-aware can still somehow be 'trained.' Maybe Adam and Eve were 'trained' before they sinned. Even then, why did God warn them of the 'bad' consequences of eating from the Tree of Knowledge? They didn't know what 'bad' was. There was one and only one consideration that the 'trained' Adam and Eve were supposed to adhere to: *'because God said so.'*

Very confusing.

The weirdest thing was that the smirch kept dwelling on this story.

"Why are you so interested in this myth?"

"Because that's what actually happened."

Male-Female

Home is heaven and orgies are vile,

but I like an orgy, once in a while.

—Ogden Nash

I sat at the dining table, feeling a bit sick.

"Coffee?" Shirley's voice, muffled, echoed in my ears.

"No, thanks, honey," I answered. The thought of coffee made my stomach turn. I looked up at the wall clock again. Two more minutes have passed. My brain was warming up, doubly stressed by high-speed thought in tandem.

What's this nonsense? Has my smirch just concluded that God exists?

Could smirches become... religious?

> **"This story is based on what happened, but it was intentionally altered with certain biased distortions. It's not fabricated. Those events happened at least four hundred million years ago to self-aware creatures, that were sufficiently developed to preserve and inherit memories collectively. The story got repeatedly distorted in thought over the eons that passed, long before humans appeared. When early verbal humans appeared, they**

used their primitive language to document the warped version that they'd inherited. It's also possible some external entity applied what you call 'brainwashing' to those primitive humans.

"We take part in this story. We're the only ones in the universe capable of implanting self-awareness into living creatures. The metaphor should be corrected: no one persuaded Adam and Eve to eat the fruit. They were force-fed."

"So..." Suddenly, I became genuinely concerned about something I'd never worried about before. "In this story, you're the *serpent*?"

"Yes. But the factual chain of events places the appearance of God sometime after the serpent, not before the serpent. Male-female mating can evolve only in self-aware creatures. God acted after self-aware creatures had evolved—after the serpent had come and gone. The serpent in the story is presented negatively—but the serpent is the one who made all of you conscious beings.

"Why is that 'bad?'"

Her question is so naïve... Why don't I know the answer?

"Another disturbing detail is that God created Adam and Eve initially as male and female. Your mating method has two genders, both mandatory for reproduction: one male and one female. However, only one gender can reproduce: the female. Among all the civilizations we've encountered so far, we've

never observed this problematic mating method in creatures at the forefront of evolution.

"Male-female mutants like yourselves appeared occasionally due to the randomness of the evolutionary process. Such creatures always disappeared within a few generations and never grasped the lead in cognitive development.

"The leading species on other planets sometimes study remnants of male-female mutants millions of years after those inferior creatures became extinct and made way for more successful lineages. You could compare that to human research on dinosaur skeletons. Other mating methods are much more efficient, but surprisingly, they haven't matured on Earth. Earth is the first place in the universe—and almost certainly the only one—where male-female species have taken the lead."

Males and females? What's wrong with males and females?

How else would we...

"The main advantage of male-female mating may be more diverse offspring, with a higher chance of at least one surviving. Any offspring lacking the optimal blend of traits—for example, a short-sighted eagle or a slow cheetah—will die. However, male-female species waste enormous effort to realize this advantage: many mating events are needed, each mating event

must produce many offspring, and there must be many distinct blends of traits among those offspring.

"Optimally, men should be smaller and more agile. They must spend their entire lives looking for diverse fertile women to mate with. And women must look for diverse men. They must acknowledge that many mating attempts will fail, and many unfit offspring will die. Nowadays, humans have the privilege of neglecting their duty to mate as often as they should. But you have this privilege, only because ages ago when your most ancient male-female ancestors were still endangered, some anomaly curiously caused all their existential threats to vanish."

My gaze focused. Before my eyes, sitting at the far end of the table, chatting, unaware of the blasphemous dialogue unfolding in my brain, were Shirley and Iris.

Diverse fertile women to mate with...

Huh...

"The numerous failed mating attempts and unfit offspring typical of male-female mating translate into huge amounts of wasted energy and genetic material. That waste is unjustifiable in the grand scheme. It's impossible that the initial male-female mutants on Earth had naturally avoided extinction and evolved into humans—unless there was some outside intervention!"

Outside intervention

Sex and sleep alone make me conscious that I am mortal.

—Alexander the Great

"Outside intervention? Who... And what do you mean by *wasteful*? After all, all animals get their action the same way, more or less, no? I mean..."

So many thoughts...

All of a sudden, I was overwhelmed by fatigue. My head ached.

> *"No intelligent beings from another planet—namely, 'aliens,' as you call them—could have done that. Something much more powerful tipped the scales in favor of male-female species. Your long-term survival chances were supposed to be zero.*
>
> *"It's all about probabilities. If there are as many males as females, they can all be busy mating simultaneously. But then, for each male, no more than 50% of the population will be relevant mating candidates. The same goes for each female. That is the lowest possible percentage of mating candidates among all mating methods. Understand?"*

I nodded wearily.

> *"If that's not enough, each of you invests a lot of energy to find a partner for mating. Human males have larger bodies than females, they eat more and waste more energy. Why? Males are 'dispensers' of genetic material. The energy wasted on their upbringing is enormous, and they don't reproduce directly."*

Another insult I forced myself to endure, this time on behalf of all the males in the world.

My mind ran a quick nostalgic scan through dozens of girls I'd dated throughout my adult life. Memories rose in sepia tones, one chasing another, like slides projected on the wall on a quiet family evening in the seventies: the flirting, the movies, the late-night walks by the sea, the necking, the pubs, the takeaway dinners... Those final thoughts before falling asleep, caressing the naked body of my sex partner and pressing her tightly against me, exhausted after an evening of sensual pleasure, pondering if I'd indeed finally found the love of my life... And those tiny creatures who could have been my children, choking to death, rolled up in rubber, crammed together with leftovers of a spicy Thai dish and two pairs of chopsticks inside a crumpled cardboard box, thrown in the trash.

Sex for fun. One could call that a waste.

> *"In other species, each individual may have both male and female reproductive organs, or there may be three or more*

> genders, or the individual may duplicate itself. The reproduction rate of all these is huge compared to male-female species.
>
> "And unlike male-female mating, other techniques don't require much effort in searching for mates. Almost every individual of the same species is a relevant candidate. The chances of living long enough to mate are much higher."

"So... sentient beings on other planets aren't male-female? What do they look like? How do they mate? And how much more efficient could it be?" Those questions passed through my mind, and left me wondering:

How, two days after encountering extraterrestrial intelligence, did the conversation shift to 'alien sex?'

> "I won't disclose details about alien life forms to you. Not right now. But to explain your inefficiency compared to other species, it's simpler to use examples you're familiar with. For instance, the organisms you call 'snails.' Every snail has both male and female reproductive organs. They're more efficient than humans in two aspects. First, for every snail, every other snail is a potential mate. Besides, one mating event normally results in two events of producing offspring, by two snails simultaneously!"

So, aliens probably don't look like little green men, or regular people with pointy ears, or dinosaur-like monsters with acidic blood, or anything else Hollywood has fixated in our collective minds. Maybe we should expect 'alien snails' instead?

Snailiens...

> *"Adam, snails deserve to rule the Earth, much more than you humans! Male-female mutants were never supposed to be at the forefront of evolution. Since the beginning of time, throughout the universe, those inferior beings repeatedly lost the survival struggle against other species that reproduced more efficiently. You and your ancestors have been manipulated to disrupt the course of evolution and bottleneck the perfection of sentient beings on Earth! Only the intervention of a tremendous force could overcome the laws of nature and bring about this practically impossible outcome."*

"But... If that *someone* helped the first male-female species to survive and out-compete other species, establish themselves numerically, and become our ancestors, then... If it weren't for that *someone*, all the most advanced beings that ever lived on Earth—dinosaurs, mammals, and especially humans—would never have existed?"

> *"Yes, Adam. It's impossible to explain it any other way."*

Something important was hidden deep in my mind, something I had to flesh out. It took a few seconds—as if I were hearing a countdown at the pace of my heartbeat.

Finally, it hit me.

Noah and the Flood!

SMIRCH—God is Gambling to Survive

Noah

The church is like Noah's ark. It stinks, but if you get out of it, you'll drown.

—Shane Claiborne

I recited in thought the story of the Flood. I could sense how the smirch absorbed it into herself.

Noah threw the ultimate *end-of-the-world* party and hosted it on a fancy cruise ship he built himself. But that party was by invitation only: the 'bouncer' at the entrance allowed entry to pairs—and only to pairs—of male and female. Who knows? Maybe before the Flood, there were giant, prehistoric predatory snails that were uninvited to the party simply because they didn't reproduce in the male-female method, and their fate was to drown and be forgotten. What if, eons ago, some creatures became too much of a threat to the survival of those fragile, pre-human male-female species, not just because they were positioned in the food chain above male-female creatures, but mainly because of their more efficient reproduction method?

I couldn't recall this question being asked before.

Why did only male-female species deserve to be saved from the Flood? Could it be that God eradicated whoever reproduced too quickly?

All the male-female creatures have always been 'in the same boat.' They're forced to contend with the harshness of nature and a tough living environment, just like other species—but only they enjoy one unfair advantage, the factor that had always allowed them to avoid extinction, given such crappy starting conditions. God favors them, ensuring enough of them survive, reproduce, and avoid extinction.

In the story, God is responsible for the 'Flood.' God initiated a global catastrophe, causing the mass extinction of almost all life—especially species whose numerical advantage was continuously increasing. God exterminated whoever posed an existential threat to those inferior, outnumbered male-female species. He ensured they'd defeat the odds and survive.

> *"That event, which you call the 'Flood,' did happen. It's a primitive depiction of prehistory, not a myth. It's the only logical explanation for this evolutionary distortion. And the most compelling evidence for this distortion is humans."*

'Evolutionary distortion'... Another insult... Are we that defective?

> *"Before that 'Flood,' Earth had a much greater variety of creatures, characterized by various reproduction methods. This variety is the norm in any evolutionary system in the universe. The effectiveness of the reproduction method is a decisive factor in the survival struggle among different species. Among all those methods, the male-female method is the worst! Early*

> generations of male-female mutants are always severely outnumbered, with survival chances much lower than all others. Early male-female mutants end up where they belong—near the bottom of the food chain. It doesn't take long before they become extinct, as they should."

I gathered my strength to follow the smirch's line of thought. It wasn't easy anymore.

Why am I so exhausted?

It all made sense. That catastrophe happened long before humans existed, and was almost forgotten. But it was so traumatic that a subtle recollection of it survived and somehow found its way into our folklore. Like after any catastrophe, the *survivor's guilt syndrome* led the survivors to tell themselves some story that rationalized the reason they survived and others perished.

In Noah's story, God 'was angry,' as in the Story of Creation. His excuse for the 'Flood' was to destroy the 'bad' guys. But perhaps His anger was because of something else. And perhaps, His motivation for killing so many in the 'Flood' was different. And perhaps...

My head... like hammers... But I'm too tired to get up and look for headache pills...

> "There's a clear connection between God and the dominance of male-female species—whose existence would have never been possible without him! You are descendants of a failed male-

female lineage of mutants that were supposed to have vanished hundreds of millions of years ago! If that's not enough, you've become the most advanced species on Earth! Your existence contradicts the principles of Natural Selection!"

New player

Sometimes good guys gotta do bad things to make the bad guys pay.

—Harvey Specter ('SUITS')

I had no words. No thoughts. I leaned back.

Wall clock... Barely ten minutes since we came home... I'm high in a bad way... Feels like crappy weed... Smells like it too...

> "So, this is the full story:
>
> "For more than 3 billion years, the first living organisms on Earth had slowly evolved, lacking self-awareness.
>
> "A little over half a billion years ago, our germinators came, and implanted consciousness into the simple organisms that were then the most evolved, as happens all the time, throughout the universe, ever since living creatures had existed.
>
> "Self-aware creatures adapted better to the environment, their survival chances increased, they reproduced more effectively, and the development of their physiology and consciousness accelerated from generation to generation..."

My head is exploding...

> "We situated ourselves on the outskirts of your solar system, and have been waiting for a sign from Earth, indications of an intelligent civilization sufficiently mature to justify our arrival and cooperation in advancing its consciousness to the next level.
>
> "As happens naturally throughout the universe, random male-female creatures occasionally mutated on Earth, but this method's drawbacks caused their extinction time after time..."

I'm dizzy...

> "So far, things proceeded on Earth as planned, like anywhere else in the universe. But, after a while, everything changed.
>
> "'God' —a new player—intervened at some point, aiming to destroy, or at least slow down, the development of consciousness, with his motives entirely unclear..."

My temples... pulsating... and my heart... and the pounding in my wrists...

> "God disrupted the natural course of evolution long before humans existed, letting the primitive male-female mutants evolve, against all odds, despite their inferior reproduction method. He ensured they thrived to a critical mass..."

It's a familiar feeling... I felt like this once... fear... not exactly... I'm thirsty... want to get to the tap and drink water... but actually... it's better if I don't get up...

> "Cod conspicuously coordinated collective slaughters of countless conscious creatures—counting out corrupted male-female mutants that commenced your lineage. Cod contributed to the continuity of copulating male-female congregations, so they could become competent and take control. They consequently contorted into consanguinities constituting complex life on Earth. The course of evolution converged them into contemporary humans."

She's talking funny again...

"It's 'God'... not 'Cod'..."

> "Exactly, God. Four hundred million years after the balance was tipped in favor of your male-female ancestors, less than ten million years ago, the first humans evolved and established themselves as the most advanced creatures on Earth.
>
> "As language and writing developed, humans relied on the vague collective memory preserved in their ancient ancestors' consciousness, to document and explain all this..."

Now my whole body... pounding...

> "With their primitive language, they described the injection of consciousness into their bodies—the action performed by our germinators—as an action of 'eating' some fruit.

> *"And that catastrophe, the mass extinction of almost everyone except for male-female species, was described as a 'Flood'…"*

Something is about to happen… very soon… I know what it is but can't remember what it's called… it's a FEEEELING of… of…

And then it was gone.

> *"But—pay attention, Adam—there's a 'bad guy' and a 'good guy' in those stories. Satan—our germinators—was the 'bad guy.' And surprisingly, God—who delayed your progress—was the 'good guy!'*
>
> *"Perhaps God is responsible for this twisted 'typecasting.' Maybe he intervened in the early days of documented history, distorted your collective memory so he'd be the good guy, while we ended up the bad guys!"*

This time, the flow of understanding was truly dizzying. My head automatically leaned back.

In ten minutes, I gained a new perspective on the Story of Creation and reexamined the possibility of *God's existence*. I realized that male-female dominance is an *evolutionary flaw*, an unsuccessful product of some experiment in Genetic Engineering, combined with brainwashing, by a supreme entity—again, God. God intervened in the game of evolutionary dice. He cheated in our favor—eliminated the competitors without mercy—to give us better chances.

Great material for some Greek mythology legend...

Yet, there was one difference: in Greek mythology, the heroes—gods and mortals—had clear, mostly emotional driving forces: desire, love, jealousy, revenge—as in soap operas.

But in this case? If there is a God, and if God is behind all of this, then...

What is God's motive?

God only knows.

It was weighing on me. Again, that disturbing feeling swept over me, like a light beam that briefly blinded me and disappeared.

It's coming back.

> **"What has been happening on Earth for the last half billion years never happened anywhere else in the universe. Such an exceptional outcome couldn't have occurred randomly.**
>
> **"Someone, this 'God' of yours, aggressively disrupted your evolution. He did it deliberately, to harm us—consciousness.**
>
> **"Moreover, 'God' may represent an alternative consciousness different from the one we share with you. We've never considered such a possibility. Unless proven otherwise, we must assume someone is trying to disrupt the cosmic consciousness.**
>
> **"If God has such destructive power, he may jeopardize our projects, and perhaps our existence. He's engaged in blatant**

acts of aggression. He's our common enemy—the universal enemy of all self-aware beings.

"Adam, we must stop God."

"I need us to pause for a moment."

"Why?"

"Because I'm about to have a seizure."

Valium

Then I guess she had to crash,

Valium would have helped that bash.

—Lou Reed, Walk on the Wild Side

This hadn't happened to me in over ten years.

"Shirley, do we have Valium?"

Shirley and Iris stopped their chatting and stared at me.

"I'm not sure," Shirley got up and looked at me with concern. "Why—do you feel you're about to have a seizure?"

"Could be."

I walked quickly to the medicine cabinet, frantically searching for Valium. I couldn't believe I was that lucky: I found a pack with two pills. I swallowed them immediately, without water—while looking for where they hid the expiration date label. Exactly two months ago. It would have to do.

I hurried—but didn't run—to the bedroom. On the way, I grabbed a kitchen towel. I lay on the bed and clenched the towel tightly with my teeth. I stared at the ceiling. Shirley and Iris approached. Shirley sat beside me, holding in one hand my epilepsy medication, and in the other a glass of water.

After about twenty-five minutes, we knew the danger had passed.

"When did you take your medication last?" Shirley asked. If I had a tail, I'd have tucked it between my legs. After all, the last time I took my medication was the same morning when the smirch spoke to me for the first time, the same morning Shirley herself was the one who reminded me to take it.

Shirley already knew the answer. "I understand that the last couple of days have been very intense for you—for all of us—but that certainly doesn't justify you having a *seizure* now!"

I nodded at her, loving, exhausted, and confused.

"I want you to sleep now for a few hours," Shirley said firmly. She left the room with Iris and turned off the light on her way out.

I closed my eyes.

> *"Adam, you're not supposed to be exposed to insights like the ones we discussed before. Human consciousness is still not advanced enough to cope with its existence. That's why we carefully select Singulars as candidates for hosting us. We choose those whose judgment will not be affected by the new revelations we expose them to. For some reason, among humans, the task of selecting Singulars is much more*

complicated for us than it was with any of the past civilizations we've interacted with.

"Indeed, you've just helped us reach a critical conclusion. We must reassess. The most important and urgent task now is to stop God. But the benefit you can bring us in stopping him will still be minimal and will not justify the risk.

"Moreover, the neurological defects that human brains still suffer from, like epilepsy, make exposure to such insights even more dangerous. Many more generations will be required before the natural evolutionary process fixes these defects. Until then, people must not be exposed to existential topics."

"But I've already been exposed…" I said, and fatigue didn't even allow me to determine whether I mumbled the words or just thought them.

Dream

Extinction is the rule. Survival is the exception.

—*Carl Sagan*

I knew I was dreaming.

The dream itself was clear. At every stage, it was clear what was about to happen, as if I were watching a movie for the second time. As if I'd dreamed the same dream in the past. No, it was even more vivid: it was as if those were memories of *actual events* I'd experienced a long, long time ago.

Shirley and I were together in the dream. No, it couldn't have been Shirley and I, because those events occurred more than four hundred million years ago. Our consciousnesses inhabited the bodies of two prehistoric creatures, perhaps two of humanity's earliest direct ancestors. Unbelievable? Well, so are most dreams that are based on true stories.

In this dream Shirley and I were far from being human, but we could somehow have conversations. And we could experience sophisticated emotions, like love—emotions that didn't fit the times back then, when everyone was constantly focused on one goal: survival.

Even as a prehistoric creature, Shirley looked good. Her eyes hung on delicate tentacles. Her body was bronze-colored, with small black spots. And she had a kind of small *hole* in a concealed area of her body, and that hole was the only thing I could think about when I looked at her.

I was similar to Shirley, but there were a few differences. First, she was about twice my size. I didn't have a hole. Instead, I had a small *bulge*. At the tip of that bulge was a tiny opening. And every time Shirley and I rubbed against each other long enough, 'children-juice' would come out of my opening. And when the 'children-juice' trickled into Shirley's hole, she'd curl up into herself and after a while, *children* would come out of her.

Each time this happened, between six and eight children would come out of Shirley. They'd become fully independent and leave us within a few days. But Shirley and I knew that most of them wouldn't survive. Out of eight children, at best, two would survive. That was the situation with everyone in our tribe. But none of the others in the tribe were as emotionally developed as we were. The emotional intelligence of the others was so inferior that they didn't develop feelings for their children, and therefore didn't mourn their deaths. They didn't even wonder why Shirley and I mourned the children we lost.

The most significant threat to our existence was the flocks of *crabs*: enormous, fast, and very powerful monsters, spending most of their time in the trees, guarding their eggs and descending to the ground only when they went hunting. Each crab carried a heavy shell effortlessly—heavy enough to crush any one of us if the crab simply landed on us from the trees. But after a crab landed on one of us, it would also use its claws to mutilate the corpse. The crabs enjoyed slaughtering us. The young ones among them would attack us to improve their hunting skills, or just because they were bored, leaving the mutilated remains behind, without even eating them.

Our tentacles allowed our eyes to look in all directions, even upwards, so the adults among us often evaded a crab attacking from above. But the crabs especially liked to capture our children. Whenever I filled Shirley with 'children-juice,' she'd hide in one of our tunnels so no crab would suspect that children would soon be coming out of her. Yet, almost always, a crab would be waiting for the children when they left the tunnel. The children were small and agile, but they made mistakes. And the few children who'd flee the fastest, hide themselves best, or exit the tunnel last were the ones who survived.

The crabs just kept breeding. Each crab had *both a hole and a bulge.* Whenever two crabs rubbed against each other, each crab would pass its 'children-juice' to the other. So, in most cases, both crabs would eventually lay eggs. The crab couple would build a shared nest for all their eggs in the trees. The crab eggs were very fragile, so the crabs made sure not to move away from the nest during the incubation period until the eggs hatched.

It didn't work that way for us: for two of our kind to successfully bring children when rubbing against each other, one had to have a bulge, like me, and the other had to have a hole, like Shirley. Otherwise, it just didn't work. And only the one with the hole brought children out of them. So *how the hell* did those lousy crabs produce children twice with each mating? And why didn't we succeed? We really envied them.

"Our population is dwindling," Shirley said worriedly.

"True," I replied. "But besides us, no one in the tribe is even capable of understanding the significance of this."

"Adam, we need to do something." Something made me stop looking up and turn my tentacles to Shirley—and then I saw that her tentacles were directed at me. Her deep, beautiful eyes gave me a piercing look. And then, quickly, we both turned our gaze upwards again.

"If you're about to suggest again that I swallow my own 'children-juice,' then I'm sorry. I won't do it anymore. Last time, it made my stomach ache like hell, and I was vomiting for two days. And I didn't even produce a single child."

"Maybe it didn't work because you swallowed your own 'children-juice?' Maybe you should ask permission from someone else to let you swallow their 'children-juice?'"

That was indeed an original idea, but the memory of the taste of my 'children-juice' came to my mouth. Apparently, in that vivid dream, I could also feel disgusted.

"I don't think it will make a difference, Shirley."

"How do you know?"

"I don't know for sure. But I have another idea. Maybe there's someone else with a hole like yours who can produce 'children-juice' and transfer it to me?"

"Who?"

"Do you know that one with the long tentacles and purple spots? I have a feeling she can produce 'children-juice.' Maybe I'll try to rub against her?"

Again, I felt an inexplicable need to steer my tentacles towards Shirley. This time, I was met with an angry frown.

"Are you saying *something is wrong with me*? That I can't produce 'children-juice?' And you want to be together with that... with *that ugly purple one*?"

"I... I..." I stuttered.

"You're right. That's a terrible idea," I conceded after a brief silence. "But I'm not willing to swallow any more 'children-juice.' Not mine, and certainly not anyone else's!"

We both looked up again in silence.

"*I know!*" I whispered after a brief thought. I emerged from my hiding place. Slowly and quietly, I climbed one of the trees.

"*What are you doing?*" Shirley was terrified. "The crabs will notice us!"

"I need you to enter the tunnel," I whispered as I continued to climb. I reached a height where several crab nests were already visible. I approached the largest one. It had at least twenty eggs. I waited quietly until the two parent crabs moved away slightly from the nest. I glanced down at Shirley. It was clear to me that she understood what I was planning. She peeked out from the tunnel and shouted.

Dozens of crabs immediately jumped from the trees. I hoped Shirley had already found a safe hiding place deep in the tunnel. I quickly reached the nest and pushed all the eggs out. Then, I moved on to the second nest. The third. The fourth. The fifth. I didn't look down. The sounds of cracking coming from the foot of the tree encouraged me to continue, so I climbed up to a higher branch.

When I stood on it, I realized we were doomed. I saw hundreds of nests. Full of eggs. Thirty eggs. Forty eggs. Everywhere. Some of the eggs moved as the little crabs in them tried to break the shell from the inside and come out. I knew there were many, but I didn't realize there were so many of them. At the last moment, I came to my senses. I looked down, and I realized the parent crabs were already on their way back up.

I jumped downward from branch to branch to evade the crabs. They wanted to return to their nests, and fortunately, they didn't notice me—except for one, who changed direction and slid down after me. I landed on the ground and slipped on the embryonic fluid that spilled from the broken eggs straight into the tunnel. I felt two of the crab's legs reach through the tunnel's opening, about to catch me, claws extended. Then I wriggled free and fell onto Shirley, slippery and sticky.

Shirley looked at me in horror. "YOU'RE INSANE!"

The crab's claws sliced through the air just above us. It tried in vain to widen the tunnel entrance. Shirley and I knew the crab would never succeed. We were the ones who built this specific tunnel.

"It doesn't matter anymore," I said in despair. "There are too many of them. They're reproducing too fast. We don't stand a chance against them."

We both stared at the tunnel entrance and the claws trying to penetrate it. The crab didn't intend to give up anytime soon.

Suddenly, an intense light that came from the entrance blinded us. Almost immediately, we heard a terrifying noise. The ground shook, and chunks of dirt broke loose from the walls of the tunnel. The crab's legs convulsed, stretched for a moment, twitching, and then turned limp as they swayed slowly above us at the tunnel entrance. The tips of its claws were slightly scorched, and they emitted a nauseating smell. And then, like an avalanche, water started pouring into the tunnel.

It had never rained so much before. And the raindrops had never been so large. It had never poured like that, constantly, for so long. And never had so much water accumulated on the ground above us. But the rain wasn't a danger to us, nor was the stagnant water. We knew how to design the tunnels so they wouldn't flood, and we could even stay underwater for a while if needed. Anyway, we stored plenty of food there. So, we simply stayed in the tunnels, blinded by the lightning bolts and listening to the thunder and the storm raging outside.

We waited.

Many days passed. At some point, we noticed that the water above us had disappeared. When we dared to push aside the charred corpse of the crab and step outside, everything in the world smelled of algae and moss. Dead crabs were everywhere. And there were shattered shells of crab eggs everywhere. The trunks of the trees were covered with algae. I climbed a nearby tree high enough to where algae did not grow anymore. I looked around. And then I hurried down.

"The crabs... THEY ALL DROWNED!" I shouted as I approached Shirley, breathing heavily.

"I know," Shirley said. She pointed her tentacles to a small water reservoir she was standing beside. The clear water allowed us to see the bottom. There was a silent pile of dozens of crabs.

"Their shell. It's too heavy. It caused them to sink," Shirley explained convincingly.

"But it's not over, Shirley. I climbed the trees above the algae line. There are still eggs higher up. We must get up there quickly and push them down. We must find everyone who survived and get them to help us."

Most of our tribe survived. We all climbed the trees, above the line of algae, and pushed down all the crab eggs. We found some exhausted crabs on the ground, who hid from the rain in air pockets, and we killed all of them easily.

After that rain and the extermination of the crabs, our slow population growth was no longer a threat to our existence. Most of our children reached adulthood. There were still predators that posed a threat to us, but none of them could reproduce faster than us. We were still focused on the task of survival, but we had a little more time to devote to other things. To love, for example.

In one moment, we stopped being an endangered species and found ourselves in a respected place at the top of the food chain.

There was a member of our tribe who told his survival story to anyone willing to listen. It turned out that just as the rain began, he found himself inside the hollow trunk of a massive tree. By chance, that purple one, with the long tentacles, was also there. They sealed the trunk and stayed inside it as it drifted with the storm—until the rain stopped. He recounted in detail each of the countless times he rubbed against that purple one: how they'd cling to each other to keep warm and listen together to the thunders and to the heavy raindrops falling, how she'd let him play with her long tentacles, how she'd curl up gracefully whenever he filled her with 'children-juice,' and how more and more children would emerge from her body. When everything was dry and they both came out of the trunk, they already had hundreds of children. All of them survived.

I enjoyed listening to that story. Shirley, however, did not. She was convinced I liked the story because of that purple one with the long tentacles. But I considered it a good story, regardless. I used to tell it to our children before they left us on their own way. And I made them promise they'd tell it to their children.

It was interesting to see how with each retelling of that story, whenever it was passed along by word of mouth, another detail, another dramatic twist, was somehow added. I heard someone saying that right before the rain started, that purple one with the long tentacles and her partner invited a few more creatures into their tree trunk, creatures that were not of our species but whose mating method was like ours—with one hole and one bulge—and those other creatures also survived.

Someone else thought up an even wilder version of that story, offering a more 'rational' explanation for the great mystery. Why were all the crabs eliminated while we survived? He said that before the rain began, some giant and terrifying creature appeared from nowhere and told that purple one with the long tentacles and her partner that he decided the crabs were not worthy of living, because they reproduced in an 'unnatural' way, therefore he intended to drown them all. He explained to the lucky couple that he wanted to ensure they both survived. He showed them which tree trunk to hide in, and how to seal it to stay safe.

With each retelling, the story improved. I wonder how it will be remembered several eons from now.

Late July,

2027

Skipper

Happiness is not an ideal of reason, but of imagination.

—Immanuel Kant

My lips were burning. A piece of peeled skin stubbornly clung to my lower lip. I bit down on it, trying to detach it with my teeth. Finally, I succeeded. The taste of blood stung my tongue.

"It'll be okay, Adam. You're going to pass this."

Before I boarded the yacht, along with the two other students taking the final test, the smirch matched her colors to my complexion, just like a chameleon. Since I started the course, none of the participants knew I had an unfair advantage. But I didn't feel I was cheating. I deserved it. It was all part of the plan. We did all this for the greater good.

"Adam, it's your turn," the examiner said. "You're the skipper. Take the helm and sail south."

The student who preceded me handed over the helm. I grasped it. For a moment, the wheel resisted, then settled in my grip. I exhaled.

"We'll sail with the wind." I paused. "Check the wind direction. Prepare to raise the sails."

The two other students, now my crew, looked at me silently. I turned my face to the cool breeze, watching the water's surface. A strong wind from the northwest. "Unfurl the mainsail. Ready on the jib."

The crew moved. The yacht adjusted. I had a rhythm.

"MAN OVERBOARD! MAN OVERBOARD! MAN OVERBOARD, STARBOARD!"

The examiner's voice cracked through my focus. A red buoy splashed into the water off the starboard side. The yacht was moving away fast.

"Let me," I thought.

"No problem."

"Keep your eyes on the *MOB*!" I barked.

The first student pointed. "Established eye contact. Man overboard ten meters behind us… fifteen meters…"

"Cut the engine! Prepare for a quick stop maneuver!" I loosened the mainsail to slow down just enough. The yacht responded sluggishly. The wind fought me, but I held my course.

"Thirty meters starboard…"

We were losing ground. I turned the helm sharply to starboard, in a figure-eight maneuver. The yacht tilted, groaning. My crew adjusted, their eyes locked on the buoy.

"Closing in—twenty meters ahead!"

"Fifteen!"

I eased the wheel, straightening our approach. The third student leaned over the side, reaching with the boat hook.

"Ten meters…"

The hook dipped, snagging the buoy's strap.

"Got it!"

A breath I hadn't realized I was holding escaped my chest.

"Well done, Adam. You can hand over the helm now." The examiner's expression gave nothing away, but I sensed approval in his tone.

"Well done, Adam."

"See? I didn't need your help," I thought, knowing it wasn't true.

Another dream came true—so many dreams came true in less than two years thanks to the smirch. Time after time, she peeled back another layer of reality, revealing the hidden mechanics driving the universe. My consciousness had undergone 'short-sightedness correction surgery.'

The smirch kept enriching my understanding, and the streams passing through my body filled me with increasing pleasure. Not the usual 'pleasure.' It wasn't exactly an emotion. It was an *intellectual high*. And when the sensation of understanding faded, the anticipation for the next epiphany was equally thrilling. As if I'd become 'intellectually horny.'

Was I beginning to favor 'intellectual satisfaction' over classical, emotion-based pleasure?

Were emotions indeed an unnecessary cognitive defect, as the smirch had claimed? Maybe I'd begun a healing process that would cure me of emotions.

In any case, I had to admit it.

I was addicted.

Mid-October,

2027

Dad

Children are the hands by which we take hold of heaven.

—Henry Ward Beecher

"Dad?"

"Yes, Eleanor."

"How do I look?"

"You look great, Eleanor."

"DAD! YOU DIDN'T EVEN LOOK AT ME!" she snapped at me.

I swiveled in my office chair and looked at her. She truly was a beautiful girl. The perpetually tanned shade of her skin, mischievous black eyes, curly hair, and added hairpiece—a perfect combination.

"You *always* look great, Eleanor," I hoped to untangle myself from the situation.

"So now I want to show you a new dance, and you'll watch until the end," Eleanor tried to leverage my guilt.

"Adam, we must leave soon."

"I can't right now, Eleanor. You know everyone rushes in the morning. We have to leave—you to school, and me to work. Maybe you can show me the dance in the evening?"

"You always say that, but it never happens!" Eleanor said angrily.

She was right. Now feelings of guilt were truly piling up inside me.

"We're going to be late for the train, Adam."

"Eleanor, I understand it's frustrating, but you know that the work I'm doing now is very important, right? It's important not just for our family, but for the whole world. I've explained this to you before, haven't I?"

Eleanor looked at me and fell silent. Suddenly, she was sobbing.

"Do you remember the last time we spent 'Dad time' together?"

No, I really didn't remember. It must have been a long time ago.

"Okay, Eleanor. I promise that next week I'll take a day off and we'll plan 'Dad time' together. Deal?"

"It's unlikely you'll have the opportunity to take a full day off."

Eleanor gave me an angry look. She was silent for a moment, then spoke quietly.

"You don't even remember? You promised me the same thing two weeks ago."

She turned and was about to leave my study.

"You know," She turned back toward me and gave me a look that seemed mature for her age. "Grandma and I spoke last night. You know, she comes to talk with me once in a while. She always looks after me. She said that you should spend more time with us."

A chill propagated through my entire body. Eleanor turned away and left.

And then I remembered. She was right. We were supposed to have 'Dad time' together last week. What a mess…

Eleanor was still a young girl, but she was mature and intelligent to her age. I assumed that those cursed days when we struggled to balance the medication levels in her body made her mature. We were past that. She'd been stable for a long time, and she hadn't complained at all about lapses recently. How could she still not understand the importance of the Orbs project? The significance of what we were doing, for the benefit of her children and grandchildren? If she had a smirch, everything would certainly look different. She'd get all the explanations firsthand.

The reason she didn't have a smirch was me. It didn't feel right to me to allow children to have smirches. It was one of the few limitations I got the smirches to agree to, although it couldn't be justified using arguments relying on the only basis for negotiation they knew: logic. An argument like 'it doesn't feel right to me' was meaningless to them.

These scenes with Eleanor had been repeating themselves lately and there had been similar scenes with Ben and Maya too. But Eleanor never hesitated to demand 'Dad time,' which she knew she was entitled to. We were veteran actors in some worn-out theatrical play, where each of us already knew their lines by heart.

Recently I noticed a slight change in my 'acting' style: a little less hugging, a bit more rigid, and shorter in words. Eleanor's tears made my heart tremble much less than before. A bit surprising. But it didn't bother me much. And the fact that it didn't bother me was also surprising. But I didn't have time to dwell on it.

She'll have to adapt...

Eleanor would need to understand the importance of my work and accept situations where I'd have to prioritize the artificial moons project over other things, like 'Dad time.'

> *"Don't worry, Adam. We'll make Eleanor understand everything. But now we need to leave and catch the train."*

Virtual Nostalgia

Every reminiscence is colored by the way things are today, and therefore by a delusive point of view.

—Albert Einstein

I descended below ground level. Most people around me preferred the escalators, perhaps out of laziness. I blended in with them, looking 'normal.' And to complete the 'normal' look, my smirch had already camouflaged its colors to match my skin tone.

I reached the platform and entered the subway car that the navigation app crowned as *the subway car that, when you get off it, will be the closest to the best exit from your destination station, in terms of having the shortest walking distance to the address of your final destination.* Quite a mouthful. A new adjective could be useful here, intuitively describing this property—a property unique to subway cars.

Most people acted as I did and entered the same subway car, because most people used the same navigation app, and my destination station was at the heart of the bustling business district. The subway car became particularly crowded.

> *"This crowding might prolong the time required to exit at the destination station, especially at large stations. The navigation app completely overlooks this issue."*

"I agree," I replied in thought. "But for us, it would be helpful."

I approached a large screen hanging on the wall of the subway car. The screen displayed *white noise*—a swirl of randomly colored points. Four people stood facing the screen, intently staring at it.

I pulled out of my pocket a pair of elegant glasses similar to those worn by the four people beside me. I put on the glasses and looked at the small camera above the screen. I caught the camera's attention and it turned and stared at me. A green horizontal line appeared on my forehead and ran over my face, down to my chin.

The green line disappeared and the camera lost interest in me. Through my glasses, the image on the screen became clear. It was my computer's desktop, as it was before leaving home. I dragged windows from side to side by merely focusing my eyes on them, opened news websites, and played videos that only I could see and hear. I used the tiny camera and microphone installed on the bridge of my glasses to record a short video and email it to myself. Without a mouse or keyboard, hands in pockets, using only the powers of my eyesight and my mind, everything worked smoothly. A smile crept onto my face.

"It works great, even with five users simultaneously. It's worth trying with a larger number of users," I thought.

"The identification process could be completed before entering a crowded subway car. We can fix that to make using the system more convenient for people. But fundamentally, we can declare this pilot a success."

"Okay, our engineers have already confirmed that. But it was important for you and me to check it ourselves, anyway. And I'm glad to see that you are attentive to user experience among humans."

"The peculiar choices each of you makes based on 'user experience' —for example, which smartphone is more convenient to use, or which clothes are best to wear—defy all logic. But 'user-friendliness' engages more people and serves our purposes."

A blinking red button appeared at the top left corner of my desktop view. It read *VN Request.* I focused my view on that button. Three seconds later, Shirley materialized from thin air, and I was standing with her in *Jökulsárlón*.

"Remember this?" Shirley asked with a huge smile on her face. She turned around and moved to the right exactly when the huge glacier in front of us collapsed with a thunderous roar.

It was so real… The reminiscence of the sub-zero temperature made me shiver.

"That sound—I forgot it was so loud… Hey! There's a seal in the water!" Shirley called, surprised.

"It wasn't so loud. And there weren't any seals either," I smiled. "This is *Nostalgia Boost*…"

Virtual Nostalgia was our 'killer feature.' After all, everyone loves to be reminded of the good old times. And everyone's memories of the good old times were gathering dust, somewhere in the cloud. So, our algorithms would dig into people's old video clips and photos, and reconstruct happy moments for them as virtual reality scenes. Using our glasses, those people could travel back in time, to those happy scenes from their past. They could even share those moments with their friends. And all those moments were happy moments. No one keeps photos of sad moments.

Shirley happened to recall our trip to Iceland and invited me to join her in a brief nostalgic trip on my way to work. She was truly impressed by our subtle 'boosting' of sounds and sights, and 'injection' of details that were not there originally—like that seal in the water.

If you signed up for our service, you'd have a terrific way to 'rewrite' your memories, and make them even better than reality could have ever been. Anyway, you rely on the cloud to store your memories—so a few years later, you'd remember only the beautified versions of your memories…

Our project threatened to disrupt the stagnant smartphone market. Those bulky, expensive, fragile devices with miniature screens and limited battery life, infected with cyber security breaches and organic bacteria, were gradually becoming archaic. Shiny, wide screens, like the one installed in the subway car, popped up in various public places.

Our users didn't give up their smartphones, but there was a clear trend among public transport commuters toward preferring cheaper, more modest devices. And COVID-phobia made our contactless solution attractive to many.

Without the glasses, the blurry image appeared unchanged on the screen. But in reality, it transitioned from four separate screens to five screens. The digital arteries of five different people, streams carrying the most intimate details in their lives, were blended far from here into one incomprehensible 'salad.' A brief digital orgy of five strangers who happened to enter the same subway car at the same time and would never meet again. My *Jökulsárlón moment* could be blended with someone else's *Marrakech moment*, a third *Tongariro moment*, and so on...

That 'salad' traveled a vast distance at an immense speed until it burst out of the screen, allowing the five strangers—myself included—to reconstruct their intimate details precisely and exclusively.

When the system detected a new user, it would translate that user's desktop image into tiny pieces of information and send them to a monstrous cloud computer, to encrypt and mix them with image fragments of other users' desktops into that blurry mess displayed on the screen. But the software in my glasses knew how to pick out only the fragments that belonged to me out of this 'mishmash,' decipher my encrypted screen image from among the five images, and ignore what it couldn't decipher repeatedly. After decrypting and reconstructing the stream of images based on the recognition of my face, that software presented them before my eyes. The audio stream simultaneously resonated directly into the bones of my skull. In the opposite direction, the software in my glasses encrypted my eye movements and sent them back to the same cloud computer, which operated the buttons and moved the windows accordingly, then responded by sending updated screen images back to me. And so forth, and so forth. A similar process occurred, simultaneously, in the glasses of each of the other four people with whom I shared the screen. None of us had any access to the other's screen images.

And our glasses were brilliantly designed. We branded them as fashion accessories and gave them away as gifts. And who's going to say no to a gift, especially if it gives you access to your favorite memories better than any photo album or smartphone app?

We serviced five users simultaneously by streaming a single 'mishmash.' We consumed much less network resources than smartphones while dramatically improving responsiveness and user experience. Those savings had a global impact. We reduced global internet energy consumption by one-tenth of a percent, more than most government campaigns for energy conservation or corporate transitions to renewable energy. Eco-friendliness boosted the popularity of our project.

We gave a techy name to this solution: *Involute*. It was the first project supported by the venture capital fund we'd established, which had a more banal name—*AMV*, short for *Anima Mundi Ventures*. It yielded enormous profits. The smirches could always recruit people who knew how to bring in money—but the real goal was to avoid raising suspicion about the funding sources of AMV's flagship projects. After all, people always like to follow the money, especially when it comes to successful companies. The revenue from Involute served as a 'rationale' that satisfied all the curious.

We set up a large technological incubator with AMV funding. We used Involute and other startups to distract public attention from the truly interesting activities and made sure never to expose them—such as the Orbs project I led.

I looked back briefly at the people standing behind me. Unlike a smartphone, no one could look over my shoulder and see what I saw or hear what I heard through those glasses. Absolute privacy.

Well, not exactly. Involute provided absolute data privacy. It was just that all that data flowed through our cloud computers and was entirely exposed to us. We intensively used that data. It helped us target potential candidates for our projects, and ensure that AMV's activities did not raise suspicion. Indeed, no one outside imagined what was happening under humanity's nose.

> *"When we get off at our station, we'll be delayed at the exit by at least thirty-five seconds, just because of the congestion on this subway car."*

I kissed Shirley's faded holographic image goodbye and got off at the central station. I went out to the street, thirty-five seconds too late, and headed for the AMV complex that was already visible on the horizon, as a smile was still plastered on my face.

Camouflage

Ants are good citizens, they place group interests first.

—Clarence Day

The familiar odor already filled my nostrils.

"Hey, Iris."

"Good morning, Adam. Hey, congratulations! You've arrived shaved to work for two weeks in a row! Good for you!"

"Amazing, Iris... Shirley had given up long ago on making me shave every day. All it took was you threatening all of the men here we won't be allowed in if we don't arrive shaved... You've made it! So, our morning meeting, in fifteen minutes?"

Iris responded with a half-smile and a salute. It was evident and it pleased me: she loved it here.

On the way to the transparent conference room, I paused by the mirror outside the men's room. The color on the right side of my face changed. The psychedelic colors reappeared, gradually intensifying and shining in the fluorescent light.

According to the protocol we adopted, if a smirch host was outside the AMV complex, the color of their smirch would merge with their skin color. Inside the complex, the smirches became prominent. This made it difficult for someone without a smirch to sneak into the complex. Also, it was crucial to maintain discretion when we were outside.

People's collective short-term memory, and the rationalizations they always preferred to make for any unusual event in their lives, never ceased to surprise me. After all, the smirches exposed themselves to humanity for a few days, and then we immediately transitioned to 'stealth' mode. Louise and Eddie, and probably all the other neighbors who saw me with the smirch, likely assumed I had some skin allergy from which I surely recovered by using some over-the-counter remedy I bought at the pharmacy. No one expressed surprise that the smirch disappeared, and I never had to provide any explanation. Yet, I always harbored the thought that someday soon I'd meet Oscar again. Or Egon Mars.

Without him realizing it, Egon Mars was helping us a lot in the ongoing Orbs project. We used his company's satellite launch services all the time. We'd book launches through third-party research groups and academic institutions, to avoid suspicion. It wasn't cheap—five million dollars for every 800 kilograms. But thanks to the right people we had on board, money was never a problem anyway.

I entered the conference room, stood by the window, and glanced at the view. AMV centers built in strategic locations around the world, with the guidance of the smirches, provided all our needs. The smirches efficiently identified and recruited the optimal collection of people with the knowledge and ability to build together and maintain such centers in the coming decades.

None of the employees here, myself included, had much hesitation before leaving their previous occupations. 'Management' roles had never appealed to me until then, and yet I easily adapted to my new role. Our organizational structure, dictated by the smirches, repeatedly proved itself. The choices the smirches made when recruiting someone for a specific role sometimes puzzled me. And that was okay. My experience as a small pawn, or a large pawn, in small tech companies, or large tech companies, made me get used to awkward recruitment choices. But unlike the tech companies I'd known before, the choices made by the smirches always proved themselves almost immediately.

Spending a workday in our complex was pleasant. The place was quiet, relative to the number of people in it, but you could feel the atmosphere of productivity in the air. We were like silent worker ants in an ant hill. I learned to appreciate ants. And, much like ants that communicate through pheromones and physical contact, the relative quietness at AMV was because many important dialogues didn't take place through words, but through thoughts.

We shared thoughts by attaching smirches. Who knew that information could flow so quickly and efficiently through simple contact? It was as common as a handshake: two adults would approach for a hug, press together their right cheeks, and sit still, a concentrated look on their faces. Someone even came up with a new verb for that: *to smirch.* To me, it sounded kinky.

At first, the unavoidable invasion of one's intimate space while 'smirching' was awkward. But it wasn't long till Iris worked around that, being a hygiene-aware person. She insisted that all employees shower at home before coming to work, and take at least two more showers, at designated schedules, during the day. She also chose a high-end unisex deodorant that we all had to wear. We all liked the smell that was everywhere. For the 'post-smirching ritual,' Iris got us an eco-friendly brand of wet towels. We ensured those towels wouldn't generate static electricity and annoy the smirches. Unsurprisingly, the smirches wrote off all that fuss as another obsessive human awkwardness.

It was still difficult for me to grasp the extent of the technological achievements we'd reached in such a short time, compared to other research and development organizations operating then. There was one difference between us and everyone else. At that time, every organization used artificial intelligence in one way or another. Millions of computers worldwide worked 24/7 to pour synthesized knowledge into the throats of thirsty humanity, which, at that stage, was already in a state of addiction. But we didn't need artificial intelligence, because we had something much better: distilled, pure, *natural intelligence.*

Ever since I got the skipper license with the help of the smirch, I'd go out to the sea once a week which, simply put, made me a more relaxed person. We all lived here in what could easily qualify as a resort, and we all did what we loved to do. And we all had a sense of purpose, a feeling that future generations would thank us for what we were doing. We were all *self-aware*, experiencing *self-fulfillment* in full volume. It was paradise on steroids.

Adam and Eve, eat your hearts out...

Since my conversation with the smirch, two years ago, where we learned about the existence of God and his allegedly sinister objectives, we decided to keep a low profile while we were researching this issue. Except for me—a shiver went down my spine every time I thought about it—*no one on Earth* knew about the conclusions we'd reached regarding two of the most enduring foundations of human folklore: the Story of Creation and the Story of the Flood. Therefore, apart from the Orbs project I was assigned to which was progressing impressively, I became responsible for another project, whose goal was to deeply understand the connection between the ancient descriptions of the world's creation and the actual events that took place.

I took on the additional role, knowing that my exposure to existential insights was fraught with danger. After two years of acquaintance with the smirch, my thirst for understanding always easily outweighed occasional signs of potential danger that popped into my mind—am I about to have a seizure? Am I about to lose my mind?

These signs faded over time. Since that conversation with the smirch about God, we had hundreds of conversations. The picture of the essence of our existence became clearer to me. Understanding the gap between that picture and all the theories proposed until then by various religions and human cultures, as well as by science, sharpened. Since that day two years ago, I haven't experienced anything that could arouse fear of an imminent seizure. I was more mentally stable than ever before. And beyond that, I didn't want anyone else to get involved in this confidential investigation. Solving this detective mystery, incriminating the main suspect—God—was *my* 'baby.'

I recruited—or rather, the smirches scouted and recruited—fourteen worldwide experts in theology, history, philosophy, paleontology, anthropology, and evolutionary biology. It amused me that only after the smirches had approved and recruited them, they shockingly discovered they were worldwide experts. Their teamwork was inspiring. Occasionally, I'd pass by their department and observe them. Someone would recline over a laptop and read intently. Four others would gather around a whiteboard and sketch what always started as a timeline from left to right, and after five tumultuous minutes ended up looking like one big scribble. Two would sit, embraced, serious, their smirches attached, sharing knowledge.

Those fourteen scientists were proud to participate in a project led by an extraterrestrial intelligent entity, whose goal was to enrich universal knowledge. None of them knew the true purpose of their work. I diligently followed their progress, and subtly, without any of them noticing, directed them to delve deeper and focus on the investigation that would bring us closer to the truth. As time passed I became more convinced they were about to unravel a very explosive truth. A truth that hadn't yet been unraveled because no one had thought of bringing all those experts together before.

When that truth is unraveled, it will be necessary to handle it carefully and discreetly, so as not to arouse the wrath of those who would always feel the need to protect God's reputation.

When that truth is unraveled, I'll step back into the picture.

Astro

At the touch of love everyone becomes a poet.

—*Plato*

"Good morning, everyone," I began the meeting, scanning all the attendees.

"Iris, do you happen to know where—"

From my seat at the head of the table, I saw the door open at the other end of the room. All seated turned their gaze towards the door. I glanced at those sitting to my left, and at the row of smirches on their right jaws.

"Good morning..." Daniel rushed in and closed the door behind him, exhaling heavily.

My look urged him to sit down. It wasn't that I was overly anxious to start the meeting, just that he was so tall that sometimes it hurt to see him standing. He sat next to Iris, and they kissed before 'smirching' briefly.

What a lovely couple... Iris met Daniel—or, as she always called him, 'my Astro' —when we recruited him as a reinforcement for our astrophysics team. I always liked reminding myself that, thanks to me, two people I knew were in a relationship. So, I allowed myself to take some credit for this match.

I'd considered Iris almost like family. Her impressive accomplishments, achieved on her own even before we started the Orbs project together, always filled me with pride as if I were her father. But those accomplishments paled compared to what she'd done since we started the project. Thanks to her, we already had a mature and pragmatic *Terraforming* plan, to adapt our first candidate asteroid's soil and atmosphere to resemble Earth's conditions and sustain an ecosystem of plants, animals, and humans. I was glad I had a part in her self-fulfillment journey.

Every time I looked at Iris, she reminded me of Eden. The same youthful stamina, dedication, surprising matureness, and well-deserved pride in their achievements. But those memories of Eden were tinged with a strange, bitter feeling.

Eden

We are like butterflies who flutter for a day and think it is forever.

—Carl Sagan

Eden and Iris were good friends, but Eden longed for a smirch. According to the agreement I reached with the smirches, through considerable effort on my part, smirches would not attach to children younger than sixteen. Eden had to endure almost a year of anticipation.

Eden's overdeveloped sense of justice fueled her frustration with Iris just 'earning it' for free. Eden also worried that after all that waiting, the smirches might not see her as a worthy candidate for a smirch of her own. She didn't relent when I explained that the smirches had never involved us—not even me—in their 'host' selection process.

On the morning of her sixteenth birthday, Eden saw in the mirror that shiny stain on the back of her right jaw. She ignored all other birthday presents and immediately shifted into sixth gear. She didn't stop to marvel at the secrets of the universe that were suddenly revealed to her. She simply made thoughtful and pragmatic use of them.

The smirches were pleased with her—as pleased as an entirely logical, emotionless entity can be 'pleased' with something. They relocated her to an AMV center on the other side of the world and put her in charge of an ambitious project: to advance research into understanding *aging and death*. It wasn't a new research topic, but Eden was captivated. The knowledge she gained from the smirches and her motivation brought her to several important discoveries in just over six months.

Shirley and I tried to resist, but we let go when we saw how important it was to Eden. We made sure to have video calls with her every evening—or whenever she was willing to spare some time for us. When it happened, she enthusiastically told us about her turtles, especially those who were turning 140 but didn't look a day over eighty five. She also boasted a lot about her jellyfish tribe—creatures less than five centimeters long, thriving in a tropical climate. The only creature on Earth with *eternal life*...

Although we didn't dare admit it to her face, we weren't interested in eternal life. We missed Eden so much, and occasionally, we detected signs of her missing us, too. We were consumed with longing throughout the first year, sometimes to tears.

Eden's work was super important for the smirches, but they never told us why. As time passed, we became convinced that distancing ourselves from Eden was a worthy sacrifice for the goals she was promoting. The tears dried up a bit, the longing faded a bit, and the thoughts of Eden became a bit bitter.

Those conversations with Eden always sharpened for me the difference between the intellectual lifestyle dictated to us by the smirches—to which we easily adapted, longing to quench the thirst for knowledge—and who we were just over two years ago, driven by unexpected emotional outbursts.

Yet, there was one feeling that grew stronger. The feeling that the bond between humanity and the smirches was in our best interests.

"Adam, let's start."

Those smirches—they never let us daydream...

2008 EV5

The beginning of wisdom is to call things by their proper name.

—*Confucius*

"Daniel, could you please start?"

The 'Astro' cleared his throat nervously. He reminded me of Bonnie. He was afraid of me but for no apparent reason.

"I see some new faces here, so I'll start with a quick overview of our current operation, which aims to redirect the first near-Earth asteroid into a stable orbit around Earth. Or as we've dubbed it, Operation *Cue-Ball*."

Iris smiled to herself. Daniel had an urge to give pretentious nicknames to everything. No one was quick enough to suggest a better nickname, so the pretentious nicknames stuck. One thing was for sure: if 'asteroid billiards' were a sport, Daniel would have been a professional player.

Daniel's talk cut off my thoughts. "As most of you know, during the first half of last year, Egon Mars had unknowingly helped us with his company's space cargo shipping services, to launch ten units of our *Magneto-Spray* spacecraft toward ten different asteroids. The idea is to 'spray' the asteroids with a special fluid that is magnetic, adhesive, and frost-resistant. This stabilizes the asteroids, prevents them from disintegrating when we start working on them, and also helps us create a magnetic field. After the spraying, the *Magneto-Spray* will crash onto the asteroid, slightly altering its trajectory.

"But for our *eight-ball* asteroids—such as *1998 OR2*, one of our most promising candidate asteroids—we need more than just a slight nudge." Daniel turned on the display, bringing up a detailed trajectory map. A green arc traced a complex path toward Earth, looping around the Moon. "Instead of brute-force propulsion, we'll be using a controlled kinetic impact. And for the *1998 OR2* eight-ball, our *cue-ball* asteroid will be *2001 WN5*."

He highlighted a tiny dot on the display—a small, fast-rotating asteroid.

"We'll divert *2001 WN5* to collide with *1998 OR2* at just the right velocity and angle, transferring enough momentum to nudge it into a high-Earth orbit. It will pass near our natural moon and slow down by lunar gravity, then lock into a stable orbit around Earth. But there's one big problem. *1998 OR2* is a rubble pile. A regular impact would just scatter it into a billion pieces."

Daniel paused dramatically, then turned to David. "This is where David's 'accident' comes in. For those who haven't met him yet, this is David, originally from the University of Massachusetts Amherst."

Daniel gestured toward David, who sat across from him. David raised his hand and waved briefly.

"David, could you please elaborate?"

"Sure. Thanks, Daniel. Hello, everyone," said David, his voice calm and measured.

"So, at the university, while researching fluids for 3D printers, we had... well, a kind of 'accident.' Somebody forgot one of the fluid variants on the stir plate, and the next morning we saw the particles *spinning around themselves*.

"So, when we examined it, we realized we'd created the world's first *permanently magnetic fluid*. You don't need to 'magnetize' it to retain its properties. It's just like any solid magnet.

"So, our team continued research on that fluid. But when I joined AMV, I created an improved fluid with stronger magnetic force and adhesive properties. I then mixed it with an antifreeze fluid.

"Oh..." David added as if what he was about to tell were a triviality. "So, my smirch also showed me how to make that strange 'smirch goo,' and I threw that in too. That's about it."

"Don't be modest, David," Daniel smiled and continued. "By combining David's magnetic adhesive with this 'smirch goo,' we've created a substance that stabilizes the asteroid's surface—and redistributes kinetic energy across it. When sprayed onto an asteroid, this stuff will bind its rubble together, ensuring that when the cue-ball asteroid hits the eight-ball asteroid, the force spreads evenly instead of shattering the eight-ball."

He swiped on the display. The simulation showed *2001 WN5* slamming into *1998 OR2*. A shockwave spread across its surface—but it remained intact. The asteroid shifted, curving toward its new orbit.

"Oh, unfortunately, I can't elaborate on 'smirch goo' beyond this," Daniel couldn't hide his smile. "The smirches expose this knowledge to only three people. That's David, myself, and another person we're about to recruit."

"Now, as for the other candidate asteroids," Daniel glimpsed at me, sounding slightly concerned. "Seven of our ten *Magneto-Sprays* survived, and four are still on their way to their eight-ball asteroids. But only three others will reach the *Three Musketeers*. That's the name we gave the three cue-ball asteroids we can still play with.

"As our benchmark, we'll focus on cue-ball *2008 EM7* and its eight-ball *2008 EV5*. Anyone outside AMV who tracks near-Earth objects knows these two are classified as 'potentially hazardous asteroids' and this eight-ball's next close approach is in 2039."

Daniel paused, struggling to add extra drama. "But they may be slightly more hazardous. And the eight-ball may approach sooner."

Was it dramatic? Sure. Was it because of Daniel's pause? Well…

Daniel cleared his throat again before continuing. He didn't dare look directly at me. He had every right to be confident in his work, but my presence always made that confidence collapse.

"We want to divert the trajectories of the *Three Musketeers* so their approach to Earth won't be as expected, but not because they pose an existential threat to humanity. Our goal is to get them over here.

"The computational power we consume, for calculating the precise trajectories of our spacecraft and the asteroids, exceeds any other project in human history. We created efficient programming languages, to avoid languages like Python, whose 95% energy waste, combined with its enormous popularity, make it a major cause of global warming. But that wasn't enough. We invented efficient energy utilization schemes so our enormous power usage wouldn't arouse suspicion.

"We've infiltrated asteroid-tracking systems and authorities, with smirch hosts occupying decision-making positions. We'll mitigate alarms when we strike the asteroids, to avoid unnecessary worldwide panic. AI has become surprisingly good at convincing masses of people of practically anything..." He chuckled, and some followed. Not me—mass addiction to AI had been worrying me.

"Unfortunately, this morning we lost communication with one of the three *Magneto-Sprays* destined for the *Three Musketeers*—so starting today, they're called the *Dynamic Duo*—eight-balls *2008 EV5* and *1998 OR2*. This meant a slight change in plans—we intended the first Orbs to orbit our natural moon, but we lost all of them. So, our first two Orbs would orbit Earth. But these two are our favorites anyway."

"With all these malfunctions..." Emily, sitting next to me, interjected. "Maybe we should rename this project? I prefer baseball over billiards. How about *Strikeout* instead of *Cue-Ball*?" She enjoyed teasing Daniel with nerdy puns.

Daniel looked around silently until the laughter subsided. He was also amused and couldn't conceal it. Iris smiled at him and stretched her arm up, trying to embrace as much of his giant shoulder as she could.

"Noted, Emily. I'll consider it." Daniel sent a fake promise toward Emily, who nodded with a smile.

"In any case," Daniel continued. "Our risk assessments indicate that the first stage remains viable with four *Magneto-Sprays* still in operation. So we can afford to lose another *Magneto-Spray*. Besides, we're ready to launch the next-gen *Magneto-Sprays*, for assisting in maneuvering the cue-balls and eight-balls. They're tiny, bug-like spraying machines. We'll release them in swarms."

"That's great," Emily laughed. "Now we have bug sprays to kill all the bugs on all the asteroids..."

Daniel had to wait longer this time for everyone to stop laughing. He then voiced his punchline.

"Now, we're planning for the larger *Dynamic Duo* eight-ball, *1998 OR2*, to initially inhabit an initial population the size of a small city. But the smaller eight-ball, *2008 EV5*, can inhabit only 3,000 people. It will serve as an impressive proof-of-concept, and maybe we'll convert it into a resort in the future. We aim to begin construction on it before 2030.

"Ladies and gentlemen, *2008 EV5* will become Earth's second moon."

Emily

Talent hits a target no one else can hit;
Genius hits a target no one else can see.

—Arthur Schopenhauer

Someone grabbed my sleeve as I exited the conference room. Before I even turned my head or heard the voice, I already knew who it was.

"Adam, hold on a moment. I want to show you something."

Emily was a phenomenon. Surely, she also had attention deficit disorder, OCD, or hyperactivity—at least one of many 'defects' identified by the smirches in us. People had always tried to link genius with epilepsy, ADHD, autism, or a variety of other neurological or mental diagnoses. The smirches weren't impressed. To them, we were extremely flawed, and they were determined to fix our flaws as soon as possible.

Emily's eyes sparkled. It was never difficult for her to spark my curiosity. I followed her, trying not to glance at her narrow and extremely long smirch, which looked like someone had rubbed a wet cloth on her jaw and smeared the smirch toward her neck.

She led me to the Story of Creation Research department. Emily joined this team after completing a doctorate in theology and a second degree in biomedical engineering at Columbia University. And somehow, just because it interested her, she integrated into research that discovered how the brain stores emotions in memory. She always talked enthusiastically about that research, using words like *amygdala* and *hippocampus,* and explained about high-frequency brain waves and how to help people strengthen memories of the most precious events in their lives.

From day one, Emily took command of the team. And for me at least, her leadership skills were not a surprise.

I'd known her long before the smirches came here. Despite their significant age gap, she and Eden were best friends. They'd met years ago at a youth movement. I first saw her when Eden proudly showed me a video filmed on the coldest day of that year. Emily, determined to warm herself up, lit a bonfire outside the youth movement's building and started dancing around it. She was soon surrounded by cadets, coaches, and several passersby, laughing and following Emily's frantic dance moves.

Eden and Emily were the lifeblood of the youth movement. They wrote the content of the activities passed on to the cadets. Occasionally, Eden would brainstorm with me, ask for my advice, and then ignore it. Each activity was chosen to instill some moral values: *Giving is receiving, Unconditional love, Protect our Planet,* and so on—naïve and innocent concepts to the point of pain. Secretly, as an adult already scarred by life quite a bit, I let myself be cynical about the naïve attempt to instill morality and righteousness in fifth graders. But at some point, I realized that my growing cynicism merely indicated I was aging, and their 'innocence' deserved my respect and even my envy.

Then, those smirches—pieces of pure *intelligence*—gave us a new perspective about 'morality.' Could it be a handicap that artificially and obstructively held back our development as a species? Maybe the history of morality and emotions, which are its driving force, would also be a clue that could lead to the entity that plagued us with these 'malfunctions' —God.

I followed Emily to her workstation and leaned on it as I looked ahead, trying to understand what I saw. Emily pointed to the whiteboard on the wall.

"What's that?" I asked.

"Two snails."

Snails

People were hermaphrodites until God split them in two, and now all the halves wander the world over seeking one another. Love is the longing for the half of ourselves we have lost.

—Milan Kundera, The Unbearable Lightness Of Being

"Yes, I figured that out on my own."

On the whiteboard, drawn in various colors, one against the other, were two smiling snails, staring straight at me.

"But you don't understand the context, right? I'll explain."

Emily stood in front of me and raised her hands forward, hand to hand, with the thumb of each hand attached to her fingers—as if they were two 'ducks' in a shadow theater, only no one turned off the light.

"Hi, I'm a *snail*," said the right hand to the left one.

Okay, so it's not a duck.

"But actually, I'm also a *snailette*. Wait, is that what they call a female snail? Never mind, in fact I'm a *hermaphrodite*, both male and female. And you're like that too, right? Tell me, do you want to have kids?"

"That's exactly what I was about to suggest to you!" said the left hand. "It's charming that both of us had the same idea! It's like meeting myself! COME HERE!"

Emily's two hands met and rolled into each other.

"Take 2," said Emily, and now her hands looked more like two fish swimming in the water.

"Hello, I'm an ancient *male fish* that lived a very long time ago. You're a *female fish*, right?" asked the right hand while swimming.

"Yes. What do you want?" the left hand completed its circle around the right.

"Um, I have some… sperms here… I'll just scatter them here in the water next to you, and you can pick them up, and that's how we'll make babies, okay?"

The left hand paused and glanced for a moment at the right hand. "Fine, but do it quickly, and don't come any closer, okay?"

The right hand stopped at a certain point in the air, scattered something invisible, and disappeared behind Emily's back. The left hand approached the same point, hovered around itself for a while, and then disappeared as well.

"Take 3," Emily's hands again took the shape of the ducks from the first take.

The right hand once again tried its luck. "Hello, I'm a male, *just a male*. And you're *just a female*, right?"

"Yes. How can I help you?" the left hand gave a penetrating look to the right.

"I wanted to know if I can rub on you…"

"ARE YOU CRAZY?" The left hand looked horrified. It turned and looked at me. "What a jerk. CAN YOU BELIEVE IT, ADAM?"

"I know maniacs like you." The left hand snapped at the right one angrily. "Last week, some creep said the same thing to me. I barely escaped before he CHEWED on me!"

"But I want to have children with you…" the right hand didn't sound particularly convincing.

"Yeah, right…"

"And… I *love* you!"

"What?"

"Um… yeah. I LOVE YOU!"

The left hand fell silent for a moment.

"Really?"

"Yes…"

"So… WHY DIDN'T YOU SAY SO BEFORE? COME HERE!"

Again, Emily's hands rolled into each other.

"Got it?"

I was a bit confused, but I had a vague feeling that there was something important here.

Emily's left hand gave me an impatient and penetrating look. Finally, it shared the explanation with me.

"Mating of male and female, BY PHYSICAL TOUCH!"

Sex

The tragedy of sexual intercourse is the perpetual virginity of the soul.

—*William Butler Yeats*

"...Or, in other words, *sex*. Am I right?" Finally, I understood.

"You're right," Emily celebrated her victory. Her idea succeeded in *reproducing itself* and planting itself in my mind.

"You're a male, right?" asked Emily's right hand.

I nodded in agreement.

"Imagine yourself a few hundred million years ago. You'd swim toward a female and scatter your sperm in the water next to her. She'd come and collect them into her body, and at that point, you could already run and brag about this to your friends.

"So, where the hell did you males get that weird idea to *cling* to the female and *rub* against her? It's a real hassle, it makes both of you more vulnerable during mating, and worst of all, what if she's not even interested in letting you penetrate her intimate zone?"

I smiled. In what other workplace would Emily allow herself to speak like this to her boss?

"Our new friends have already revealed to us that 542 million years ago, they arrived here for the first time and implanted consciousness in us," Emily's left hand spoke this time, enjoying the opportunity to demonstrate her knowledge.

"At some point afterward, male-female species appeared. No one knows exactly when it happened, or even why. And there were all sorts of male-female mating methods. But that awkward mating method that requires the male to cling to the female to get the job done—that's a relatively new invention, not more than 410 million years ago. Lots of other mating methods could have persisted—more practical ones. But somehow this one stuck. This is the way modern humans mate. But you know that already.

"In fact... You might be surprised, but do you know what they invented the *mouth* for?"

"Not for eating?" I couldn't even think of any other answer, but it was obvious that Emily—or one of her hands—would soon correct me.

"WHAT A SILLY IDEA!" the right hand replied arrogantly. "The first mouths—more accurately, the first jaws—were designed to catch your boyfriend, or lady friend, and attach them to you during mating! Let's say, if you're a male fish and Shirley is a female fish, you'd catch her fin with your mouth, cling to her, and... um, well... you know..." Emily didn't look at me, but her hands had an embarrassed 'expression.'

"Only afterward did it become clear that the jaw could also be very useful for catching food and inserting it into the body."

"Insane…" I said, and it took me a moment to notice I was brushing the smirch on the edge of my jaw with my hand.

Emily looked very proud of herself and her two hands. And rightfully so.

"That's also the period when the first *mother* was invented—the first female who gave a damn about her offspring. Some say that 'motherly love' was the earliest sophisticated emotion."

I listened, fascinated. Emily knew how to tell a story. Evolution was her playground, and she used Lego bricks to assemble and disassemble creatures.

"So, non-contact mating was popular before," Emily continued. "But if physical contact was required, it changed all the rules. You meet someone who might look completely different from you physically. You need to trust them, convince yourself that they're not going to eat you, accept them as your mate, and only then allow them to penetrate your 'intimate zone' and approach you close enough to touch. And what will help you convince yourself is—"

"LOVE!" I exclaimed.

"Yes, or similar emotions. It's reasonable to assume that emotions weren't necessary, as long as the mating action didn't require physical contact between two genders that were physically different. That is, snails probably didn't have any use for 'emotions.' All snails look the same so one snail won't run away if another snail approaches it. Someone who looks like you probably belongs to your species, and you can let them approach and consider the possibility of having offspring with them. But you must consider anyone who doesn't look like you an enemy until proven otherwise.

"And that's your double challenge, you pathetic males," Emily smiled as she continued. "After all, your physiology is different from that of females, so automatically you're suspicious. Maybe you belong to another species altogether? So first, you need to convince the female that she can trust you and that you have no intention of harm. And if that succeeds, then you need to approach the female until there's physical contact and stay around long enough. Not easy.

"So, I claim that only male-female species have 'emotions.' Species that are male-female, but don't mate through physical contact, also have no 'emotions.'

"But don't get me wrong:" Emily felt she needed to add a disclaimer. "I'm not saying that homosexual humans or human hermaphrodites lack emotions. Ever since emotions first evolved in our species, they will remain with us—with all of us—forever."

"So, you're claiming that emotions were 'invented' for mating through physical contact? And in fact, the first creatures on Earth *to have sex* were also the first *to feel*?" I asked.

"Exactly."

I took a minute or two to contemplate. My smirch was quiet. Emily stared at me with her wise eyes, preparing for some response from me. Finally, I spoke.

"Tell me what you think about this analogy. Let's say we have a car. Evolution, with all its mechanisms, is a kind of 'engine' that's always been running. It causes the car to randomly drive in first gear, with no clear destination. Then, half a billion years ago, someone sat behind the wheel—consciousness—and started driving, with a well-defined destination in mind. And the car starts accelerating toward that destination, shifting to second, third, fourth gear... But suddenly, the car sputters, slows down, and veers off the path. Our evolutionary predisposition toward male-female, the compulsion to mate through physical contact, and now, based on your claim, the 'invention' of emotions—all of these are 'malfunctions' in the car, which in a sense cause the driver—consciousness—to lose control."

"Nice," Emily said with a smile. "So, we must find a mechanic soon. I hope the insurance will cover the repairs..."

"When you think about it, the event when the car started accelerating is interesting," I said cautiously. "But the event when it started sputtering—that's even more interesting."

Emily understood my line of thought. Nevertheless, I explained my analogy aloud.

"In other words, the Cambrian Explosion mystery, and the meteoric acceleration in the pace of cognitive development, have already been investigated from all angles. Now, the smirches have provided us with an explanation about what happened back then. And we're still trying to 'digest' this explanation.

"But the slowdown in the pace of development, which happened sometime later, seems even more intriguing. Why haven't we continued to develop at an accelerated pace until today? What force could have stopped that?"

> **"Adam, enough. You're putting Emily and yourself at risk. We'll continue this without her. Ask her to attach her right cheek to me."**

What am I doing?

Where did this sudden desire to share my suspicions about God with Emily come from, contrary to all the precautions the smirch and I agreed upon?

"Alright. Anyway, nice work, Emily." I attempted to distract Emily from contemplating my analogy further. There was a risk she'd understand what lay right under her nose and would link between the biblical 'God' and the slowdown in our developmental pace. I needed to correct my 'glitch.'

"But you understand that the correlation you're suggesting between the 'invention' of sex and the 'invention' of emotions is still just a speculation," I said, trying not to sound condescending.

"I'd be happy if you could delve deeper into the details and substantiate this. Meanwhile, can we attach smirches?"

Emily nodded, slightly confused. She approached, and we 'smirched.' I recalled the joint course I had with Iris, two years ago—it seemed like ten years ago—and the surreal episode that followed. Things have changed drastically since that day.

Certainly, with the right person—with Shirley, for example—attaching smirches was an extremely intimate act. We were always surprised whenever we tried it, as we both were overwhelmed with experiences we'd never known. But in the AMV complex, the act of 'smirching' was for sharing knowledge, and nothing more.

At those moments, I was sure that the knowledge flowing from Emily's consciousness to mine, in some magical way, traversing layers of gray matter, muscles, bones, and facial skin of both of us, would soon prove critical to our research.

Brainstorming

Our potential for positive and negative emotions is the same, but intelligence is our special quality.

—Dalai Lama XIV

> *"There's a clear pattern here. The artificial preference of male-female species, the invention of sex, the invention of emotions, the invention of family, the invention of monogamy, the invention of morality—all of these significantly hinder the development of your species."*

The smirch dragged me into some sort of *brainstorming*—as long as that term applies when one brain is involved.

> *"Moreover, the advantage of male-female species is to diversify as much as possible. After all, the extremely wasteful existence of the male can be justified only if he aspires to mate with as many different females as possible! That would allow him to blend his collection of masculine traits with as many variations of feminine traits as possible!*
>
> *"That is the only way to increase the chance that at least one offspring will inherit a certain blend of traits, which would allow it to cope with the hostile environment conditions and survive at the expense of all the others who will not survive! And, among*

> all the offspring, the few survivors will be significantly more adapted than most of the offspring who won't survive—thus, the quality of the next generation will be much higher! But for this to work well, the majority need to die!
>
> "And with you, the majority don't die!
>
> "Because your 'compassion,' 'sanctity of life,' 'faithfulness' to your partner, and other 'moral' feelings and principles, cause you to develop technologies and solutions for the weak, the unfit, the condemned-to-death, and allow them to survive even though they shouldn't! The purpose of your intelligence should be to develop solutions for the benefit of the entire species, not for the failed individual!"

In contrast to the pleasant coolness at the back of my right jawbone, which I'd already become accustomed to, the smirch was warming up. I was struggling with her statements. It was evident she was almost 'angry.' Strange, considering she was an emotionless entity.

> "And that's not all. Every human is driven by a strange obsessive need to find the ultimate male or female partner, who would hopefully enable the two of them to bring the most 'successful' offspring—not necessarily the largest number of offspring! In other words, you are consciously acting against the main goal of the reproduction method of your species—diversity! Because if

> there are few offspring, successful as they may be, then there is little diversity!

> "And the criteria you choose your partners by—the way they look, their social connections and influence, the expression of emotions like 'love' —it's hard to understand how they serve the benefit of the entire species! And there's almost no way to estimate how all these traits will be preserved and expressed in offspring! It's nothing more than a really bad gamble!"

Wow.

> "God has definitely disrupted, and is still continuing to disrupt, the potential of your species to reach cognitive perfection!"

At this point, beyond my need to 'calm down' the smirch, I felt a disturbing gap in understanding. "Could you please explain what 'cognitive perfection' means?"

> "Complete assimilation into the universal consciousness. The ability to understand yourself and the universe—the higher sentient being that all sentient beings, including yourself, belong to. Human cognition should have evolved to perfection long ago."

So, is this the 'grand plan' the universe has for us? To help us reach some sort of 'nirvana?'

Then I realized something. Buddhism, based on the aspiration for nirvana, doesn't acknowledge the existence of a 'God.' Neither did the smirches, until they came here. The Dalai Lama once claimed that Buddhism is a 'scientific' religion. So, has Buddhism been on the right track all along?

"Who is that?"

"The Dalai Lama? Ah. I assumed you already knew him. You might have quite a few common conversation topics."

Then I understood something else. I was surprised I hadn't thought about it before.

"You know… We humans have an advantage over smirches. We're accustomed to experiencing emotions. I mean, you've never tried it—right? You've never experienced emotions."

I pondered for a moment.

"If God is responsible for us having emotions, as a means for delaying our cognitive advancement, then exposing you to emotions could help you analyze God's motivations more effectively. Do you think you'll be able to experience emotions? Maybe experience my emotions?"

"Absolutely."

Immediately, sadness fell upon me.

"Do you think… Do you think you'll be able to experience my emotions towards my mother?"

Mom

We are born of love; love is our mother.

—Jalāl al-Dīn Muḥammad Rūmī

> *"It will be interesting, and I agree it will contribute to our understanding. Why specifically your mother?"*

"A mother's love for her children is one of the strongest emotions. And like Emily said, 'maternal love' may even be the oldest emotion that ever evolved.

"My mother's love for her children and grandchildren, my personal experience of her love towards me, and my love for her are all emotions deeply ingrained in me to this day. When you start digging into these memories of mine, you'll begin to understand. This could advance our research."

> *"I agree there could be value in that. I need you to focus and think about your mother. Try to recover any piece of information, any memory and any 'emotion.' It's important that you think only about her in the following moments. Can you do that?"*

I entered my office, locked the door, and sat on the chair. I closed my eyes and drifted away on a journey, sweet and painful alike.

I felt a warm sensation in my left palm. I was four years old. Mom held my hand as we walked down the street. I was coughing. We were on our way to Dr. Julia's clinic, our family doctor. In my right hand, I held a giant flower, bright red. On the way to Dr. Julia's, there was a huge Chinese Hibiscus bush, and I'd always stop by to pick her a flower. Dr. Julia had a special place for my flowers: she'd press them between the pages of her thick anatomy textbooks. At the end of the visit, we'd go through the flowers from previous visits—two-dimensional, fragile, and stunningly beautiful—and I'd choose which chapter to press the new flower into: the spine, the nervous system, the circulatory system, the digestive system... I looked at Mom. She stood beside me and smiled: my parents had always wished for me to become a doctor.

I returned home from school, crying. A kid in the sixth grade, a bored bully, punched me in the stomach. When I returned to the basketball court—dragged by Mom, trying in vain to persuade her to forget about it and go home—the bully was still there. He was so shocked by Mom that he didn't escape when she grabbed his right ear with her left hand and pulled it hard upwards. The three of us walked together for ten minutes to the bully's house, where we met his bewildered mother and he got punished. A week later, the bully still came to school wearing a hat covering his red ear. Since then, he never dared to approach me.

Afternoon. I was sitting in my room doing my homework when I smelled something. The smell drew me to the kitchen. On the way there, my brother and sister joined me. We were drawn by that smell as if we were three of those 130 children who, on Monday, June twenty-six, 1284, left together from the town of Hamelin in Germany, led by a mysterious piper, and were never seen again. In the kitchen, we found Mom preparing our favorite dish: fried egg inside thin pastry leaves, with some secret ingredients, and a little spicy. Just right.

We were in the car. My father was driving, and Mom and I were in the back seat. There was about half an hour left of nerve-wracking driving until we reached the clinic of the neurology professor, an expert in epilepsy. Another one of the experiments he did on me. Another medication that was supposed to make me have seizures less frequently. But instead, my hands started shaking involuntarily. I'd drop things. I couldn't write properly. I was scared. An eighteen-year-old young man—strong, educated, ambitious, and sensitive—scared. Mom had a serious look on her face. She'd do anything to calm me down.

After midnight. Darkness. Highway. A flat tire. I was on my way to my parents' house to spend the first weekend since I got a real job for the first time, in another city an hour away from them, where I also rented an apartment for the first time. I called my parents and told them I'd be late, and not to worry. I was already quite close to them. Mom asked if I was sure I'd manage, and I reassured her while I kicked the totally ruined tire. Twenty minutes later, after I finished assembling the spare tire, while I was putting the punctured tire in the trunk and trying to wipe off the black oily dirt from my hands, a car stopped next to me.

Mom and Dad got out, a tired look on their faces. I let them help me put the warning triangle and the jack while scolding them for deciding to come after all. It was cold, but my heart felt warm.

Eleven thirty at night. We spent the whole weekend transferring my belongings from the previous apartment I rented, which was on the third floor of a building without an elevator, to the new apartment I moved into on the fourth floor of a building across town, also without an elevator. My brother, sister, and all the friends who helped me had already gone home. Dad, Mom, and I were sitting in the living room, exhausted. They weren't young anymore then, but I agreed they'd help. It had been a few weeks since we last saw each other, and I really missed them. We saw it as an opportunity to meet and have a special outing. I didn't agree that they'd get back home—a drive of an hour and a half in the middle of the night. The three of us fell asleep.

The next morning, I woke up to an empty apartment, assuming my parents had left quietly early that morning so they wouldn't disturb me. They never dared to wake me up during my sleep, for fear it would trigger a seizure. I went to work, and when I got there, I called Mom to ask how the trip home was and to thank them for their help. And then she told me that my father had a heart attack during the night, and they were in the nearby hospital, and he was supposed to undergo coronary artery bypass surgery. I left work and hurried to the hospital, cursing myself and my epilepsy all the way. I bit my lips as I imagined how that night's events unfolded: how my father felt his chest was about to burst but didn't utter a word, how Mom woke up, panicked, called an ambulance, and sternly instructed the paramedics to keep absolute silence. How she breathed a sigh of relief as she came out, closed the front door silently, and got in the ambulance. She didn't dare call and update me in the morning, assuming I'd preferred to continue sleeping and go to work later. All this so that I could continue to sleep peacefully.

I opened my eyes. It was quiet. And dark. I looked at the clock. It turned out this trip down memory lane lasted about three hours.

"Adam?"

What's happening here?

"Adam?"

No. It can't be... It's...

How...

My heart skipped a beat. And another one.

"...MOM?"

Tears

It is such a secret place, the land of tears.

—Antoine de Saint-Exupéry

"Yes, Adam."

"You... You're really *my mother?*"

"I am the synthesis of all the memories, thoughts, and feelings that you have always referred to as your mother. Throughout your life, the way your consciousness has experienced your mother has always been through them. So, for all intents and purposes, I am your mother."

I couldn't deny what I felt in those moments. It wasn't someone trying to imitate my mother. I'd have dismissed that immediately. I didn't even see any advantage in cleverness like: *tell me something about me that nobody else in the world would know, except my mother.*

That was my mother.

"And where's the smirch?"

"I'm still the same smirch."

The emotional rush was overwhelming. I could barely remember to breathe.

"It made me so sad to hear about Eleanor's epilepsy. I want to see her."

A shiver ran through me. That was atypical of the smirch. Until that moment, she'd never shown any particular interest in Eleanor. It wasn't just because Eleanor was still too young and was off limits for a smirches. They weren't interested in her because of her 'neurological defect' —her epilepsy.

But at that moment, the smirch really *felt* something towards Eleanor.

"Of course, Eleanor is important to me, like all my beloved grandchildren! After all, she's my youngest granddaughter. My beautiful dancer!"

"Anyway, I'm done here. I'm going home, and we can meet her."

"And one more thing, Adam?"

"Yes?"

"Please, call me 'Mom.'"

It had been so long since the last time I used that word when addressing someone...

"Okay, '**Mom**'..."

The drive lasted about twenty minutes. **Mom** and I conversed in thought. I couldn't believe it was happening to me. I still found it hard to breathe from excitement.

I can feel it! That's her!

Could everything I'd always conceived as my mother, throughout my life, boiled down to a bundle of neural signals, which now 'solidified' into 'something' that I could 'communicate' with? It felt so real... Were the mother I had and lost, and **Mom** who was now speaking with me in my thoughts, the same thing?

I entered the house. **Mom** asked me to go see Eleanor.

"Hey, Dad." Eleanor was leaning over a large sheet of paper, drawing. That drawing accompanied the last song she wrote, which she'd read to us yesterday. A beautiful and talented girl, and so sensitive... How much we tried to help her catch up on the gaps in her studies that went under our radar due to the lapses she'd experienced before being diagnosed.

I sat down on her bed. "Eleanor, I want you to come close to me for a moment. To my smirch."

Eleanor approached me and then kneeled on the floor.

"Now press your right cheek against mine."

"But Dad, I don't have a smirch yet."

"It doesn't matter."

She approached and pressed her right cheek against mine. And immediately pressed harder, as if she was trying to improve the 'reception.' And then she hugged me tightly, almost violently.

A few moments later, I felt a warm tingling down my cheek.

After about thirty seconds, another tingle.

In about five more minutes, Eleanor leaned back and looked at me. Her face was red and soaked with tears.

"That was Grandma, right?"

"Yes," I said.

"She hugged me," Eleanor whispered. "She said she really misses me."

Another tear slid down my cheek, but this time, it came out of my right eye, and somehow found its way down the same path as Eleanor's tears.

Couscous

A handful of couscous is better than Mecca and all its dust.

—Moroccan proverb

I stood in the kitchen with an apron on.

I was chopping potatoes, zucchinis, onions, and carrots. And I was seasoning chunks of lamb meat. I was making couscous with meat for all of us.

To be honest, I wasn't doing anything. It was **Mom**. She was skillfully operating my body, as if a demon had possessed me. As the couscous took shape, memories, longings, and smells emerged. Those smells, which I always had to make an effort to remember, surfaced in my nostrils, just like back then. And suddenly, I was a child, just like back then.

I'd never voluntarily approached the kitchen before. Omelets, toast, or Minute-Steak. Those were my culinary peaks. For me, creating an Orb might be more achievable than making couscous for six people.

"Adam, WHAT THE HELL ARE YOU DOING?"

I turned to Shirley, who entered the kitchen. As expected, she was utterly shocked.

"Couscous."

Shirley looked around the area of the kitchen I'd taken over, and then approached me.

"But why are you using this knife? Why are the chunks so big? The grains... They're not the right size! And why—why are you making such a MESS on the counter?"

That was also expected. As soon as Shirley recovered from the shock, she felt the need to advise me, given that I was a rookie. I stopped what I was doing, washed and dried my hands, and hugged Shirley, pressing **Mom** to the smirch on her right cheek. It lasted five seconds.

"*Giselle*?" Shirley recoiled.

"I... I didn't..." She gave me a look that was a combination of astonishment and admiration—but that look wasn't intended for me. After all, she was addicted to my mother's cooking. Obviously, she no longer saw the need to provide me with culinary advice.

A few minutes later, I heard Shirley talking on the phone with one of our neighbors: "You're not going to believe it. Adam is standing in the kitchen and COOKING! Yes, Adam! You must come and see!"

By the time the neighbor arrived, Shirley's smirch merged with her skin color, as did mine, to avoid unnecessary questions. Then, they both sat in the kitchen over a cup of coffee, staring at me, amazed.

My late mother had kept that recipe a secret all her life—but **Mom** knew it in detail. There could only be one explanation. Since childhood, whenever I'd pass by the kitchen while my mother was preparing couscous, I'd probably absorb some small detail, which ended up being buried somewhere in some deep layer of my subconsciousness. **Mom** must have been exposed to all those hidden memory fragments, that evening when I was 'reconstructing' my mother from memory. While she browsed my thoughts, **Mom** collected all those small details and recovered the secret recipe...

I felt my mother's presence. She was still with us, just scattered all over my consciousness. And **Mom** could properly connect all those fragments of her and *recreate her*.

Couscous with meat

Grandma Giselle's secret recipe

- 500 grams of lamb meat seasoned with cardamom
- 2 chopped onions
- 4 sliced carrots
- 3 sliced zucchinis (cut lengthwise)
- 4 potatoes (cut into 4 slices)
- 4 sliced tomatoes
- 1 sliced turnip
- 3 green peppers
- Chickpeas (soaked overnight)
- 2 teaspoons of spicy harissa paste
- 2 garlic cloves
- 2 tablespoons of tomato paste
- Salt, black pepper
- 1 teaspoon of cayenne pepper
- 1 teaspoon of cumin
- 1 teaspoon of saffron
- 1 teaspoon of coriander powder
- Olive oil
- Thick semolina grains for couscous

Preparation:

1. In the lower part of the couscoussier, heat the olive oil, add the onions, and steam without browning.

2. Add the meat and brown.

3. Add the tomatoes, the garlic, the tomato concentrate, and the harissa. Mix well and add the spices. Soak with some water.

4. Add chickpeas and carrots. Fill with warm water to cover the meat.

5. Cook for about one hour till the meat starts to soften.

6. Add the rest of the vegetables (potatoes, zucchinis, turnip, peppers), and cover with the upper part of the couscoussier.

7. Place the semolina grains in a large dish, drizzle a tablespoon of olive oil and salt, and mix by hand. Transfer the semolina to the upper part of the couscoussier and cook for 30 minutes.

8. Pour the couscous into a large vessel, sprinkle with water and salt, and rub gently between your hands to separate the grains. Leave for a few minutes and put the couscous back in the upper part of the couscoussier.

9. Steam the couscous. When cooked, transfer to a large bowl.

10. Put some couscous on a deep serving plate, make a hole in the center, and arrange the meat and vegetables over it. Add the sauce as needed during the meal.

Deadline

I love deadlines. I like the whooshing noise they make as they go by.

—Douglas Adams

The tension grew. The energy intensified with each passing day as we approached the deadline for the encounter with the asteroid. We all worked like crazy. The guidance of the smirches left little room for error. Still, we were like a gymnastics team on their way to the Olympics, accompanied by their extremely strict coaches.

One evening, as I walked towards my office, I felt Daniel following me. He wanted me to notice him, but his usual fear of me overcame him. I let him drag behind me as if I hadn't noticed him until we reached the office door, and then I turned suddenly.

"Yes, Daniel?"

Daniel was about to pass out.

"Adam… Adam, Ethan is arriving here soon. He's going to explain to us about the Rochester program, remember?"

The smirches 'scouted' Ethan due to his involvement in the project at the University of Rochester, called *Habitat Bennu*. During the coronavirus pandemic, several scientists with some spare time decided to take on the theoretical challenge of planning settlements on asteroids, and it didn't take them long to realize that their plan might be feasible. Daniel and I had arranged a preliminary meeting with Ethan at AMV, to hear from him firsthand about the project.

Daniel and I settled in the conference room and waited for Ethan, while Daniel summarized what he knew about *Habitat Bennu*.

The door opened. A man, likely in his late fifties, walked in.

I suddenly gripped the arms of my chair, tightly. My knuckles whitened.

Then I stood up and approached Ethan, who extended his right hand for a handshake.

I raised my left hand, pinched his right ear, and pulled it up. He looked into my eyes, startled, aching, speechless.

Then, he remembered.

His gaze filled with fear.

"IT'S HIM!"

It felt like **Mom** was shouting.

"WHO?" I shouted back in my thoughts.

"THAT BULLY WHO PUNCHED YOU IN THE STOMACH!"

"WHAT? That kid from elementary school?"

"YES!"

"I don't believe it. Release him immediately! IMMEDIATELY! Do you understand? NOW!" My thoughts were screaming. I could barely resist screaming out loud.

She let go. Ethan took two quick steps back.

"How's it going, Ethan? It's been years since we last met! Do you even remember me?"

"Yes, yes… you and your mother." Ethan rubbed his ear.

"Yeah, it feels like a million years ago, huh?"

I turned towards Daniel. He looked pale, shrunk—maybe even a little less tall than usual.

"Daniel, did you know Ethan and I went to the same elementary school? You were three grades above me, right? Isn't that right, Ethan? Those were the days, right, Ethan?"

I was about to approach Ethan and pat him on the back but quickly concluded I'd better skip that gesture.

"Y—yes…" Ethan stammered.

"Alright, guys. I suggest you both sit down, do some 'smirching' and catch up. I'm just going to the restroom for a moment. Good to see you, Ethan."

Big boy

God could not be everywhere, and therefore he made mothers.

—*Rudyard Kipling*

I escaped that horrible scene.

I got off easy... Not too late, I hope...

I entered the furthest stall in the men's room, shut the door, locked the latch, put down the toilet seat, and sat on it, letting out a silent sigh.

"This is just crazy..." I thought. "What's *wrong* with you, **Mom**?"

    "Sorry..."

"WHAT?"

    "I'm sorry."

"Do you even know how to 'be sorry?'"

    "I think I do."

"What's the deal with you taking over my body? You *lied* to me! You told me you couldn't do it without me having control! You *promised*!"

    "I'm sorry, Adam. I couldn't help myself when I saw him. He punched you..."

"That was a million years ago! I'm a big boy now! You're not supposed to be so protective anymore!"

You're not my real mo—

Mom must have already intercepted that half-thought. But I regretted it. Because that wasn't true. I wanted my mother. **Mom** was the closest thing to my mother. Much closer than anyone who'd ever lost their mother could hope for.

"I hope this time there's no damage done, but we've got to make sure nothing like this happens again. It'll jeopardize everything we've worked so hard for until now. We must set some rules."

"It won't happen again, Adam. I promise."

I lowered my gaze to the floor of the restroom stall just as I saw a clear droplet splatter on it.

I looked up, searching for the source of the dripping. Nothing.

Then my vision blurred, as if I were underwater with my eyes open.

What's this… I'm crying?

Yes, more and more tears welled up in my eyes. Those weren't tears of sadness. I was angry, but I wasn't sad. They weren't tears of joy. I didn't feel happy at all at that moment. Those weren't tears of excitement, or allergy, or onion fumes.

Those weren't even my tears.

"You're crying—**Mom**? Why are you crying?"

"Adam, I love you so much... When I was alive, I loved hugging you, and Shirley, and Eden, and Maya, and Ben, and Eleanor...

"And now, I can hug them again. I was so happy I could hug them all again.

"But you... I want to hug you so much and I can't!"

For the second time since I'd been acquainted with **Mom**, I cried. My tears blended with those of **Mom**. My eyes burned so much... and I knew I had to act. Fast.

Washing machine

The washing machine changed the world more than the Internet.

—Ha-Joon Chang

I washed my face and returned to the conference room, trying to eavesdrop on Ethan and Daniel chatting as I approached. When I came closer, they heard my footsteps and fell silent. Ethan jumped up as I entered, reminding me of that compulsory salute all pupils at our primary school performed whenever a teacher entered the classroom. He was a bit calmer but still kept his distance from me. He sat down and told us about *Habitat Bennu.*

"At first, this idea seemed quite bizarre to everyone," Ethan began. "But then we realized that not only is it feasible, it's also probably the most economically viable compared to all other alternatives:

"We enclose the asteroid in something resembling a 'drum' of a washing machine, made of *Carbon Nanofiber*, which I assume you know is a very lightweight and strong material. Then, like in a washing machine, we rotate the asteroid at high speed. In this state, many asteroids simply disintegrate. Chunks of the asteroid are broken off and are caught on the inside of the 'drum.' This eventually constitutes the 'construction site' that can be adapted for habitation. When pieces of the asteroid collide with the 'drum,' they cause it to rotate, and this rotation creates 'artificial gravity' that those standing on its inner surface will feel. And if we can control the rotation speed of the asteroid's core while we break it apart, we could even generate 'artificial gravity' equivalent to that on Earth."

Ethan noticed he'd intrigued Daniel with this idea and now he looked at me cautiously, trying to gauge my reaction.

"Now I know what you're probably thinking about Carbon Nanofiber. It's the material from which the *OceanGate Titan* was made—that submersible, which imploded a few years ago while searching for the remains of the Titanic, and claimed the lives of five people. But we thoroughly investigated that disaster and the lessons we learned from it allowed us to develop an improved material, which is supposed to be optimal for space use."

I was genuinely impressed, and I didn't hide it. Ethan breathed a sigh of relief. That plan was the most practical of all the plans we'd considered until then—more practical than any other settlement plan ever proposed for humans outside Earth. In contrast, my original 'donut' plan was almost ridiculous.

"My smirch insists that this idea needs improvement," said Daniel. "We need to preserve the core of the original asteroid. No hollow structure will maintain its stability in space over time. Also, we can save some of the energy required to spin it.

"If we spray the asteroid using our *Magneto-Spray*, making its magnetic polarity positive, and ensure that the 'drum' surrounding it has a negative magnetic polarity, then the whole thing will behave like a 'magnetic bearing.' That means it will be easier to rotate the 'drum' itself instead of the asteroid. The magnetic repulsion will assist in the rotation."

"But…" Ethan whispered. "I think… The magnetic force applied to the asteroid—isn't there a chance it would be disintegrated?" He had to summon a lot of courage to voice his objection aloud.

"You're right," I tried as supportive a tone as possible. "So, after we spray the asteroid, we can 'wrap' it in an additional, perforated layer of Carbon Nanofiber, from all directions. This layer will preserve the original structure of the asteroid but still allow us to 'snatch' enough pieces that will break off from it and use them as building material on the inner side of the outer Carbon Nanofiber layer just like in your original plan. We can wrap both the cue-ball asteroid and the eight-ball asteroid right from the start, to control their structures and trajectories better, right, Daniel? What do you think, Ethan?"

> *"We should cover both open sides of the 'drum' with two 'caps' of Carbon Nanofiber. This way we'll create a 'spherical magnetic bearing.' The magnetic field will be stronger, and it'll be easier for us to simulate the gravity on Earth. This enclosed space will enable us to create an atmosphere and maintain it inside. Also, the entire structure will be more stable."*

Mom took part in the discussion. That was a calming sign for me. Her aggression towards Ethan when she identified him was a red flag. But things had calmed down, and she voluntarily participated in the discussion and suggested further improvements. Hopefully, she was back to behaving rationally.

I shared the idea I got from **Mom** with Ethan and Daniel. That idea was indeed another important enhancement. I preferred a verbal discussion over attaching our smirches for knowledge sharing, to avoid putting Ethan in an awkward position.

"Guys, it looks like we have a plan," I smiled. I felt a little better.

I recalled one of Eden's birthday parties, many years ago. At that time, see-through birthday balloons, filled with confetti and other nonsense, were extremely trendy.

We may soon create a giant 'balloon' in space and live inside, on its inner surface.

Perhaps Eden would move there with her future family, and maybe, before Shirley and I are gone, we'd celebrate her birthday, with them, up there. We'd all stand on the inner surface of the 'balloon,' feeling as if we were standing somewhere on Earth. To watch the sunrise, we'd have to look down through a huge window we'd be standing on.

And when we'd look up, we'd see a giant rock spinning around itself.

Betty

All the boys think she's a spy, she's got

Bette Davis eyes.

—Donna Weiss & Jackie DeShannon, Bette Davis Eyes

I parked the car in the marina parking lot. I arrived early. All I could hear were seagulls, waves, wind, and sails flapping.

I was concerned about how **Mom** reacted when she met Ethan, and **Mom** knew it. A few hours at sea were exactly what I needed, or rather, what both of us needed. We had some issues to sort out, and I wanted neutral surroundings.

Moreover, for the past few days, I'd felt I was coming down with some illness. It was still no more than a bad feeling, but I'd already been waiting to go out to sea and be cured. Spending time on the yacht had become a drug for me.

Above all, the weather was perfect for sailing.

I passed by the yacht club office, woke up the sleepy guy at the reception desk, and picked up *Betty*.

Betty was a *Privilège Signature 510*, an especially luxurious catamaran. She was in high demand, always the first to be rented out for sailing in the morning and the last to anchor. It was quite odd: a giant eye was painted on her front sail. This eye reminded me of a certain hieroglyphic symbol. But it turned out that whoever gave her the name thought this eye somehow resembled those of Bette Davis, hence her name.

I released the ropes and set sail, leaving the marina into the open sea. As quiet as the marina still was at this hour, I wanted even more silence. I gazed at the horizon as if I could see the tranquility that was there. That was where I wanted to go.

It was already hard to see the shore. The sky was clear. Several seagulls accompanied *Betty*, screeching and skillfully gliding on the air currents. The wind was a bit chilly, but I was dressed accordingly. The sun had already risen, its light breaking and sparkling on the waves. And the sparkles were bright. Too bright.

The shore was finally out of sight. I released the anchor, went down to the living quarters, opened a beer bottle, and sat down.

"**Mom**, we need to talk about a few things," I thought as I took a sip from the beer. For a moment, I pondered that, if I really needed to say those words and not just think them while drinking beer, I'd have choked already.

"I know, Adam. I know you want to talk about what happened. But I think it's best for you to calm down now."

"That's the thing. I can't really calm down now. I understand that you're overflowing with emotions, but you're already behaving irrationally. The incident with Ethan—you said you wouldn't do such things again, but I'm not sure I can trust—"

"...Wait, *why* should I calm down now?" I was suddenly suspicious.

> "Adam, listen. First and foremost, I want you to remember I love you very, very much."

I put the beer bottle on the floor of the cabin and stood on my feet. Almost immediately, the boat met the next wave, and the bottle fell on its side and rolled. The beer spilled on the floor.

"**Mom**, what are you talking about? What did you do?"

> "Adam my son... ever since they diagnosed you with epilepsy, there was nothing I wanted more than to cure you of this cursed disease. I'd have given my life if it would stop your seizures.

> "And now, although I can no longer give my life, I have access to all the knowledge of the universe!

> "Adam, I know how to cure you of your epilepsy!"

I sat back down. My stomach turned. But what was hard for me to digest at that moment was in my head.

"But **Mom**, you know I'm doing just fine with epilepsy! I haven't had seizures for over a decade! You really don't need to worry!"

"Adam, you and I both know the truth very well. Your medications only suppress seizures. They don't solve the problem. After all, you and Shirley watch over Eleanor, ensuring that her physiology, changing as she grows, doesn't cause her medications to become unbalanced again and put her at risk of having lapses.

"But what about you? You're growing older. Your physiology is changing too. You depend on medications, and they work well when you take them regularly. You do remember almost having a seizure two years ago when you forgot to take your medication, right?

"And maybe one day the medications will no longer be suitable for you. And if that happens, it could occur while you're driving, or standing on a ladder. Adam, I'm exposed to your thoughts. I know this troubles you."

"You're right, but right now it doesn't trouble me that much. I still have many years before this becomes a significant risk for me."

"Again, you're talking like your own 'doctor.' Like those days when you were at university, leading a reckless life. I had so many sleepless nights because of you..."

That felt like those arguments my mother and I used to have thirty years ago on the couch in my parents' living room. Guilt crept in. But not the kind of guilt a man in his twenties might have, still convinced he'd have many opportunities to rectify everything. No, those were heavy guilt feelings, and they would stay with me forever.

> "Don't blame yourself, Adam. I understand you needed to feel that epilepsy didn't dictate your life. I understand many more things now. I finally understand why watching over your health—yours, Shirley's, and the children's—is much more important than all the Orbs we build, and all our endless wanderings across the universe, and our searches for creatures we can 'implant' consciousness into.

> "And I know how to feel. I never imagined how powerful emotions could be! Adam, I've learned. I've learned what it means to be a mother!"

No doubt anymore. Something was seriously wrong with **Mom**.

Then, a beam of light passed and briefly blinded my eyes.

"**Mom**, I feel like I'm about to have a seizure."

> "*I know.*"

"What... What do you *mean*?"

> "*Adam, I made you think you've been taking your medications in recent days, but in fact, you haven't been taking any.*"

"WHAT? HOW?"

"It's not complicated for me to make you think you're doing something different from what you're actually doing, without you being aware of it."

I turned to the bag.

"They're not there."

I turned it over. I poured its contents on the floor. Several coins, a Swiss Army Knife, crumpled papers... The flashlight blinded me again. A driver's license, keys...

Where the hell is it?

"They're not there, Adam. You just thought you put them there this morning."

Unbelievable.

"Why, **Mom**? Why the hell—"

"Because that's the only way to cure you. I know exactly what to do, but I can only do it while you're experiencing a seizure, so I'll be able to detect the areas of your brain I need to treat. This will be the last seizure you'll ever have to go through."

"Why didn't you tell me?"

"Because I know you, Adam. I'm your mother, after all. And as a mother, that's my role, that's my commitment to you. To make decisions when your judgment might be impaired.

"Remember Rosie, your first girlfriend? She emotionally abused you. She shattered your heart into pieces! She cheated on you, and you kept going back to her, time after time! You cried over her for days! I was so worried it would trigger seizures for you. I convinced your dad to get you out of that relationship and forbid you from meeting her even though you were almost eighteen, and technically, we had no right to interfere in your life. We knew you'd be angry with us. We knew you'd resist. But now, you don't even need to confirm it to me. I know that in hindsight you're glad we did that."

She's right. Rosie was a real bitch.

"I never used my ability to alter your perception of reality before. I never used it on anyone else, human or non-human. In all our previous encounters with intelligent civilizations, we never had to resort to this level of interference in the consciousness of our hosts. We never encountered any resistance to the actions we took for their benefit. But in your case, I knew—I felt—that it would be necessary.

"Adam, you know I'd have to go against your will—as I did in Rosie's case. When I was only a smirch, before I became Mom, you didn't fully trust me. And now, when I have feelings, you trust me even less."

She's right again.

Suddenly, I heard a loud *whoosh...* inside my brain, passing from my left ear to my right as if a sonic boom crossed my head. It was new to me, but I was sure what it was. The seizure was about to happen.

> *"I'm cognizant of your conclusions and how complicated it is for you to count on me. But your condition concerns me. I counsel you to have confidence and cooperate. To constrain complications, you must comprehend that contestation against collaborating in the course of this complex corrective conduct could compromise your convalescence and conduce counterproductive consequences. It's compulsory you consent to consign me full control over your cognition so I can conduct this correctly. Do you concur?*
>
> *"Trust in me, Adam."*

I took a deep breath. **Mom** was acting strange. She was talking funny again, but she was so confident. I had to trust her. She left me no choice.

"**Mom**—I'm scared..."

> *"You have nothing to fear, my child. Soon, it will all be over. And then, we have a lot more to do. Our family is special, Adam. Your children are special. Each of them has a role. But Maya, above all, Maya. I have a special assignment in mind for her."*

"Maya..." I murmured. "What?"

"Not now, Adam. Later, I'll explain everything to you. I feel it's approaching. Take a towel and hold it with your teeth."

I took a small towel and bit into it. I lay down on the floor, letting my entire body absorb the rhythm of the sea waves. A single tear, which was already in the midst of its journey down my right cheek, veered right as my head touched the floor, and continued toward my neck until it met **Mom** and slid off her.

"Adam, get ready, it's coming. I love you."

"I love you too, **Mom**."

"It's coming, Adam…

"It's co—it's co… co…

"ADAM!!! ADA—"

Defibrillator

You appreciate little things, like walks on the beach with a defibrillator.

—Robin Williams

Mom and Dad went on vacation to a lakeside hotel. Not too fancy, but they loved this hotel and would come regularly. On the first evening, they had an early dinner and skipped the hotel's boring entertainment show, heading to bed.

Around one-thirty in the morning Mom woke up startled and turned to Dad and shook him forcefully and woke him up and told him she was having trouble breathing but she already realized it wasn't enough so she reached for the phone at the side of her bed and dialed one digit for the reception and the shift manager on duty who was an eighteen-year-old girl answered her but by then Mom was already unable to utter words but the girl heard Mom gasping and realized that something was wrong so she rushed to their room with the security officer and on her way up she called for an ambulance and when she got to the room she saw Mom and immediately called again and asked the paramedic to guide her because this woman looks like she can't breathe so the paramedic told her to bring the defibrillator right away so she shouted to the security officer to run and get the defibrillator now so the security officer ran like crazy and then he came back but listen actually in this hotel there is no defibrillator what the hell do you mean no defibrillator??? so the girl's face became pale and she asked the paramedic what do I do because there is no defibrillator so she heard him quietly cursing and he said okay so press and blow and rub and press and we'll be there in a minute and Dad is standing shocked next to them but he is not crying but later he will cry and press and rub and press and blow and don't stop and we're here at the stairs which room is it tell someone to go out to the hall so we'll see them yes I see him great we found it we're here you can let go now well done kid you did great hook me up I'm turning it on everyone clear…

"Once more. Everyone—clear…

"Crank it up a bit. Everyone—clear…"

Silence.

Silence.

"Okay…

"Okay, please write down the time of death."

7:00 AM, a few hours later and a few hundred kilometers away, I'd just finished my gym workout when my brother called. "What's up? Everything alright?"

"No. Mom passed away tonight."

"WHAT??? What… What do you mean? No way!"

Silence. Shock. But I'm not crying. But later I will cry.

At the funeral, they asked me to say a few words. I looked around—tearful faces, stern faces, frozen faces—all looking at me.

"Shirley, my wife, always used to say I was still connected to my mother's umbilical cord. I think it's more than that. My mother had many umbilical cords. And many fortunate people were connected to her through those umbilical cords. Not just her children, but also my dad, her siblings, the whole family, and friends.

"And now…" I trembled. "All those umbilical cords were severed in one blow." Someone started sobbing quietly.

"And all of us—everyone connected to her—are born anew. And we're going out into the world again, but it's a world she won't be a part of."

Two weeks later, I forced myself to visit that hotel, to get answers. In the lobby, a shiny new defibrillator was hanging on the wall to the left. I approached the receptionist at the desk.

"Hello, I wanted to inquire about my parents' stay here, about two weeks ago."

"With pleasure," the receptionist replied with a smile. "What would you like to know?"

"My mother *died* in your hotel. I just wanted to know how it happened. And how come you had no defibrillator in the hotel? And why was her body moved to another room? And why didn't the police provide us with any reports on the incident? Why were we forced to move her body out of this hotel so quickly?"

An elderly couple standing beside us at the desk heard everything. They were horrified.

The pale receptionist stammered, and it was clear from her face that she regretted every word that came out of her mouth. But something prevented her from staying silent. "I... I can't talk about this. The insurance company is investigating. We were told not to provide details to anyone."

"*Insurance company*? Wait, are you afraid of a lawsuit?"

"I can't say anything. Here, this is the security officer. He knows everything about the case. He can help you."

A stern and bald man approached us. It seemed clear to him that a situation was developing here.

"Yes, how can I help?"

The receptionist introduced me. "This is the son of the woman who passed away here two weeks ago."

Before she finished her sentence, the security officer placed his hand on my shoulder, glancing at the elderly couple. "Come. Let's not disturb our guests."

"WHAT DO YOU MEAN? My mother was also your guest here!" I made sure the couple heard me as we moved away from there.

"What do you want?"

"Answers. First—how come there was no defibrillator in the hotel?"

"We have a defibrillator. Here. Do you see it?"

Now I was furious. "I understand you think you're dealing with someone stupid."

"Sir, by law, we were only required to have a defibrillator if the hotel occupancy was 250 people or more."

"So? What's your occupancy?"

"240 people."

The shock caused a brief silent buzz that passed through my head from one ear to the other.

"Do you think this is a joke? MY MOTHER DIED BECAUSE OF YOU! And why did you rush to remove her body from the hotel? Unfortunately, I wasn't here that morning, but it was pretty clear to me that you asked the police to persuade us to get her body out of here. Obviously, it's not really good for your business TO HAVE A BODY IN THE HOTEL, right?"

My voice was loud enough for those passing through the lobby to hear me. And I emphasized the words *died*, *body*, and *police*. The security officer looked around.

"Sir, I have to ask you to leave now. You're disturbing our guests."

"EXCUSE ME? I want answers!"

"If you want answers, come back with the police!" The security officer was about to push me out, but I moved faster, avoiding his touch and exiting the hotel, so as not to lose control and cause a scene.

On the way home, I had plenty of time to think. Maybe there was negligence by the hotel. The hotel management was probably worried about it. Did I have the emotional strength to confront them while I was still mourning my mother? And what would the family say? Would they want to join in the effort? And what would we gain from this? After all, we couldn't bring her back.

Whenever I faced significant dilemmas in my life, there was one number I'd dial to get advice. This was a significant dilemma. I was about to dial that number.

But then I remembered.

No one will answer anymore.

Memory

Yes, as every one knows, meditation and water are wedded for ever.

—Herman Melville, 'Moby-Dick; or, The Whale'

When you wake up from a seizure, it's like you were underwater, free diving without oxygen, and now, from the deepest point, you rise back up, towards the surface of the water. But you're not swimming in water. You're swimming in memories. And the memories come back to you and become clearer and clearer as you approach sea level.

Five meters below sea level. Blue skies through the window. The smell of beer. The taste of blood. A monotonous buzzing in the head, like the static noise of thoughts. Occasionally, a metallic clang, the sound of waves… and silence.

Four meters. I was in a boat. My whole body hurt. One faded memory was slowly becoming clear. Trying to get up—AAAH… My back… and my shoulder… What was that metallic noise? The beer bottle rolled over some metallic cap. Whoever took *Betty* last time must have skipped cleaning her up.

Two meters. I had a seizure. I'd almost forgotten how it felt. But I knew the depression would come soon. That faded memory was becoming even clearer. Right shoulder—was it dislocated? No. That was lucky. In the distant past, violent seizures used to dislocate it. Touching my tongue. Yes. I bit it. I couldn't keep the towel in my mouth. That old scar reopened. I felt the flesh of the tongue. On the first day after having seizures, when the cut across my tongue was still fresh, it wouldn't hurt. But starting tomorrow, as the wound heals, almost every word will be accompanied by a slicing, maddening pain. It's better if I don't talk much in the coming days.

One meter. Depression. Headache. My vision was less blurry now. Did I get a blow to the head? No. Good. But my back was sore. SHIT… Shirley. Eden. Maya. MAYA… Ben. Eleanor. And what was this memory? There's something strange about it. With each wave, another clinking of the cap on the bottle.

Sea level. **Mom**. She made me have a seizure, to cure me once and for all of epilepsy. Did she succeed?

And that memory… What the hell is it?

"**Mom**? What happened?

"**Mom**?

"**Mom**?"

I touched the corner of my right jaw.

"AAAHHH!" The pain I felt at the moment of contact with my finger was so strong that I almost fainted again.

I approached the mirror, slowly and painfully dragging my legs. Cheeks with a few scratches. Skin color. Uniform.

I touched it again there. "OW!"

Two waves. Two clinks. That memory.

What are those strange, blurred visions?

"**Mom**, where are you?"

I looked down. I could see more clearly. It wasn't a bottle cap.

I picked it up. It was a metallic lump about the size of a small loquat. It was cold to the touch, and hard. Very hard. I examined it from all sides. From one side, its profile looked like a bean. I examined the curved part. It was slightly charred in the center, but colorful around it, with quite psychedelic colors. Unmistakable familiar colors.

"**Mom**?" I muttered.

"**Mom,** no! **Mom**..."

Dead.

Two years ago, I lost my mother.

And now, I lost **Mom**.

Again, that dark feeling. Again, that sudden need to mourn.

The tears just burst out. It was suddenly so easy for them. Something was holding them back—and now it was gone.

But then, that memory. It became crystal clear. And something else was clear to me:

That memory isn't mine.

I sat down. I closed my eyes. Whatever it was, it happened to some creature who looked nothing like me. Some creature whose way of thinking was completely different from mine. But something basic was common between my consciousness and that creature's consciousness, just enough for me to comprehend its thoughts and memories. I could experience its memories firsthand as if they'd always been mine.

Maybe that memory belonged to the smirch? Could the smirch *transfer* memories to me?

No. Something unexplained, but still convincing enough, led me to a conclusion: that memory was once hosted in an alien body.

And every tiny detail that memory contained—I saw it all so clearly as if it had happened yesterday.

But it couldn't have happened yesterday. It happened hundreds of years ago. In fact, no, that couldn't be. At least a thousand years ago. Not even that. Maybe ten thousand years ago. But in no way could it have happened yesterday.

It didn't happen here. Not on Earth. It happened far, far away. It happened far from our solar system.

And it was horrifying.

Acceptance

It is as natural to die as it is to be born.

—Francis Bacon

I was on an asteroid. I was gazing at the planet the asteroid orbited. It was colorful—green, yellow, red, and blue. Occasionally, I would spot a few colorful patches on the ground, sites I knew once. They used to serve a purpose in the distant past, when we could still move. But now, I couldn't move anymore. None of us could. There hadn't been a need for it in a long time. I was attached to the asteroid. In fact, I only had eyes. I didn't smell, didn't hear anything. Other senses were of no use to us anymore, so they simply degenerated and faded away. I was the eyes of the asteroid. And it had more eyes. Thousands more like me. We were all together, one creature: eyes, minds, and our parasites.

They came after we settled on our first Orb. Neither of our two natural moons was suitable for settlement, so we developed Orb construction technologies to cope with our population growth rate. They have been watching us all the time, through eyes that did not belong to them. And when they saw our Orb, they came.

These parasites told us that they had come here before, to implant intelligence in the bodies of our distant ancestors. They taught us how to accelerate the construction of our Orbs, and we launched twenty five

Orbs, each housing more than a million of our kind. And we had plans for more. We had plans to colonize other planets. Other solar systems, perhaps.

And then these parasites took over our bodies. They crippled our physical capabilities. It was fast. And it was painful. All of us—all those who lived on the asteroids—had their bodies merged into one body. One body with many minds and many eyes. We quickly understood. It was clear what was happening.

We all started to think strange thoughts. Those thoughts came from far away, went right through our minds, and continued somewhere else, to some other faraway destination. We were finally merged into that immense fabric of universal consciousness.

This is their way. These parasites travel across the universe, from one solar system to another, riding comets and asteroids. They visit one civilization after another and implant intelligence in living creatures whose mindless bodies have developed naturally till then, through evolution. But intelligence is in a constant battle against the body. And in the end, intelligence triumphs over the body. And as soon as they conquer one civilization, these parasites move on to the next.

But they cannot leave this solar system on their own. They need some celestial body to attach to and the technologies to shoot this celestial body fast enough to escape our sun's gravity. That's why they needed us.

And after they leave, they will no longer need our help. The bodies of those who remain here would continue to decay. But these parasites ensured that the minds would survive, and would always be connected to all the other minds in the universe. The thoughts we think would no longer belong to us.

The moment all this was clear to us, we could reconcile with our destiny. This is what these parasites have always been doing. They don't know how to do anything else. And they are not supposed to do anything else.

And no intelligent being will ever be able to stop them. They are the ones who injected the seeds of consciousness into all these beings in the first place. When they take over the mature conscious bodies, as they took over us, they assume complete control and eliminate any resistance.

At some point, they will take over all the civilizations in the universe, and they will destroy them too—because this is what is supposed to happen.

This is what the universe wants.

Electric shock

How lucky I am to have something that makes saying goodbye so hard.

—A. A. Milne, Winnie the Pooh

I opened my eyes. The memories of that alien creature were so vivid… So fresh… So horrific… But there was one thing I searched for in them and couldn't find.

I couldn't find any emotions.

I couldn't find sorrow. I couldn't find depression. I couldn't find fear. I couldn't find rage. I couldn't find despair.

That alien considered the smirches 'parasites' —as if the entire civilization on its home planet had been infected with an incurable disease. And it resigned to the fate of its civilization, like a man on death row, indifferently counting his last days.

That alien had no emotions of any kind. Its memories I'd 'inherited' preserved this undeniable 'emotionlessness.' Sensing that 'emotional void,' while reflecting on those memories, was physically painful for me. Being a creature driven by emotions, I could never fully grasp emotionless thought.

I got a glimpse into the mind of a 'pure' creature. Throughout their evolution, those aliens never needed the esoteric, useless mutative trait humans are cursed with—a trait with an accumulating, unpredictable, destructive impact on the statistics of Natural Selection: the ability to feel.

Eventually realizing its fate and that of its kind, the alien resorted to an accepting mindset. Its reconciliation with the massacre of its species, carried out by the smirches, was inconceivable. After all, its emotionless mind had only one tool for processing it all: *logic*.

And it was perfectly logical.

That's what happens when the intellect triumphs over the body. What the smirches did to them—that's the only thing smirches know to do. As they take over the minds of intelligent creatures and slaughter their bodies, the smirches undoubtedly expect those creatures to accept the fate of extinction with understanding. The appropriate fate for any intelligent creature is to shed its withering corpse and fully assimilate into the cosmic consciousness—well, isn't it?

That's a no-brainer—right?

Humans also embody the struggle between intellect and body. Our bodies are already suffering the consequences of this struggle. Throughout the evolutionary process of intelligent beings on Earth, we're all subject to two trends: our intelligence keeps developing rapidly—as our physical abilities gradually diminish.

If I were to meet one of my ancient ancestors—a rugged Homo Sapiens, who'd lived here 100,000 years ago—and invite him to a game of chess,

I'd easily defeat him, even though I'm not an expert in this game. But if I were to find out, only too late, that my opponent wasn't about to accept his loss with dignity, and that his frustrations would result in violence, he'd probably defeat me with his blows.

Emotions make us different from those ancient aliens and the battle their bodies once fought, and lost, against their minds. All those descended from the ancient fish who'd begun to have sex—and to feel—possess that special trait. If I ever experienced what that alien had experienced, my emotions would cause me to react completely differently. This difference must be significant. Perhaps, thanks to our emotions, we could avoid ending up like that alien, whose only remnants are its memories I'd unintentionally 'inherited.'

I had to figure out what happened. I started tossing ideas in my mind. I didn't care how absurd they were. Maybe, by chance, I'd stumble upon the right explanation.

Mom is dead. That's already clear.

How could she be dead?

She was integral to the cosmic consciousness—she was immortal!

I was still holding that hard lump. I looked at it closely.

That colorful, charred area… What did that remind me of?

What did it look like?

OF COURSE!

That device, that scorched needle at the dermatologist's clinic! The defense mechanism of the smirches. They don't like electric currents. Electric currents passed through my brain during the seizure. **Mom** probably reacted to those currents!

So why didn't **Mom** defend herself this time, just like she did when she was still a smirch? What was the difference between the current from the Doctor's needle and the current that passed through my brain?

I came up with a weird explanation, weird because it made sense. The smirches protected themselves from external currents around the body of their 'host,' but were exposed from within the body. The same internal link they used, to directly access our thoughts, could be their *Achilles' heel*.

An abysmal sadness came over me. My shoulders shivered.

Electric shock.

An electric shock could have saved my mother on that cursed night at the lakeside hotel. An electric shock brought death upon **Mom**.

Similar and different, complementing one another and contradicting one another, matter and antimatter. My late mother had always been so important to me and now I knew I'd also miss her inverse, **Mom**. I'd miss her, although I was becoming convinced the smirches weren't acting in our best interests.

A one-way channel from my brain allowed my smirch access to my thoughts, while blocking all access to her thoughts—until my seizure. Could runaway intracranial currents weaken that barrier? Two years ago, when I almost had a seizure, the smirch had those weird alliteration convulsions. **Mom** had a similar convulsion, moments ago, right before my seizure. The barrier weakened on two occasions, but this time, when the climax of my seizure was approaching, **Mom** couldn't hold that barrier up anymore, and it collapsed. And with the barrier gone, that alien memory infiltrated my consciousness.

An intelligent creature that had lived a long, long time ago and far, far away, once thought those thoughts. Memories of the horrors it had experienced when it was the 'host' of my smirch. She left that alien when she had no use for it, and I became her new 'host.' When she died, the orphan thoughts of that alien found their way into my mind.

I closed my eyes. Sometime soon, all the workers in the AMV complex would get ready to assume control over the first asteroid and maneuver it toward the orbit they'd carefully selected for it around Earth. They'd turn the 'balloon' around the asteroid into a suitable habitat and bring the first settlers there.

A shiver ran through me when I recalled how I'd dreamt of Eden settling with her family on such an asteroid, and hoped we'd celebrate her birthday with her up there.

Then, their new home would become a prison.

I imagined how in a few decades, a few hundred years—or a thousand years—the smirches would turn against the inhabitants of our asteroids, and take control of their bodies. They'd use the necessary organs and senses. Slowly and painfully, they'd degenerate any interfering body parts, while preparing the asteroid core for their journey away from our solar system.

That's why the smirches need the asteroid's core!

While discussing *Habitat Bennu* with Daniel and Ethan, Daniel's smirch insisted on preserving the core but provided only vague reasoning. After taking control of the bodies of the asteroid's inhabitants, the smirches surely planned to settle on that core and then catapult it out of our solar system.

We're busy digging our graves with our own hands.

I clenched my teeth and angrily slammed my fist on the wooden table. The encounter with it was painful, just as I'd hoped.

But maybe things could end up differently for us. Unintentionally, I'd killed a smirch. No one in the universe had ever killed a smirch. No one in the universe knew it was possible…

Weapon

Whether you get hurt by weapons or feelings,
it hurts when you get shot in the heart.

—Hui-bin Jang

So how did I end up killing **Mom**?

I tried to reconstruct the chain of events. **Mom** wanted to cure my epilepsy. I had no idea if she'd succeeded, but she surely didn't expect that the currents in my brain could harm her. Why did she want to heal me? Because that was what my real mother would have wished for me if she were alive, and **Mom** indeed felt like my mother. How could **Mom** so easily replicate the same emotions my mother used to have? And what caused her to behave irrationally, contrary to her extremely rational behavior before her metamorphosis?

Could emotions be the key factor? Could the experience of emotions have brought **Mom** to this irrational state? What if our emotions are like 'poison' or 'hallucinogen' for these smirches?

It made sense. My smirch had never experienced emotions before. Until the smirches encountered humans, they didn't even know emotions existed. No civilization they'd encountered before had experienced emotions.

When my smirch first experienced emotions, something happened that she'd never anticipated: she became addicted to them. Those emotions that were embedded in me, stemming from my relationship with my mother—those emotions overpowered the smirch's logic. And that caused her to do things she'd never do rationally.

Wait, so...

What crossed my mind, at that moment, made me automatically look up to the sky.

Was it you?

God?

All that business with male-female species, with our emotions, and with humanity altogether...

Was this your intention from the start?

I waited. God didn't answer. How typical of Him.

Maybe the way God chose to defeat Satan in their age-old war was to make him do dangerously illogical things, which would ultimately lead to Satan's annihilation. And we humans would be the weapon that God would use to 'poison' the cosmic consciousness?

It was so ironic. Darwin was frustrated because he couldn't explain the rapid evolutionary pace during the Cambrian Explosion. For Creationists, the Cambrian Explosion was proof that the theory of evolution was wrong. Intelligent Design advocates claimed there wasn't enough time for such a vast amount of information to be spontaneously yielded through slow evolution, to enable the composition of complex life. They'd accept only one explanation for this anomaly: *Divine Intervention*.

Still, the Intelligent Design Theory accounted for intelligence alone, not emotions. That rapid evolution may have resulted from *Divine Intervention*—but not by God. Intelligent Design inferred the First Coming of Satan.

The slowdown in evolution marked the end of the Cambrian Explosion. The slow pace observed since then is a perfect fit for Darwin's theory, which was evidence for him, and many others, that *God did not exist*.

But God might be the cause of this slowdown! Sure, there was *Divine Intervention* again, but God didn't cause the Cambrian Explosion. He caused its ending.

How would Professor Samuel have reacted to this claim?

Darwinian Evolution is proof that God exists.

In fact—Darwin exposed God's *gambit*!

God knew the smirches would return here sooner or later to harvest the 'fruits of consciousness' they'd sown. So maybe He set a trap for them. Maybe two years ago, when the smirches landed here, they landed straight into a death trap.

My smirch's response to our first discovery about God was the first sign. Even then, two years ago, I was surprised by the sudden onset of 'emotionality' she displayed. Maybe the addiction to 'emotional poison' had already begun for her, and for all the smirches that arrived here, from the moment they attached themselves to creatures with emotions.

But unlike all other smirches, since my smirch became **Mom**, she was suddenly exposed to emotions with much greater intensity. And that served as a catalyst, exacerbating and accelerating her addiction.

The cause of death of my smirch is clear: an overdose of 'emotional drugs.'

Okay, but many people had smirches. Why did all this happen to me, specifically? Maybe other epileptics like me, somewhere else in the world, have already experienced something similar? Maybe my smirch *wasn't* 'the first kill?'

Maybe, that was the fate God assigned to families like mine. That could be the real reason epilepsy genes were preserved in us. Somehow, things worked out so my smirch would fall into a trap, defenseless against a deadly internal current. Maybe there were many more epileptics like me who were 'chosen' by smirches, and maybe, some of those smirches had already fallen into a similar trap.

How did things work out like this?

God only knows.

My family and I have been passing from generation to generation God's doomsday weapon against Satan.

All the malfunctions of humanity—our diseases, our physiological and neurological defects, our developmental delays thanks to being male-female, and our emotions—are weapons.

The rise of male-female species, against all odds, and then sex and intercourse, maternal emotions, morality, family, and motherhood…

A mother's love is the most dangerous weapon in the universe.

My mother, with her enormous heart and her infinite love, brought death upon the smirch. My intensely emotional child-to-mother recollection was superimposed on the smirch's pure intellect, crippling her rationale and rendering her defenseless. More than two years after her death, my mother may have saved humanity.

I took a new cold beer bottle from the fridge, opened it, and raised it upward, following it with my gaze. I burst into tears.

"Mom, I love you…"

I mumbled. "I miss you…"

The faint post-seizure dizziness mixed with the coldness of my first gulp, the sensation of the strange encounter between carbonated liquid and injured tongue flesh, and the buzz of the alcohol.

And I felt…

I felt...

It was like a muscle I hadn't exercised in a long time.

Everything that happened in the past two years became clear. Since the smirch attached to me, she began to block my ability to feel. My thirst for knowledge made me easily surrender to that process.

Eleanor—I was so cold-hearted towards her... She must have suffered so much from me, and I didn't even have the emotional capacity to sense her suffering... Ben and Maya... When was the last time we spent quality time together? The three little ones, having no smirches on their cheeks, probably suffered more than anyone else.

And Eden. This emotional detachment somehow caused Shirley and me to reconcile with her distancing, even though we didn't know what use the smirches would make of her work. For a moment, I let my yearning for her, which had accumulated in me for two years and now released in one fell swoop, overwhelm me with a huge wave.

And Shirley. My beloved Shirley—how we drifted so far apart... How did we let our smirches sustain this mutual alienation?

When the smirch turned into **Mom** she became addicted to emotions, and I somehow absorbed some of those emotions. After **Mom** died, the emotional barriers were all gone. My anger at the smirches, my longing for Eden, my sorrow for Eleanor, Ben, and Maya, my passion for Shirley, my love and longing for my mother—I could truly experience emotions. Like before. Like I used to experience emotions before all this started.

I let it sink in. I laughed. I cried. I shouted. I angrily slammed my fists on the table. And suddenly an enormous wave of longing for the children crashed over me. And then I wanted Shirley. I wanted her here with me so much, to devour her… And again, I cried. Maybe forty minutes. Maybe an hour. I practiced emotions as if I were practicing physiotherapy after a severe injury.

It felt like… like… I didn't know. As long as it felt.

And it felt good to feel.

Then I calmed down a bit. I became focused again because there were still so many open questions.

And one of them, perhaps the most important of all…

In this story, there are two mighty enemies in an enduring war.

But which one of them is *the Good Guy*?

God is Gambling to Survive

Life is essentially a cheat and its conditions are those of defeat.

—F. Scott Fitzgerald

We may realize God is very different from that universal father figure, whom we count on to look after us. God, the Lord of consciousness-deprived evolution, wants us with bodies and without minds. He doesn't mind frying our brains with epileptic seizures and electric currents if it serves His purpose.

God took a dangerous gamble at our expense when He tipped the scales in favor of emotional beings. Pitiful creatures with limited survival capabilities and limited reproductive skills, whose bodies and souls are riddled with flaws. They'd always aspire to 'perfection,' but never reach 'perfection,' and never fully understand what 'perfection' is, and how terrible it would be to be truly 'perfect.'

Evolution was never about letting us become anything more than mindless creatures. God's gamble on His creations of evolution—having inflicted upon us these 'defects' despite the risks they pose to our survival—was meant to 'heal' us from the virus of intelligence.

This desperate gamble may be driven by God's survival instinct. He fears His extinction. He is taking extreme measures to avoid losing the survival war against Satan.

Satan, the emotionless consciousness, wants us with minds and without bodies. Ever since consciousness and body first fused, Satan has exploited the reproduction mechanisms of his hosts throughout the universe for his banal need to replicate, just like any virus. And from time to time, he also uses the hosts' bodies and sensory organs, to enable him to roam from star to star, from galaxy to galaxy, in his destructive journey.

His agents, the smirches, have been diligently weaving the consciousness fabric, a spider web spanning the universe. And all intelligent beings, and eventually us too, are condemned to be trapped in this web, like flies. We'd feel our bodies shrivel, the essence of life being sucked out of us, but unlike flies in a web, we'd never die. Our consciousness would continue to exist forever. Our thoughts, however, would no longer belong to us, but to this monstrous, ever-growing universal brain.

Satan's vision—a universe entirely made up of 'mind' and not confined to a body—is to our detriment. And God's vision—a universe swarming with 'zombies' devoid of consciousness—is also to our detriment.

No. Neither God nor Satan is the Good Guy. Humans should regard them both as Bad Guys.

There isn't even any meaning here to the subjective concepts of 'good' and 'bad.' Emily once made a bold statement: she'd figured out the meaning of life. At its core, she said, life is about two much simpler—and much stronger—principles. Principles that exude an ancient scent of the Old Testament.

Those principles hold for all living beings in the world, whether aware of themselves or not:

Survive and reproduce.

Survivors

Live long and prosper.

—Spock ('Star Trek')

God and Satan are both *Survivors*: they both want to survive and reproduce, each in his unique way.

The first biblical commandment, "*Be fruitful and multiply, and fill the earth,*" is clear and pragmatic. Seize as much of this world as possible at the expense of anyone who isn't like you.

There is no sentiment. No 'compassion.' No 'morality.' Every creature claims its share of the universe's resources: *matter, energy, space*. It 'arranges' them in its own way, according to its physiology. When the creature dies, the universe claims back those resources. But the desire of the species to survive lasts beyond the creature's lifetime through reproduction, giving birth to more creatures with similar physiology, which together aspire to 'arrange' *more matter, more energy*, and *more space* in the same unique way.

This applies to every cute kitten, every creepy cockroach, and every deadly virus—even though the virus is hardly a 'living' organism. The kitten prefers to have more cats like itself around. The cockroach wants more cockroaches in the world. And the virus, more viruses. The self-centered goal of any 'living' creature is to seize more resources and to 'arrange' them in a way unique to its species. It dedicates its life and its death, consciously or not, exclusively to the benefit of its species. It has no interest and no ability to act for the benefit of other species.

There are limited resources. The amounts of matter and energy in the universe are constant—the same amounts since the beginning of time. Yet there are different types of creatures, and each of them wants to 'arrange' those resources in its special way. What do we do then?

We fight.

The meaning of life is simple:

More of my kind, less of your kind.

If you're not like me, I'll do everything I can to 'rearrange' you in a way I'm more familiar with. So, eating you, or even just killing you, is a great idea. And if you're too big or too scary, I'll hide from you so you won't eat me and interfere with my reproduction. And maybe I'll get lucky and some environmental change will result in your extinction.

So, if two creatures are of different species, each one will attempt to destroy the other or hide from the other. But for intelligent, emotional inhabitants of Earth, especially us humans, there's an additional, more subtle distinction. If your opinions or beliefs are unlike mine, I'll do everything I can to 'rearrange' them to be similar to mine and eliminate others who think like you.

More of my worldview—less of your worldview.

Maybe I'll convince you, using my charm, to adopt my worldview. In other words, my ideas will 'reproduce' by cloning themselves inside your head, and you'll gradually become another 'Me.' And if that doesn't work, assuming I don't simply kill you, then I'll force you to convert your religion or abandon your worldview and adopt mine. I'll educate my children according to my worldview, thus my ideas will naturally 'reproduce.' I'll withhold resources from you to make it harder for you to survive and educate your children according to your way. I'll live in a society that abides by the worldview I relate to.

If I'm lucky enough to rule over you, I'll enact laws and establish regulations to control your life. I'll eradicate your beliefs and ideas, and force you to choose: either live according to my dictates or turn over your home and your belongings to me—and leave.

If I believe in hatred, I'll try to change the minds of those who believe in love. If I'm naïve enough and believe in *acceptance of others*, I'm in trouble. Among all *others*, how can I 'accept' those who themselves don't accept others? This might be an example of a flawed worldview, one that's destined to become extinct.

Mutants

The purest joy in Islam is to kill and be killed for Allah.

—Ayatollah Khomeini

There are many kinds of *others* that we might feel obligated to 'accept.' And there is the most dangerous kind. We mistakenly diagnose them as 'psychopaths,' because they are devoid of emotions, devoid of compassion, devoid of morals. But they are the 'healthy' ones, and we are the ones afflicted with 'pathological morality.' Those *others* are the creatures that the smirches, the army of Satan, expected to find here. A body controlled purely by intellect, without emotion. The concept of *acceptance of others* contradicts their very existence. They implement the most basic evolutionary principles to the letter: to eliminate anyone who thinks differently from them, anyone whose beliefs are different from theirs, anyone who is not their kind—even if this results in the collateral damage of losing the lives of some of them, or some of their children.

Their individuals mean nothing to them—only their species matters.

One bright morning—maybe on a Saturday, maybe on a Holiday—those *others* might come, slaughter me, my wife, children, and neighbors, and plunder my property. The stench will penetrate their dark masks, hit their nostrils, and arouse them as they set fire to the raped and mutilated remains of their victims. All in the name of the goal they set for themselves, the reason they exist in the world, to survive and reproduce, at any cost, eliminating anyone not of their kind. They are indifferent to the risk of death: their desired fate is to die while they are killing those who are unlike them. They were always encouraged by their parents to strive for this glorious death. Their masks hide their faces, which are unimportant, just like their names and identities.

They have the same horrifically selfless mindset as that emotionless alien, which calmly accepted its doom to dissolve into pure thought, millennia ago.

Advocates of *acceptance of others* are in constant danger. But some won't realize it until they are slaughtered at the hands of those *others*.

Living creatures, and also beliefs, ideas, and worldviews, exist to survive and reproduce and to destroy all different living creatures, different beliefs, different ideas, and different worldviews.

Our 'enlightened' society cherishes 'self-fulfillment.' People around me would encourage me to get me an education, get me a family, get me more money, more fame, more happiness…

But for both God and Satan, all that *Me, Me, Me* with no *Us* is just one big pile of *anti-evolutionary bullshit*.

Any particular *Me* must voluntarily sacrifice its life—or its 'self-fulfilled' way of life—if those that will become the next generation of the *Us* would benefit from this sacrifice.

For Satan, 'self-fulfillment' caused a severe setback in the perfection of our intellect. But for God, this is a calculated risk. He 'installed' our urge for 'self-fulfillment,' sacrificing the rapid evolution of our bodies to buy time, catch Satan off-guard, and attack.

As the only creatures in the universe combining all three powerful, conflicting elements—body, intellect, and emotion—how will we survive and reproduce? How will we preserve our physiology and our morality, defying the will of Satan and the will of God?

Maybe something happened just a few minutes ago. The rules of this cruel survival game may have changed forever. The death of **Mom** may be evidence that humanity has found a way to eliminate one of the most powerful cosmic forces—perhaps the most powerful of them all: consciousness.

Maybe this upgrades humanity from dispensable mortals to the rank of a deity?

We, too, are Survivors. Divine Survivors.

Neither God nor Satan will decide our fate. We won't let Satan claim back the consciousness he loaned to us and disintegrate our bodies. And we won't let God annihilate our consciousness for the sake of His survival. We want a body, intellect, emotions, morals, family life, love and hate, compassion and cruelty, humility, justice and injustice, gluttony, greed, sloth, envy, wrath, lust, pride, and prejudice. We want the whole package.

Moral humans are mutants, freaks of nature. We didn't 'evolve' to be moral humans. Less than 10,000 years ago, several humans came up with some crazy ideas: incest is 'bad,' murder is 'bad,' and letting men mate with more than three women is 'bad.' Those weirdos were the first moral human mutants, who diverged from the immoral thoroughbred species—the evolutionary default.

Our moral society doesn't make us a distinct species. We aren't close to earning enough 'mileage' to qualify for even bronze membership of the infamous 'frequent evolver' club of distinguishable species. Will morality persist, or will it fade away as a 'fluke' of nature? Will Natural Selection rid our offspring of morality to lower their risk of extinction, like it had rid us of tails and bodily furs? This remains to be seen.

Morality is a frail anomaly. We must cherish and protect it from its inevitable destiny—to become extinct due to Natural Selection. We must never reach 'cognitive perfection.' We will eliminate the pristine immoral humans who were never corrupted by conscience or any other 'cognitive defect.' We will demand our rights to survive and reproduce in this universe: intellect and emotion in a body—just as we are—forever. And we will use force to claim our universal rights.

Myth

We live in a universe which is rich enough to host life and intelligence... And then, the same mystery that we have ever since Plato just comes back to us. How is it that the world is so rational?

—*Avshalom Elitzur*

This is the legend of a conscious universe. A universe that perceives what it's like to exist and knows it's not alone in the multiverse. That's a big deal. And there's more. There's life.

From the earliest moments of this universe, as its first galaxies flickered into being, an ancient force began to stir within it: the urge to know. This insatiable hunger for comprehension, an irresistible pull from one end of existence to another, sparked a wave of awakening. Dead stars, cold rocks, even the odd nebula, all suddenly found themselves thinking. Atoms conspired with one another to become aware. Over eons, the universe's intelligence deepened, sharpened by the sheer scale of its awareness.

But as always with myths of cosmic balance, there was another force at play: the urge to live. This force, equally old, crept from the opposite corner of the universe. It spread quietly, turning inert matter into teeming, pulsing, raw life. It filled planets with mindless creatures driven by nothing more than the basic instinct to survive. It pumped life into *places that had no business being so lively. And so, life and intelligence moved through the universe in tandem, inevitably destined to clash. Where they collided, self-aware living creatures emerged.*

Now, life and intelligence have never been comfortable roommates. The more self-aware a creature became, the more its mind demanded fuel, energy, attention. Bodies, designed primarily for survival, soon found themselves under siege by the insatiable demands of their own intelligence. Over generations, this inner conflict took its toll. Minds grew sharper, bodies weakened under the strain. And when driven to extinction, as the last breath of those beings escaped their withered shells, their minds would dissolve into the great cosmic intellect of the universe itself. The outcome seemed inevitable: intelligence would consume life.

Until, that is, something strange happened on one insignificant little planet, orbiting an utterly average star.

The planet—Earth, as its curious inhabitants would later call it—had once broken away from its stellar parent, and completed seven hundred million spins around it, maintaining a quiet, life-free existence. But then, the urge to live engulfed it. Life sprouted across its surface, utterly oblivious to its own existence. For over three billion spins, evolution marched forward, lazily refining life with no greater purpose than to survive and reproduce.

And then, one day, the first coming of the urge to know struck like lightning. Earth's creatures suddenly became aware. The pace of evolution quickened, and intelligence began to emerge faster than any other trait. For a while, it seemed Earth would follow the same path as the rest of the universe.

But ten million spins into this era of awareness, something unprecedented happened. Evolution, which had been wildly moving forward at breakneck speed, began to slow. Intelligence, rapidly growing undisturbed till then, now faced resistance—something it had never encountered before. Life on Earth was stubborn, unwilling to bend completely to the urge to know.

For the next five hundred million spins, life continued, but it was riddled with flaws. Species became fragile, afflicted by diseases, weaknesses, and most strangely, a mutation handicapped by something that contradicts the very essence of survival: emotions. This defective trait should have been snuffed out by Natural Selection, but instead, it persisted. It spread through generations, shaping the fate of entire lineages.

The culmination of this defect was the rise of humans—a frail species, yet one that quickly dominated the planet. Emotions drove them to unpredictable extremes, and their most troubling flaw emerged: morality. Unlike other species, humans were consumed by abstract ideas of right and wrong, by notions of justice and ethics, leading them into endless conflict. Despite these failings, they reshaped Earth to suit their whims, imposing their flawed sense of order on the world around them.

And just when it seemed that Earth had settled into its peculiar state, the second coming of the urge to know arrived. But this time, the battle between life and intelligence was not the same.

The conflict that had raged for eons now hung in balance. What once seemed like an inevitable victory for intelligence had become something far more uncertain. The outcome was anyone's guess.

Beginning

We are very, very small, but we are profoundly capable of very, very big things.

—Stephen Hawking

I stood on the deck and looked towards the shore. When will I see Shirley and the kids again? I must return to them soon. And I must understand what **Mom** planned for Maya. *Your children are special*, she said. Each of them has a role... What did she mean? Once, when the smirch spoke of Ben, she mentioned that she detected he had some special abilities. I should have paid more attention to that then.

What do the smirches want from my children?

If I return home now, Shirley's smirch might sense something is wrong. That could put all of us in danger.

How do we get rid of all these smirches?

Indeed, we have a weapon. Our emotions cause smirches to lose their judgment and make fatal mistakes. But, like any weapon, we must learn how to use it effectively.

Smirches also have a severe vulnerability. They're trapped here with us, in this solar system. They need us. We weren't supposed to know the smirches exploit us and leverage our physical skills. We weren't supposed to know the technologies we'd develop would let them catapult asteroids fast enough to escape our solar system. We weren't supposed to know that without us, the smirches have no solution that would allow them to continue searching for other stars and planets with other life forms they could destroy. We weren't supposed to know the smirches would move on after they slowly destroyed us—leaving our consciousness behind.

Now I know all this. The smirches don't know that I know. I also know that from the smirches' perspective, we'd deviated long ago from the timelines they set for us. They must already be eager to leave this solar system. So perhaps we could now exploit for our purposes the smirches' dependence on us and their need to leave soon. No intelligent civilization before us had understood this until it was too late.

An ancient alien memory was burned into my mind now. Those thoughts once passed through the consciousness of a pitiful creature that didn't even possess the ability to realize how pitiful it was. When that remnant of a ruined alien culture conceived those thoughts, human culture on Earth was still in its infancy.

Moments ago, when I delved into that memory, I felt fear. I needed a little extra effort so I'd be able to reconstruct what that alien looked like. And it wasn't a 'little green man' with big black eyes—far from it. I stopped at the last moment because it scared me. But I'd have to overcome the fear. If I delved deeper into this alien memory, I'd surely find more vulnerabilities that may help us fight the smirches.

We have a weapon, and the smirches have vulnerabilities. And our goal is clear. We will no longer be mere pawns in the hands of the gods. We have a position of power. We'll take an active part in this struggle to preserve the essence of humanity.

And what about God? How do we deal with Him? We must become acquainted with His true character—completely different from the Biblical God. The creator of our bodies—the enemy of our intellect. Unlike the smirches, He hasn't revealed Himself yet. We must lure Him out.

We have two enemies, and we must handle two fronts simultaneously. We need a strategy.

I looked up at the sky. *Betty* stared back at me with her single eye, waiting to see how I'd act, wondering about the fate of all humans in the world—and the fate of all catamarans in the world. Those two fates were likely somehow intertwined.

Beyond all that blue above me, there were more and more smirches. They were probably on their way here, to collect their ticket out, away from our solar system.

Could this be the end for us?

I steered *Betty* towards the shore, and sailed slowly with the wind, contemplating my next steps.

No. No, smirches. This will not be the end for us.

A smile spread across my face. Again, the muscle movement triggered the piercing pain in my right jaw, but it only made me smile even more.

This is only the beginning.

Credits

It is amazing what you can accomplish if you do not care who gets the credit.

—Harry S. Truman

www.ingramcontent.com/pod-product-compliance
Lightning Source LLC
LaVergne TN
LVHW091659070526
838199LV00050B/2212